Ben drives west. Sunlight streams through his back and left side windows. This is the kind of day that memory detaches from time. On the stereo, Michael Roe sings about how long a day it is from Heathrow to Humboldt Bay.

West is toward the ocean, though he might not drive that far. It's too beautiful a day to stay in the city. The late May weather is the kind of perfect that lasts through August, except for the seven or eight days every year when the temperature suddenly jumps into triple-digits and everyone prays for rain. He still feels the urge to drive, to go, to shrink his own world to the cab of his truck, alone with his thoughts, as the world unwinds in a thin black ribbon of asphalt, one curve at a time.

He's as light as he's ever felt. Even as he fought to leave town, up and over the mountains to the west (he avoids the tunnel, when possible, preferring the detour through and around the park), he found everything beautiful as it is. He crossed a bridge over a creek and looked far to the left in the leaf-covered banks to see a sleeping bag and a folding chair tucked away under a tree. The image remains; he sees it when he blinks. It is peaceful and serene as the notion of sleeping on a discarded refrigerator box under an evergreen tree during April rains. It's a beautiful ache.

GRAVITAS

S. CHRISTOPHER

Gravitas
by S. Christopher

Copyright © 2007 S. Christopher

First Edition: June 2007

Published by Onyx Neon Press
www.onyxneon.com

Editor: Allison Randal
Interior design: Rachel Elizabeth Dillon
Cover design: Allison Randal
Front cover photograph: Holly Ng
Back cover photograph: Shane Warden
Logo design: Devin Muldoon

ISBN 10: 0-9779201-0-0
ISBN 13: 978-0-9779201-0-5

Thanks to Kate Agena, Emely Amaya, Melanie Ash, Ann Barcomb, Esther Chung, Miranda Opell, Aleatha Parker, Allison Randal, Katie Roberts, Kirsten Thorsteinsdottir, Eva Vecsernyes, and Vanessa Wojtas for manuscript advice and suggestions.

Wild Thoughts

Ben

Wᴵᴸᴰ Thoughts is a terrible place to discover yourself.

Ben stands outside the shabby bar at 11 pm on Tuesday. He holds a bottle of domestic beer for a twenty-something casualty of the human condition who has bent over the scabbed bike rail, with a cigarette in one hand and his long hair, slicked at the top and stringy in the back, in the other. Ben very politely looks away—more out of self-interest than sympathy—as the other coughs up bar peanuts, the warmer half of the cheap beer, and a few gooey strands.

Discovering other people is much easier. At least, it's easier to discover the kind of other people that frequent grungy bars on weeknights in the city.

The city loves neighborhood bars, but Wild Thoughts will never appeal to its young urban scene. It's actual, not faux-dive. No one spent a lot making its new interior look shabby. Smoke-stained walls and beer-stripped floors have absorbed twenty years of psychic stains

1

from true tales of woe and conflict, and the harder to detect effluvium of human lives winding down to slow whimpers blowing bubbles in glasses filled by three dollar pitchers every Tuesday night from six 'til nine. It's too *genuine*.

Ben grimaces with cold glee at the irony of the name every time he thinks it. It's not wild. It's predictable. On any given night, in any given bar off of the main street, in any given major metropolitan area of a million people or more, the same characters play out the same dramas. With wigs, thousands of dollars of dental work, new wardrobes, manicures, a higher class of problems, and half a jar of petroleum jelly smeared across three camera lenses, you could film a week's worth of soap opera there every night.

He's not sure what's sadder, the stark view by sunlight or the ineffective rage of beer-sign neon against the night. The street's residents shiver in their plaster and concrete bungalows, with sycamore trees on the patchy lawn strip between filthy sidewalks and skinny two-car streets. If they ever look out at night, they never really see. Yet there are few bikers or vagabonds or fistfights. When the serious gaze of the sun falls on this street again, it reveals only a tired stretch of road, a wrinkle on the face of the city, littered with uninteresting cigarette butts and bottlecaps.

Besides a bar, the houses mix with some kind of hippie craft store that brightly proclaims "Fire Your Own Pottery!" and a laundromat that could only be more depressing if all of its cheap fluorescent lights worked. If he ever wants to turn his whites gray, he knows where to go.

The eructating stops and the smoker straightens to wipe a thin black velvet overcoat sleeve across his mouth. In the hazy cone beneath a sodium light, the smear of mucus gleams like the cuff links his outfit should have included. He coughs again into a fist framed in what looks to Ben like a lace doily emerging from the sleeve, then croaks "Thanks, man," and reaches for his bottle.

Ben shrugs. No matter how many times a stick-thin vampire dressalike takes advantage of his proximity to raise an undead meal, it's always disturbing. It's an insult. No one would ever ask a stranger "Mate, can you hold my excess baggage while I lighten my internal load?" but too few people think twice about making a new pal prior to a little rumination. Yet he offers a tiny blinking nod. "Good luck."

The anthroponoctule yanks open the bar door. Determined vibrations from the truly awful cover band escape out into the night air. It could have been anything from classic Stones through the entirely forgettable '80s. On any given night, the world's best rock band isn't playing at the Wild Thoughts of the world. They're lucky to have never-will-bes.

Ben ignores the question of free will versus his personal every-Tuesday gravity of standing just outside the bar. There's nothing on TV, of course, but he wants to think that there's more to his life than silently insulting end-of-the-road-in-the-middle-of-the-week bar patrons in the middle of absolutely nowhere. He could read a book— even self-help or philosophy—to sip orange juice from a wineglass and wiggle his toes inside lambskin slippers as a fire cackles in the hearth and a bloodhound naps on the rug.

He has the orange juice and the slippers.

Ben won't admit that he's waiting for magic to strike again. The thought dances on the edge of his mental movie screen, but he's afraid to look directly at it. If he stares, will he go blind? Will it drop its metaphoric pants and blow him a mental raspberry as it skips off frame, out of sight, and into the category of things the Universe uses to taunt him?

On any given night, just outside any given shabby bar, in any given major metropolitan area (except possibly Houston, which he hates enough to believe that magic won't ever exist there, no matter how its residents point to Galveston Bay as a shamanistic token), someone'll slip the bonds of the weight of the world and drift upward until he sees the kind of big picture view that puts all of life into perspective. From there, everything is and is only exactly what it all is. It's a map. It's better than a Mercator projection. It's a globe flattened out to two dimensions with big white labeled arrows standing out in three.

Ben repeats this sometimes, when he lets himself dream. It's happened to him before. Sober.

When he closes his eyes and really *remembers* the sinking feeling of a peculiar gravity in his chest, really allows himself to reach the point of tears, he can replay the entire scene well enough to produce a filmable storyboard. He tries to avoid it. Tonight he's tired enough to let himself go.

Ben floats now, hovering just above and behind his body. He sees himself hunched over with too much seriousness and too much responsibility. He sees it all now. Every burden he's taken on and every implied debt he carries draw lines of pain and worry on and through him.

He also sees every good thing in his life. Brilliant lights try to move around and over and under and through the mountain of guilt and pain and fear. Few do. He tries to reach down and reshuffle the baggage and his grip, but his hands slip.

Something pulls him backwards, up into the sky, and he sees the entire neighborhood. Dozens of houses full of bent-down people carrying their own burdens store a hundred stories and a thousand pains and fears. Everyone lives in weighty shadows where the light seldom breaks through. There are more patterns there. Everyone looks around when no one else does, to gauge the angles at which their backs bend relative to each other. No one mentions it. Perhaps no one ever realizes it.

He flies further and sees the entire city in its districts and neighborhoods and suburbs, divided by raised freeways and rivers. It rolls up and down hills and through tunnels and spreads out slowly, as if something poured all of this life into place. A million tiny lights wink on and off, individuals who move together in clumps and clusters. He can't see the drops of water in the rivers or lakes or ponds or puddles, but every person weighed down is a candle's light. They all follow the same rules.

He sees the pattern in himself, his own behavior played out script-like countless times by the tiny lights beneath him. All it takes is a shrug. He could stand up straight, dump off everything he doesn't need to carry, and reach out to the little lights beside him to share every burdens. He sees her face and her hand, and he stretches and strains toward her.

It all fits. He traces the line back from her to where she was and where she is. He tastes the shape of the words in his mouth: the seven words he can say to erase his mistakes and the nineteen words he can say to win her forever. He begins to speak and his heart lifts and he feels a weight on his shoulder, dragging him back down as the city rushes up, then the neighborhood, then the street. He sinks back into his own body again.

It never gets any clearer. It stabs.

○ ○ ○

Matthew

A curious nose pokes into view two doors down.

Ben doesn't mind the chill. It's November but it's not cold yet, not enough to bore through thick jeans, and chill the steel toes of his boots. His socks are thick and gray, neither matching nor clashing with his blue flannel shirt and nondescript motorcycle jacket. He doesn't have the motorcycle yet (if ever), so why go crazy with patches and studs? It's cold enough that he'll see his breath if he sticks around for another hour and concentrates on his breathing, if he doesn't cry uncle and let the truly hideous cover band insult what good taste the idea of opening that door again hasn't already chased off. Maybe they unknowingly swapped drummers with another band in another bar, with each playing in time with the wrong playlist. That's assuming that there are two drummers in cover bands simultaneously able to read playlists and not notice that something has gone too wrong even for rock and roll.

These lines of thought make his hands tired. The alternative, though, is giving that fool leprechaun the satisfaction of knowing that he sees it. It'll taunt him for sure.

To his credit, Ben doesn't jump when he sees forty pounds of highly dubious dog sit and watch him. It looks like an English setter: a mottled face and dark ears paint over a white base. The distinctive wispy hair sprouts from its chest. There's something else Ben can't place. This particular dog isn't quite a puppy—it has markings already—but it's not full grown either. The dog cocks its head like the spaniel breed's name implies and stares, full-on, with large hazel eyes. Ben imagines suddenly a sandwich.

The dog is clean, well-fed, and apparently intelligent. The occasional car zipping by doesn't shift its attention from Ben as the only point of interest on this backwater street in the city at 11 pm on a Tuesday night.

Dogs remind Ben of Emily, and he tries to stop before her name can throw him to the ground. He swallows, both in his throat and in his heart, a wrenching motion as much physical as emotional, and really looks at the dog again. Satisfied it only wants to make friends, Ben squats and holds out his right hand, back first.

That's enough encouragement for the dog, who reveals his gender by ambling over for a friendly sniff.

Wild Thoughts

The dog's nametag says "Matthew" and gives an address just down the street. 1734. The house is dark. Though there are two cars jammed into the makeshift bar parking lot in front, it looks like no one's home; it's good courtesy to leave your porch light on for the nightly parade of revelers. Better, it's a way to keep light-sensitive drunks off of your lawn, if you care anymore.

Ben lets Matthew sniff his hand for a moment, careful not to push too much eye contact. This habit he learned from standing outside Wild Thoughts, where it applies equally well to the kind of people who haven't yet discovered that the truly adventurous parts of the human condition don't care much for ethyl. He still ends up holding a beer or a cigarette more often than necessary, though.

Matthew moves on from sniffing to fishing for a good ear scratch. A spot just behind a little stub of cartilage on his left ear needs some attention, and with an uncharacteristically cat-like motion he convinces Ben to knead it idly while pondering the relationship between brand of cigarette and brand of domestic beer. He's never figured out where people who buy their own tobacco and roll their own smokes fit in. In his judgment, they ought to brew their own beer—if you're going to skim from the margins of cigarette sellers and possibly ignore the whole purpose of filters, you might as well control the toxicity of your own brew—though the argument against blowing up your garage or shed is compelling. A friend once offered "freshness" as a reason, but he couldn't defend the taste there either.

Ben tends to write about a dozen research papers in his head at any given time. He draws and labels axes meticulously, imagining the shapes of curves as he scatter-plots his thoughts.

The night is clear. Pedestrians who've avoided low-warmth sodium lights casting stark shadows in back alleys and those hideous blue car headlights can look up a few miles into the thin air. A lazy satellite drifts across the sky. It winks as it falls endlessly, just high enough and just fast enough to stay in orbit as the earth rotates beneath. The last time Ben flew up and out of his shoes (metaphorically speak-

7

ing), he had to duck out of the way of a cellular phone antenna. He didn't have time to read the label. He vowed to give it a good kick next time, ignoring questions of ballistics, coverage paths, inertial forces, and metaphor.

Matthew drinks up the attention, eyes rolled back and long pink tongue dangling precipitously. The bar door opens again. A guitar solo limps outside, but the drummer is almost four seconds ahead, which means he'll be back on the verse before the guitarist has had a chance to mangle a series of fingertaps on just three notes. Ben envies the lower-mammal capacity of shutting off all higher brain functions. The dog's ears twitch, apparently registering only an unpleasant but minor audio stimulus.

He ought to be able to hear the dull thumping of a bass drum complaining for arrhythmic double-kick abuse and losing an argument with the bass guitar over how many eighth notes should be in a measure. One of Ben's closest friends in college took a music minor, with music appreciation and sight-singing classes burning in tradition guised as theory, and the second-hand snobbery has only grown in the years since. Despite believing so strongly that 4/4 time is a fixture of Western musical literacy as much as the equal temperament system by now that this cover band actually produced mild physical pain, he can't stop his runaway brain. Ben once calculated that they kept slipping to three-and-seven-eights/four time with a curious anti-swing beat that drops the endings off of measures, in the same way that lip-syncing pop stars never seem to sing ending consonants except for s yet still manage to make r and n into holdable vowels.

Then again, when he signs his name, he mostly gets the first letters of each name shaped correctly and ends with scribbles.

Privately, he's not sure whether it's a good thing that the music industry prefers tiny young blonde slutlettes to the ugly but honest garage band fronts who'll grow up, if they're lucky, to be as hideous as Steven Tyler or Mick Jagger. Sure, it's creepy to use a seventeen-year-old's burgeoning talents (Ben's roommate Randy's euphemism) to push an ultimately forgettable disc full of exhortations to dance and either call or don't call. Still, there are bands so bad that he can't help but remember their work so far as to figure out how this particular drummer and bass player consistently finish just under six seconds apart for a three minute song.

Ben wishes he'd seen the Beatles perform.

Now he's lost his place in the library of his mind. As his eyes focus again on the now, he forgets the totemic raven-headed coyote gamboling and making obscene gestures, hears distantly the drummer drop a stick he tried to twirl to make up for speeding up, and good for him for finally noticing, feels the sloppy pink tongue lap sticky cheap American beer from the palm of his hand, and sees himself sort of through the eyes of Matthew the dog and sort of from behind. He's 30. He's cold. He's tired. Some drunk has subjected him to a half-galloping guitar solo in Eleanor Rigby. He ought to be home in bed, or at least unfolding a real pair of pajamas, with buttons and maybe stripes. He hasn't decided yet.

Matthew whines as Ben straightens to leave, but the click-click of toenails on cold sidewalk lasts for only three or four steps before the dog has reached the limit of his familiar haunts. A small, unselfconscious part of Ben's mind otherwise carrying enough preoccupation to fail a job interview from overqualification hopes that the dog doesn't regularly imprint upon strangers. Strangers outside Wild Thoughts tend not to be any sort of positive impressive.

It's 11:10 pm and magic won't strike tonight. A sudden exhaustion takes him, and he hates himself again for succumbing to wish-fulfillment fantasy.

o o o

Midnight Walk

It's not far to Ben's three-bedroom house, but the bus ride would take over an hour, counting waiting and transferring once. He prefers to walk. It's only a couple of miles and the air's clean enough that it won't do any permanent damage. He noted that in the benefits column for living on the west coast outside of southern California. The pollution of the city does add up sometimes, but a zephyr soon carries it along to the invincible desert.

The streets of the city, at least in the southeast neighborhoods, seem cramped at night. It's partly the lack of garages, partly the lack of tree prunings in the past decade, and partly a wordless community agreement that streetlights would ruin their character. Cloudless nights always trigger latent claustrophobic twinges in Ben. Hunching over and twisting sideways to duck bare branches starting to drip with what will become dew—or fog, lately—makes it worse. There's an odd aural dampening too, like someone could sneak up behind you and you'd never hear him. He feels safer with cloud cover, when far off lights or moonbeams light up the whole sky way past sunset and ambient noise bounces off the mother-of-pearl domed ceiling back down to earth. It's then ethereal and otherworldly, as if he moves slowly and deliberately and gracefully.

The sickly yellow-green fire hydrants always break the glamour. They save lives and property values, but for a town that claims to value aesthetics as vigorously as this one does, he would have chosen robin's egg blue.

Sometime tonight it will rain. From October through April, good paperboys here always add an extra plastic bag before leaving the whole paper in a puddle. Ben can think of few things less appetizing than soggy newspaper to go with his breakfast. Most come from babies or untrained pets.

The vacant lot just down the street from Ben's house is still a pile of well-intentioned construction materials. Its chain link fence lately sags in polite rebellion. Loose dirt leaves muddy smears all the way to the runoff drain every time it rains. It'll be a set of apartments that would look out of place anywhere from here south to Los Angeles. The last thing the city needs is yet more too-adorable townhouses marketed as in the middle of a neighborhood "with character" with a rent set too high. The owners will plant plastic signs to offer two months free on a year-long contract with other useless amenities rather than dropping the rent to something commensurate with, perhaps, the general property values of the rest of the houses on the street, let alone the entire neighborhood.

Ben hasn't finished the math, but has a short list of better ways to tie up half a million dollars over the next five years—his own mortgage, for example.

Forty minutes from the bar, he walks up three concrete steps barely too narrow for matching stone lion sculptures. The closed plastic blinds on the front window flicker bluishly. Randy must be watching TV with the lights off. Ben sighs and heads for the kitchen door instead.

o o o

Randy

The kitchen's around the side of the house, hidden from the street by a tall, almost fluorescent, green bush. Ben wants to slip in and up the stairs without Randy noticing he's there; he's not in the mood to watch the best moments of Japanese humiliation game shows or whatever fills the gaps between infomercials in the nosebleed seats of midnight cable. He seems to remember a show with skinny young men drinking pot after pot of tea, stripping down to their underpants and socks, and sitting in snowbanks to win prizes, but Ben's never asked around if anyone else remembers a televised bladder control contest. It may have been a dream.

Ben grimaces at the image of a nearly naked Japanese man in glasses running and slipping in slush to reach a portable toilet probably full of eels and flips through his tidy keyring by memory. Friends and acquaintances have carried little rubber chickens and big carved wooden ovals and powerful LED flashlights as gewgaws and might-need-it-someday fetishes. He can never remember how useful the light sounds when he's near a useless gadget store, but has likewise never figured out how such a mess of things poking in all directions fits a normal pocket. Maybe it's harder to lose two pounds of incidentals connected to the one key you absolutely need at the moment, but if you can always fit them into the same pocket why do you need help not losing them?

Fortunately, the deadbolt doesn't stick and Ben makes it inside quietly. He closes and relocks the door, fiddling in the dark because the frame's just a little crooked. He resolves yet again to take a screwdriver to the hinges in the hope that that's all it is. He reaches to undo his boot laces, but can't recall the last time anyone has mopped and suspects that the cold floor also has crumbs and tiny rosettes of what everyone hopes is salsa or spaghetti sauce. He has almost made it to the stairs when Randy yells "Ben! Check this out!", and the game is over.

Randy lies on his left side on the couch, propping up his head with his left arm and clutching a round throw pillow to his chest with his right arm. The remote is on the floor, not flying idly through the air, so Randy has stuck with the current program for quite a while now. Ben shuffles to a wall where he can lean back, fold his arms, and ignore the waves of pure psychic glee. Every seventh sentence or so, Randy produces a tsunami.

"They're making supermodels eat bugs. Madagascan giant hissing cockroaches."

Ben shifts the weight onto his right leg and thinks "*Grompha-dorhina portentosa.*" The second word bothers him more than involuntary Latin. He starts "Some people keep them as pets," and fully intends to ask about the cruelty of digging up a box full of bugs just to gas them and feed them to people who don't eat anyway, but Randy has already grinned and started to speculate on exactly which supermodels he'd like to keep as pets. The cockroaches are hideous. The supermodels aren't much better, though they look a lot better wearing normal clothes and vaguely annoyed and horrified expressions as opposed to the normal runway pose. Ben can't rephrase "I started thinking that I'm so much better than you but the shiny lights distracted me and I forgot to change my facial expression" in monosyllabic words that they could remember.

The guest host of the show is an ex-model turned mommy and author. Her presence is apparently to promote a book about motherhood, describing how she ballooned out to 130 pounds in her third trimester, and somehow managed to make it back down to 118 in just two months while still working in at least ten minutes of baby time every day or so. Ben's not an expert but he can roughly gauge the size of a newborn's head against a human being on the television. He inadvertently visualizes fat kids plugging up water slides when similar thoughts escape Randy.

"What is it about women and kids anyway?"

Randy just shares sometimes, with no particular intent. Ben shrugs, all shoulders and no arms. It's almost time to refold them, though changing to a more open conversational posture might only encourage Randy, not that he needs it at midnight. Ben considers trying to turn it toward biological versus cultural imperatives, but there's no good direction this conversation could take. At least the only loser in that debate is the clock and not good taste.

"Seriously, they really do all want to have children. What's the deal with being afraid to be a mother though? Oh, 'I love children, I can't wait to have them, I have their names *all* picked out and

I just want to dress them up in cute little outfits and those darling booties... and I know I'm going to be a terrible mother and will spoil them rotten and let them walk all over me and...'" Ben stops listening before it spills into multiple paragraphs. Nodding and making little "go on" noises neither encourages or discourages Randy. Ben's current tactic is to shift uncomfortably and use his best baleful expression and hope that Randy comes up for air sooner or later.

Ben has long since realized that his parents did the best they could while having to figure out him and his brothers. That thought scares him a little, but it seems perfectly reasonable, though he imagines himself giving this mysterious everywoman some brilliant advice. If you're not sure you'd be good at something, listen to your doubts but try it out, maybe once a little bit. That'll give you some evidence to decide if you really want it enough to fail for a while and eventually maybe become better at it.

"...and she was mad then because I told her that and it was a rational thing to say. Why be afraid of what you want?"

Apparently Randy actually *did* just that with his characteristic grace. Ben's too tired to explain again his dual idea that a) women talk to express their feelings, not to solve problems and b) it's not wrong for people to have different opinions from you. Next time he'll try a nice contrapuntal arrangement of the male versus female conversational motivations talk to see if the novelty breaks through.

He scowls at the irony of this conversation.

"She's nice but she can be so angry sometimes. She won't even tell me why."

At least Randy has muted the TV. The guest host yells into a red windscreen-tipped wireless microphone as a huge Coast Guard Reservist speeds a jet-ski in some sunny bay somewhere. Ben finally decides on a little aikido.

"Did you ever notice," he starts, walking slowly but deliberately over the stacatto of Randy's choppy sea, "that they only invite guest stars who want to hawk a movie, TV show, book, or album?" The old hobbyhorse still bucks. Randy stops, mouth open mid-rant. You could fit three full-grown Gromphadorhina portentosa in there.

"Just a little anti-corporate propaganda to keep in mind," Ben calls as he walks up the stairs by force of will. He could sleep for a week.

o o o

...Doesn't Stay There

Breakfast

HE always feels awkward when he awakens, especially from the wedding dream. It's not for grown men to dream about churches and bells. Only little girls should spend their entire childhoods planning this dress, that color of flowers and the beautiful surprise of swans in a pond behind a fake gazebo or diapered doves flying overhead.

Randy is characteristically late for work. He sits at the kitchen table in an undershirt, blue boxers, and a thin plaid flannel bathrobe. A pale leg juts off of the side of the chair to bounce up and down in time with the nervous rhythm in his cerebellum somewhere, and his robe has loosened far too precariously for Ben's comfort. He's unshowered and unshaved, with a distracted bird's nest of short brown hair and blush crescents under his eyes resembling severely hypothermic lunulae. February is The Human Body, in the Increase Your Vocabulary 2003! calendar.

16

He won't make it to the call center by 9:30 am again and so he'll spin an interesting story for his boss, as if she cared. Ben's sure it will have some thematic connection to the maze on the back of the cereal box Randy must have read a dozen times already this morning.

"The paper's on the doorstep, if you'd rather read the comics than help the bee find his honey." Ben sighs inwardly. If Ben hadn't accidentally locked himself outside, again, he'd surely inadvertently amuse the neighbors whom Ben actually likes despite the fact that they find nothing amusing. Randy's a special kind of nothing; he wraps so far around the spectrum as to make "amusing" completely "unamusing".

For example, Ben wasn't happy with *how* he learned that you can order custom-made frisbees of your own design. Randy's post-surgery Pamela Anderson blank-bee—the euphemism changes as Randy's creativity fires again—remains perched against Mrs. Truesdale's chimney. A good windstorm will drop it right in her lawn. Fortunately, he moved on to other hobbies before mangling the phrase "flying disc".

Randy grins, showing a smear of chocolate across his right front tooth. "I'm deconstructing the subtle consumerist messages the back of the box activities send to unsuspecting children. If you compare this maze to one from 1981, just after the Soviet-U.S. hockey game in the Olympics, you'll see a gradual shift from communism as a bogeyman to body-conscious imagery. F'r example, the bee's escaping a bear in the 1981 version and now he's going for delicious and nutritious honey with the losing conditions being a doughnut and rocks and twigs. Apparently that represents a mueslix."

He has printouts of the previous box cover. Ben can't decide if he feels more disturbed that people on the Internet have scanned cereal boxes from the '80s or that Randy cared enough to download them to read over breakfast. He pours a glass of orange juice and lets the idea flow through his brain, hoping it'll wash out the other side. Leaning back against the sink, he can't help but respond.

"How about 1989, with China and the Berlin Wall?"

Randy tends to think after he starts to answer. "Ooh, good question. Are you expecting a dragon motif for the one and maybe a hammer for the other? That's good iconography. I like that a lot."

Ben pushes. "Also look for the bee riding a camel or buzzing around near the Sphinx or great pyramids in 1981. It's clearly a reference to Sadat—but pro- or anti-Israel?" He used to see how many times the family dog would chase the tennis ball he pretended to throw. Randy, ostensibly capable of pattern recognition, never apparently notices. He's moved lately more into semiotics and iconography than deconstruction, but that's the kind of sloppy thinking that you expect from second-tier phone support powered mostly by sugar and, before 3 pm, caffeine.

The look of the soggy mess in Randy's cereal bowl raises the idea of omelettes in Ben's mind. It always starts the same, with a thin base layer of granola, with almond slices and hard clumps of dessicated raisins. Then comes a level of filler cereal, some sort of flake or wheat shred, always with frosting. Next are the marshmallowy tiny leavings of toy commercials. Finally, Randy sprinkles a handful of miniature chocolate chips as a garnish against the evil-but-healthy spirits of the corn, wheat, and oats lurking elsewhere.

At least he's stopped using chocolate milk.

Ben has occasionally considered replacing the miniature chocolate chips with miniature carob chips, just for laughs, but he's never found them anywhere, not even the yuppie grocery store with a dress code. Also, he's not really that cruel—but that level of sincerity requires a little tweaking now and then.

A proper omelette requires preparation. You can't just throw eggs in a pan and pretend you're scrambling without actually scraping a spatula to churn soft yellow hills. Ben removes four large eggs from the fridge, leaving one. One hand keeps them from rolling off of the counter while the other writes "eggs" in patient lowercase letters on the blue shopping pad. He taps a small dent into each, then opens the shell with his thumbs to drop the gooey little suns into a bowl. He adds a dollop of milk, a dash of salt and pepper, a good shake of garlic powder, and a trace of chili powder. He beats the results—with a wire whisk, by hand—into a soupy goop with small translucent floaters by the time the pan on the stove has warmed.

In goes the egg mixture. Then he rushes to chop a tomato and a green pepper and the black olives he noticed while rummaging in the fridge. Sadly, there was no Canadian bacon. It does not go on the blue pad.

The real trick is flipping the omelette over at the right moment. Ben removes the pan and tilts it. As the omelette starts to slip, he flips the pan just so that the top of the eggs fold over, and he slides the results onto a plate. From there, it only takes a few strokes of a grater with medium cheddar to make a breakfast worthy of the term.

Moisture seeps onto the plate. He winces; he should have cooked the vegetables separately. Still, it's a worthy attempt and he resolves, as he does every week, to do it right next time.

Suddenly, Ben leaves his plate on the stove and starts to scrub down the counter. There's a bit of dried jelly and spatterings from pork chops the night before. A mood has struck him and he just wants his kitchen clean and his life ordered. It's strong this time; he eyes the microwave suspiciously and wonders if he has a spray bottle full of bleach water.

Randy's seen this before. "Ben, what's up? You want your chair?" Ben reads the comics over breakfast. The seat at the head of the table offers the best room longitudinally for lying down newsprint while avoiding the crucial sun-in-the-eyes moment for late-risers.

With three nascent cleaning projects in process (the kitchen itself has six: clean the counters, empty the dishwasher, rinse out the sink, mop the floor, scour the microwave, and the less said about the nether regions of the third shelf of the fridge, the better), Ben stops, scrubby sponge in hand. "I had the oddest dream. Do you have vivid dreams? You wake up and you're feeling what you would have felt in the middle of the dream and you don't know for a minute if it really happened?"

Randy shrugs. "Slept like a baby."

Ben sips his orange juice. "I was in San Diego, fighting aliens."

"Punching aliens. I like that one. You should make it into a video game."

"Right. We were throwing pistachio shells at the head alien, parabolas over palm trees into a hotel or restaurant or some sort of game—simple ballistics, and then I walked into a restaurant. A different restaurant. It was dark and narrow, twisty halls, like a buffet restaurant, with wood paneling and a California blonde server girl with dark roots, hair pulled back, in a white blouse and dark pants handing out menus. She asked my group to follow our waitress and I knew her."

"Who was she?"

"Well, I don't *know*-know her, but I knew her in my dream. She was my ex-fiancée. Uh, in my dream. She didn't recognize me, so she led us down a long hallway. The paneling was gone; it was a normal, off-white textured wall again. We went through a door to the right, a heavy metal exit door, like for a theater or a restaurant. I was alone then. She was gone.

"I was outside, in a small town in Oregon, I guess, though it could have been Idaho."

"Long tunnel."

"Right. The door was still open though, so I walked back inside, trying to figure out what was going on. I walked up three steps and onto a stage inside a church. It was a wedding. The waitress, my ex-fiancée...in my dream, was walking up the aisle with her father."

20

"You went from punching aliens to a wedding?" Randy sounds wistful for the violence of the start.

Ben hasn't finished. "I was behind a baby grand piano on one side and a big wooden beam on the other. No one else could see me. She looked at me and smiled and kept on walking. The groom was waiting beneath a garden lattice, indoors for some reason. That's when I woke up."

Randy looks like he wants to laugh, but Ben takes it as a sort of uncomprehending sympathy. "That's messed up."

"I woke up thinking, 'No, this isn't right! This can't be happening!'" Ben still has to fight his desire to sweep and maybe mop behind the fridge. "I had this profound sense of grief, of loss, and I don't know what and I don't know why."

Randy sucks on his spoon and sweeps by Ben to reach the sink. "My advice is to let it go. Dreams don't mean anything. You'll drive yourself crazy if you analyze the colors of flowers on the trellis versus the time on the clock on the wall. Stick with the dreams of punching aliens. I'm telling you, there's a video game in there. I'll draw something nice and drooly for you while I'm at work."

Randy tightens the knot on his belt for emphasis, then dashes up the stairs. He has 12 minutes to shave, shower, dress, and drive to work. He's early, if only per his normal schedule.

Ben turns back to his omelette. At least the cheese has melted now.

o o o

Emily

Ben takes over one of the few square tables in a coffee shop on February 18th. He's written the date on a fresh legal pad in pen. The store is empty enough to consider it empty at 11 am on a Tuesday. Behind the counter, a cute little blonde girl fidgets with the busy-work that earns her $6.90 an hour plus tips. Toward the back of the store, a businessman, judging by his off-primary-color dress shirt (the two top buttons open, with no tie) and charcoal pants with dark socks and nice shoes, nurses a mocha in the back corner with the Wall Street Journal; perhaps he's headed to a meeting later. An older couple, presumably mall walkers on the late shift, have just left.

Outside the sky threatens to spit again. On the way here, Ben kept flicking on and off the wipers. The lowest setting was still too aggressive, making rubbery scraping noises like a senior citizen too old to care about decorum sucking little chunks of roast beef from between her bicuspids. It left long, slender puddles by the curbs that chased Ben from his office to somewhere decorated with human touches—and, hopefully, humanity.

He has two text books: one pre-calculus, one physics; the legal pad, three pages marked with polynomial refactoring problems and the rest blank; two pens; a couple of general interest magazines he didn't bother to return to the faux-African basket by the door when he sat down; and half of a tepid apple cider with cinnamon and a dash of caramel. It improves as it cools. He's doodled a little graph of temperature versus pleasure, conjecturing a causal relationship between the melting point of the caramel and the texture of the drink.

The blonde girl finishes wiping down the espresso machine and rinses her cleaning rag. It'd normally be time to mop the bathroom before the early-afternoon college student study break rush, but she pulls the rarely-used-on-other-shifts stool (tasteful red vinyl cushion, four lacquered blonde wood legs) from beneath the cupboard and

22

perches on it to thumb through an overpriced undergraduate biology book. Ben tries not to notice the gap between her navy shirt and khaki pants in back, just beneath the tidy red apron ties.

It's been six or seven long years since college math. Ben remembers not particularly caring about the areas under curves, though the idea that you can measure a curve by measuring an infinite amount of straight lines of infinitely small length still fascinates him. There's little call for calculus in the universally understimulating backwaters of business software development.

He admits again that he's not much interested in calculus for calculus's sake.

The businessman folds his paper and tilts his drink way back, making a whistling-sucking sound. He crumples and discards the empty cup on his way out the side door. He must have an 11:30 meeting. Ben has ignored the same problem for ten minutes and by now can only remember a general feeling of satisfaction from not working on it.

It's just another two-variable polynomial with cubes. He's done a dozen more just like it, numbers 11 through 35 inclusive, successfully—according to the back of the book answer key. It's not the difference of two cubes, so there has to be a common factor somewhere and somehow related to the denominator of the first expression. He holds his pen backwards in his right hand and notices himself tap his thumb against the table. He leans back in the chair again, but can't see the blonde girl out of the corner of his eye: a display of coffee-and-chocolate gift baskets blocks his view.

Also, she's pulling out the chair next to him at the table. "Math major," she asks, then turns the physics book to read the title, "or physics?"

Ben thumps the two front feet of the chair back to the ground and stares. He had already noticed the gentle curve of her bob, sweeping just below her ears, but not the faint freckles across her nose. Now

23

her smile reaches all the way to a pair of clear green eyes—she *liked* surprising him.

"Uh, philosophy, a couple of years ago. This is. . . a side project."

She skips away with the advantage. "Ambitious for a philosopher. They've already refined gravity at least twice." She drinks in his eyes with her own for a moment, all serious. Her smile returns as she laughs and ducks her head—shyly?

"I'm Emily. Pretty slow in here today. I noticed you were studying about as well as I was and thought maybe you might like some company in your distraction." She's leans over the table slightly, resting her arms on the full pages and knitting together her fingers. This is the charming posture of a good listener.

"Ben. And you're right." He tears off the neglected top paper, matching its corners carefully, and makes a precise crease with his thumbnail. Now it's a bookmark. He nods toward the stool. "Undergrad biology?"

Her face is squarish. A strong but cute jawline drops straight and solidly from her ear. Ben can't help but trace it all the way to her round little chin as she talks. "It's a required class for undeclared students. Midterms aren't too far away. The first semester was tough."

"There are advantages to studying dead Europeans who didn't know what they were writing either." He tries to keep his delivery dry, but the smile he can't keep out of his voice gives her away. He's usually good at telling jokes, but the only one he can remember right now involves cows and helicopters and is too appropriate, if contemporarily topical.

"That's next semester. I'm sure it's very practical. What does a philosophy major do, besides math problems in pen?"

It's not time to tell the grand story of How I Learned To Love Being an Unemployable College Graduate and Found a Real Job Anyway. The more often Ben tells it, the more he takes the capital letters seriously. "I write business software" often summarizes sufficiently. He's not sure if she's given him an opening or just wants something to do besides watching the big hand creep around to 12 again.

"That sounds inappropriately dull, but less messy than dissecting a lamprey." She can make no facial expression at this point that's anything but adorable, even with her nose scrunched up, eyes squinty, and a tiny triangle of pink tongue sticking out of her mouth.

"There's a surprising amount in common, really." He likes the attention enough to swallow his rant about the Rube Goldberg-as-a-caveman state of software development these days. If she actually has an interest in the conversation, she'll follow this line. He hopes.

Her best BBC World Service voice is pretty good. "Dead, slimy, and possessing a delightful aroma of preserved fish?"

Ben's full smile shows four of his upper teeth on the right side and three on the left. He's only noticed recently that everybody else is crooked and talks or sings more out of one side than the other. He can feel the long dimples on his cheeks now. "Don't forget a pile of ugly guts. I don't know if you had to put your lamprey back together, but we usually end up with parts left over." Halfway through the sentence they're both laughing, him for the uncontrollable rightness of the image and her, he starts to believe, because she's enjoying that he enjoys it.

He notices her hot cocoa. "Not a coffee fan?"

This is her chance to look a little guilty, as she rolls her eyes and shrugs. "If you weren't already a fan, you'll become an addict or a teetotaler, working here. I still love the smell, but the taste ungrew on me."

Ben worked briefly in a roastery which grew the profitable afterthought of a coffeeshop, in college. The first handful of chocolate-covered espresso beans he ate lasted for a very long time.

"I know the feeling," he says. "I'd wake up to the smell of coffee and bacon any day, but I never make either."

Her eyes flick toward his empty left hand. He's already catalogued her ring finger; it's a simple class ring. "Your roommates don't cook?" she guesses.

Ben laughs. "Randy's idea of cuisine is macaroni and cheese from a box. It's comfort food, yeah, but it's not the kind of meal I'd willingly choose on a regular basis. Oh, and yes, just the one roommate. We've been friends since college. How about you?"

"Three. Dorms: two to a room, four to a suite, one bathroom per suite."

"Cozy."

"It's an improvement over freshman dorms, with shared bathrooms for the floor."

It's Ben's turn to guess. "Junior? Kinda scary to be undeclared then."

Emily deflates a little. She slouches in her chair and stares between her arms at upside-down math. "First it was political science, then pre-law, and now I don't know what. Whatever's the easiest way to graduate next year. Anything but, you know, Communications!"

Apparently that's the last refuge of the indecisive here, too. Ben takes a pause to gather himself. "Sorry. I didn't mean to bring up the painful subject, um, of subjects."

This olive branch is enough. He watches her purse her lips into a cute little rosette before she pulls it together, with a tiny sigh.

Emily looks at him again. "No, it's watching you here working and thinking that I should be doing the same. This shift is great; it's slow and it's not full of other students but... something's missing, I guess. I'm not sure why I'm even in school anymore. I'm there because I started. Why should I finish? What's the point? What's the plan?"

"There has to be a plan?"

"Shouldn't there be?"

Ben shrugs. "I have a degree in philosophy and I write business software to move data in and out of databases. It's honest work. It pays the bills. Maybe it's not my life goal, but maybe it's what I need to do for now." He leaves unspoken how glad he is not to work any of his college jobs anymore.

She shifts in her chair, sitting up a little straighter. "For now?"

"I'm 27. It seemed old when I was 21, like the age when you have everything figured out, but every year I learn a little more. Randy and I were talking the other day about the stupid things we did in college. I wouldn't do half of those things again. In five years, I'll probably feel the same way about things I'm doing today. Oh, Randy's my roommate."

Ben has the feeling of being a very exotic bug on the floor in front of an adolescent housecat. He can't decipher the look before the way she brushes her hair back behind her right ear distracts him, and doesn't she take advantage of that? "You don't change much anymore?"

"I don't change as fast, or dramatically maybe, as I did in college. I still change though. I'm sure you'll learn more quickly than I did."

She laughs and relaxes. "You have the utmost confidence in someone you just met."

Uh oh. "Just asking the question is a good sign. Remember Socrates. 'The unexamined life is not worth living.'"

"The college professor's motto." Seeing the puzzled look on his face, she starts again, "Because they give...."

"Exams, right! Very clever." It's a moment; it's their first shared joke. His stomach flutters, roller-coaster-wise, at the thought of forever playing the straight man. He balls his left hand under the table and concentrates to fight the temptation to ask her when she works; it's always present in the presence of a beautiful woman's smile in restaurants, coffee shops, and even grocery stories. He bats away the lingering what-ifs with lonely logic: that being nice and pleasant to people is part of the job, especially when it comes to tips. Even real nuisances get at least cordial service. There's no sense in taking it for more than what it is.

Emily just stops for a second, head tilted and a faraway look in her eye over his shoulder. "Can I do something bold?" She gives the words a head start.

Ben nods. Can she read minds? "Yes," he pleads inwardly.

She reaches for his hand, and pauses! Then a shy index finger taps the pen between his thumb and forefinger. She raises an eyebrow and meets his eye. Ben nods again.

"I'm going to give you," she says, as she scribbles on the corner of a blank piece of paper, "my phone number," with her first name in cursive and underlined, "and say that I'll be free between seven and ten tonight," and tears off the corner and holds it out, "if you'd like to call."

Ben catches her very serious expression. There's uncertainty maybe, again mixed with the daring. He sees himself stand, put one hand on her shoulder and the other on her hand and promise that everything will turn out for good, but instead he says only "I would like that."

Emily pushes back the chair and stands. She pauses, holding the paper for a moment, and then tucks it in to the forgotten math book. "We'd both better get back to work, okay?"

A pair of young mothers pull open the door. Emily turns and smiles expectantly, heading barrista-casual back to the counter as they approach.

o o o

Patience

Ben lies on his bed with his left arm across his eyes. The evenings stay light longer now, just a little bit, but it's still too dark to see the magical corner next to his cell phone. He tries to burn away his nervousness with shame.

A dozen years of memories don't help: the only dance he attended, a high school sophomore standing in a corner without even his buddies to talk to. There's no greater sense of isolation for a clever 15 year-old boy than to realize he's in a situation where he has never belonged. He consoles himself now by promising himself that the only guys who didn't feel awful there will probably spend the rest of their lives looking back favorably on those days as they wait for their old men to die and leave them the deeds to the family car dealerships. At least, that's what happened with Todd Something-or-other, a weaselly little bucktoothed fellow who paid too much attention to clothes and had an awkward weak-wristed jumpshot.

Ben hasn't thought of high school in years, but trying to understand the mind of a woman always throws him back in time to 1989.

Life would be a lot easier if he found flawed women as endearing as Randy does. At least then he might not cling to the hope that

29

they have plans and goals and execute them flawlessly and deliberately. Fiercely green-eyed Elizabeth is the latest; she is a testament to human indecision in the wrong cases and stubborn decisiveness in others. When she first appeared giggling on Randy's arm, she introduced herself as "Libby".

Ben put on his best polite face to say "Hello, Libby. It's a pleasure to meet you."

In retrospect, watching her come unwired actually was a pleasure, though Ben'll never forget the disturbing and dopey "Ain't she cute in her own way?" look from Randy.

She, he learned, has a complex set of rules and protocols governing who can shorten her name in very specific circumstances. Parents can do what they want unless she has some petulant and momentary grudge, in which case her mother almost always uses the formal "Elizabeth", though it usually infuriates Elizabeth anyway as she finds this forced matronal formality condescending. "Libby" is always too informal and her mother wants to do the best friends forever, more like sisters, thing. Her father usually used puddin' which was good in private but in public you really can't pull it off without a Southern accent which he is definitely not good at in public.

"Lib" is right out.

Ben's not sure how Randy qualified to use the "Libby" moniker, unless the two met at an unholy Viking consecration ceremony on a full moon fifth Tuesday or something. In private, he thinks of her as "Lizardbreath" in memory of the older sister of a childhood friend. In very private, he replays the entire naming speech with her wearing the head of a Gila monster.

Wherever Randy finds these women, they don't last long. It's not that he loves inveterately, but he can apparently only talk about the weather or what happened at work that day or, worse, *shoes*, for a couple of weeks with any one person before the glamour fades and he's off like a mosquito at a nudist convention. Ben's also never seen nor heard an actual argument between Randy and a romantic interest on any subject that might possibly matter such as children or houses or finances or goals or even which movie to see. The bubble floats too high and pops, but there's more dish soap in the jug and everyone gathers around again to watch sunlight distort in oily rainbows floating, floating, floating....

If Lizardbreath had ever given Ben her number, he twists his mouth, he'd never have had his current dilemma. What would he say? What would he do? Should he continue the conversation about philosophy? Is this her way of hinting that they should meet somewhere outside of work? Might he rather visit her coffee shop again? Is he becoming a work-dodging, coffeeshop-lurking yuppie?

Breathe in and think rationally again, at least compared to Lizardbreath, who for all her faults is an endless source of schadenfreude to winch him away from wincing at the antics of years past. Emily's given him a, for now, preferred communication vector. At worst, she can only yell at him for calling.

It's ten short digits. He's closed his door. There's nothing on his schedule tonight except delivered Chinese food, if Randy doesn't de-carton all of General T'so's chicken while punching aliens downstairs on the big TV. Ben hopes again that he'll show the decency to use a plate instead of sucking it out of the carton as a chunky, boxy, high-protein drink. It's worse watching Randy do that with rice.

Something roils in his stomach. Is it the thought of hot, salty chicken, egg rolls, egg-fried rice, and curry vegetables—his favorite is water chestnuts, but even broccoli goes with the spicy green sauce—or the unshakable impression that he's seen Emily before?

Was it a dream? Was it a daydream? Is he slowly going crazy and imagining that he's imagined things before? He has almost convinced himself; the image is too persistent: a seated woman leans forward, with her hands clasped and her elbows between her knees. She smiles—at him. Her chin-length hair is honey-blonde, simple and straight. She has it pulled back behind her ear on the right. She wears light blue or gray—he can't tell in the photograph-flash of the vision—cotton pants, a white undershirt, and a checked, perhaps woven, jacket.

The image feels weighty, as if it's held him for years. Did he insert Emily's face as a very convenient lie? Has he fooled himself into seeing visions or thinking that he's seen visions?

It's 7:15 now, hot-smack appropriate, time-wise. It's would seem too interested to call right on the dot, but it's rude to be late, and he always hates himself later for trying to sound too casual. Right. It's time to dial.

Ben flips on the light, panting from both from nervous excitement and from sitting up so suddenly. He forces two deep breaths as he dials. He hears his heart pound in his ears; is it loud enough for the tiny microphone to broadcast the rhythm? Three rings don't help. A fourth drills through his head before voice mail clicks and chimes. A bland female voice annouces that an "Emily" (her voice on the name, for real) is not available.

Yet another familiar dilemma edges into the hollow of the first. Should he try back in a few minutes? Should he pretend he hadn't called, hoping that she has no visible logs? Should he leave a message and give her the responsibility and frightening power of calling back?

Politeness wins, if only because the beep interrupts his juggling of decision matrices. "Hi Emily, this is Ben. We met earlier today; it was a real pleasure. It's, hmm, a quarter after 7 on Tuesday." He leaves his number and hangs up, glad to have it finished but secretly wishing for the power to rewind time, practice twice, and record it again. All he really knows is that there actually was an Emily there. At least it seemed like the right number.

He toddles inwardly at the Descartean point of doubting everything except his own doubt, then forces a reset-button toggle and rolls to the right side of his bed. There's no denial possible; it's night now. He swings his legs and feet to the floor and stands, holding on to the mattress for a moment while red blood cells grudgingly start enforced mingling.

Now he knows he was hungry.

o o o

The Waiting

Randy sits on the floor with his back against the couch and his legs splayed roughly toward the TV. Only his hands move, to punish a purple game controller. On the screen, a black-clad ninja dodges fire- and acid-balls while rushing up to punch obnoxious green aliens in the face.

Some aliens are larger than others. The most bloated and monstrous rides a hovering saucer. This lovely character has slimy tentacles and an annoying tendency to cackle. Though the cackling presages a barrage of belly-launched missiles, it fortunately also leaves said alien open to punches, kicks, and what appears to be a wedgie, however out of character it seems for both ninja and alien.

The goal of the game, as Randy plays it, isn't to save Earth per se, but to punch as many aliens in the face as possible. Apparently shame is the primary motivator for the alien invasion. When the ninja so rarely fails to crush an alien's cranium with a powerful forehand finishing blow, the vanquished foe slinks away, rubbing sarian jaws and mumbling imprecations.

Ben flips the lightswitch. The standalone halogen lamp buzzes as he turns the dimmer to full power. Conic sections of light cast up to and across the corner of wall and ceiling. Randy glares over his shoulder at the light, blinking to adjust both depth perception and pupil dilation. He touches his ears to his shoulders, right first then left, then his cervical spine gives off sharp popping noises and he winces sheepishly.

A plate on the floor to his right hosts a half-eaten pile of egg-fried rice; the little hillside strip-mined by a merciless fork operation faces slow erosion from sweet and sour sauce. Chopsticks are no prime delivery vehicle for the discerning alien-punching ninja, though a fork is more hardware than Randy uses at the moment, both in and out of the game. A grain of rice dots his chin.

Ben has long had a soft spot for the Duke Nukem games, which feature similar plots. The primary story motivation is that aliens want to steal Earth women, but this game seems like a cheap knock-off. He prefers astronauts versus cavemen. He feels ready to make the argument that some cavemen would probably never use cudgels, though he can't defend the idea that a well-stocked shinobi might occasionally choose a blowdart, katana, or kodachi as necessary. In fact, the ninja *does* have access to a full range of powerful weapons, but Randy seems to be playing on a higher difficulty level with less available ammunition, more powerful and plentiful monsters, and gorier animations. Also, the latest Internet rumor promises a particularly violent chainsaw somewhere on this level.

Randy shakes out his fingers, once and twice, then returns to the game. Ben crosses behind him to the kitchen. Fortunately and half-uncharacteristically, Randy has left the boxes on the counter there along with lonely grains of rice, a single large serving spoon used in both the white rice and beef and broccoli, though perhaps in reverse order, given gray drops of gravy in the previously pristine rice, and a forest green thumb print that matches absolutely nothing in the meal or the house.

Ben wants a fully balanced supper, more than rice and whatever sauce comes with the chicken these days, and so digs a hearty helping from the nearly-full vegetable crate. Miso soup sounds good too. Though it's normally an odd dish to take out from a Chinese restaurant, the city's eclecticism has added a dash of pragmatism to local restaurants. Ben's never noticed strict distinctions between Mandarin and Szechuan styles, for example, anyway.

He pulls open the silverware drawer, then pauses over a fork before choosing chopsticks. It's not a matter of principle or an attempt to impress people. It just feels right. An odd feeling of aliveness buzzes in his head as details assault his brain; they ping off his retina and tear down optic nerve pathways and he'd like to stop or slow down but there's so much information, so much that he just can't think about phones or voice mail or hear the metronymic tick-tick of the analog clock just around the corner as the night and his appointment slip further away into memory.

Ben returns to the living room and sits on the couch to Randy's right. The coffee table is way off center; he puts his feet on it anyway.

Inside a warehouse now, Randy fights leather-clad robot female assassins in addition to the normal crew of aliens. This level has the requisite features of any violent game of the first-person perspective: muted shades of gray with occasional tans and blood reds, hundreds of identically empty crates—as the revolution always begins in the shipping district of an interchangeable major port city—and bad guys who either go down after a couple of solid hits from a decent weapon or mostly-indestructible bosses with more firepower than brains, for which evidence the games present that the winning solution is always discernible by studying the unskippable introductory animation to find one vulnerability under armor/hide/forcefield exposed when the boss cackles maniacally, ferociously regenerates powers by eating mushrooms or harvesting magic crystals, or preparing an overlong and overdramatic magic spell.

In reality, real German commanders with machine guns for arms might have given 1941 Moscow some real trouble.

"This would be a good level to hunt vampires," Ben suggests. "You could kick them through crates as finishing moves and try to make them impale themselves on the shards."

He can accept syncretism as artistic if it includes care and precision to smooth out ideas kept rough by plot and story. He likes steampunk, with its merging of cyberpunk technology and attitude with Victorian settings and sense of style. On the other side, Randy claims that taking mere entertainment things too seriously removes the fun from it.

They've had this conversation before. Ben once argued that Randy's particular line of thought would lead to situations such as ordering an ice cream sundae and receiving the wax replica shown in the commercial and having to eat it anyway or risk apparent hypocrisy. Afterwards, they merely nodded while passing in the hallway for two days.

They both agree that superhero movies rarely make for good art. Ben claims that it's mostly the sloppiness, in everything from concept through script to execution and editing—and even sometimes special effects, that plagues modern American action movies. Randy swears that very few appreciate the depth of the characters. Somehow, they've always avoided a separate debate about exactly how subtle an unshaved man in a trenchcoat can be while giving a voiceover narration about feeling conflicted about acting on his darkest urges. Ben often has to bite back the analogy that, compared to a Dick and Jane primer, Hemingway seems florid, but no one with any literary experience will confuse him with Joyce. He takes pride in his restraint: if he'd thought of it in college, he'd have won two more arguments and lost another friendship.

These water chestnuts are unusually delicious tonight. The strangely uniform one-and-a-half inch by one-and-a-half inch by three-quarters inch tofu squares are less interesting. They occur with alarming frequency from this restaurant, where he'd expect more carrots, peapods, celery, baby corn, or other vegetables besides bean curds. The cashew chicken, named not in descending order of relative ingredient volume, remains delicious. Some of the real self-crowned connoisseurs of all things Asian argue that the only passably decent

Asian food in the whole city sprawloplex is Thai. He yawns inside around snobs.

Randy's echoic memory rummages through its outbox for a crumpled scrap of paper reading "While You Were Out" and dated only moments earlier. "There's already a level with vampire aliens or something. They suck your life force, not your blood. You have to kill the invading Captain because they're a hive-mind pack. If you're fast, you can kick his head down the central staircase."

"Is the whole point of the game to throw together any possible culture-pop reference into a giant stew to see what the collective Internet can decipher in the next ten years?" An idea tickles Ben's curiosity.

"The aliens watch a lot of television."

"It's a postmodern deconstruction of consumerist culture with faux-literary digressions, full of ironic in-jokes because irony is hip, not because it's bringing to light a serious discussion or fulfilling a higher purpose?"

"Ben, you could analyze my sock drawer. No—*your* sock drawer. I've seen you hang and re-hang jeans fresh from the dryer in your closet according to what you think your weekly schedule will be."

It's true but it's not funny. He starts, "Anything worth doing is worth thinking about," but on screen now, Randy's ninja rides a jet-ski around a giant squid alien attempting to eat Atlantic City, as if anyone could tell if it succeeded. Apparently the shadow wasn't over Innsmouth at all. For this level, at least, there's no punching. Instead, the ninja throws mutant starfish. The squid blows bubbles of oil (not ink) that make the ski spin out treacherously. If Randy can throw starfishes into all of the squid's bulbous eyes, the monster will reel back in terror, allowing him to crash the ski into its maw in a death-defying leap-aside-at-the-last-moment oily explosion that will destroy the monster.

Ben's second attempt fares better. "Words mean things. If you're not going to be sincere, why be amusing? Why bother saying anything?"

"Not everything is as serious as you make it."

Ben's pants starts to vibrate just then. At first, he thinks that the giant squid has grabbed the gold ring on an ancient Lovecraftian carousel, but after the second ring he digs in his pocket for the phone. The number looks familiar, and he dashes up the stairs, plate in hand precarious, to answer. "Hello? Emily? Yes, this is Ben."

o   o   o

Thor's Day

Ante Meridian

THE bi-annual science fiction and comic book convention attracts several hundred devoted fans to a meeting center just north of town in the river delta to the east of I-5, where traffic never seems to move faster than 15 miles per hour. Ben wears a simple, pocketless black t-shirt, black jeans, and hiking boots. He feels warm, relaxed, and peaceful, almost dreamlike. He weaves his way through crowds wearing everything from actor fan club t-shirts to full book, comic, movie, and TV show costumes. It's not always pretty. Men outnumber women by twenty to one, but a naïve count based on apparent gender of outfit skews the numbers toward an uncomfortable detente.

Many of the attendees wear effectively-the-last-woman-on-earth goggles, too.

The big draw this demi annum, apart from the chance to hunch over a table full of collectible game cards, collectable miniature wargame tokens, or uncollectable but still awfully expensive imported German board games with your closest friends is the zombie Alec

Guinness and some guy who played a robot or alien in some film. Otherwise, it's exactly like normal Friday night plans, except that it's in a larger space with more people and it's daylight. Ben can't decide if expanding the coverage to include the recent trend of syndicated half-fantasy action shows is positive. Though there are often more women present—however prurient he knows it sounds, he primarily thinks the general crowd behaves slightly better with an improved gender ratio—the question and answer sessions often degenerate into asking the guest for hugs and half-panicked queries if the guest remembers the questioner from a previous con where she wore this or that costume or asked this or that stupid question.

Positively this does afford the guests plenty of opportunities to demonstrate their underappreciated acting abilities. That is, actors lie.

Ben avoids the merchandise hall passionately. Sometimes an indie company will release a new book, comic, *collectable*, but usually it's an excuse for sneering hobby store regulars to harass someone new and for bookstore owners to argue with their distributors. If you need a fresh pack of collectable gaming cards to play in a tournament, and the rules are exceedingly clear that you do need many fresh packs, you can so fortunately buy them at just over cost in the exhibit hall. Some of the booths do have autograph sessions, and if you're fortunate enough to have someone who loves fans as much as Neil Gaiman or Jeff Smith, it's worth braving the mess to spend a few moments with someone who can appreciate the magic of the moment from both sides, at least if you can avoid being squished between two sweaty comic shop employees.

Ben avoids the deliberate mondegreen of the filk sessions too, about which the less anyone says, the better. He tries to push "Paint it Black" out of his head, but keeps hearing "dwarf" instead of "door" and shudders.

One of the big auditoriums right now hosts blooper reels from some random television show. They're interchangeable; a door fails to open or an actor forgets his line and swears and the crew laughs and the audience falls out of their chairs and rolls in the aisles as if it weren't exactly the same as a M*A*S*H blooper reel from 1982—the tenth season, not the eleventh—except that the Alan Alda counterpart wears half of a puppet on his face. People pay \$45 per head per weekend for this sort of thing, though there's a sizable discount for multi-headed costumes, says a sign by the door. Ha ha. For a group of mostly adolescent males bonding over the pain of society's misunderstanding, they're surprisingly non-speciesist.

The other large rooms have their own problems. Costume contest? No. Snow White didn't have to shave his legs, but definitely earned that title for his lily-white skin. Live Action Role Playing is a vampire game. Ben can't imagine standing around in velvet and fluffy poet shirts to misquote Blake, whom he likes. Even if he felt like chatting cheerily about how depressed and disaffected he feels, he fears that he'd giggle every time someone addressed him as Greatlord Ryvenclawe Wolfensbane.

The only remotely interesting event right now is a comic session. It would be fine without the fans.

The striations of comic fan culture are endlessly fascinating as twisted reflections of the feared and hated mundane world. The bottom end of the mainstream is all the 12 year old boys who still care about the surface stories of superheroes. This is the church of the rising action, where there are no beginning and no endings, just good guys chasing bad guys perpetually and ineffectively.

Next come the 15 year old boys who've bought into the idea that a flawed superhero is an inherently interesting concept, having apparently never read multiple ancient Greek tragedies. They use this idea as a "you must be this sophisticated" shibboleth to prove their superiority over the younger group. There's *violence*, for example! Real violence, and swearing!

Ben appreciates how clever it is to market to the disenfranchised outcast, full of hormones but too skinny to get dates and too awkward to play any sport with a ball in it. There's no shortage of artists who can transcribe softcore scenes from dubious exercise videos, exaggerate human features of the bulging or bouncy kind, and steal plots from whatever soap opera's on at the time. You can almost change the yacht club into the Fortress of Justice and names such as Tiffani Vanderthorpe into Evilina Octopusgirl. Mix in a spine-crushing amount of violence without apparent consequences.

The only real source of innovation in the comic world is the rule requiring at least four variant covers for every special issue.

Manga fans sit somewhere to the left of and above the wish-fulfillment groups, mostly because the traditional difficulty in finding good imports means that only the dedicated can find anything good, but also because it's such a broad category. Ben hasn't cared enough to notice the social strictures there but suspects that giant-robot-only fans fall somewhere near the bottom of the cultural ladder.

It's not clear how to treat the people who collect little girl comics. The writers are rarely women. They're more often old men who think that kittens, rainbows, and enough pink to look like an explosion in the Valentine's Day factory will somehow attract little girls.

Finally, there's a group of mature, intelligent people who prefer comics that actually take advantage of the medium to tell literate and interesting stories. Any of those fans who've read original source material—Lovecraft almost counts, Chesterton counts, Tolkein ought to count but is pretty mainstream, and being able to quote Ambrose Bierce should count double—can make for decent conversation, though you definitely want to avoid fanboy topics like, say, variant covers and whether the black and white indy market still has value.

You can throw out easily half of this group by asking if comics are a genre or a medium. Ben always slowly backs away from anyone who seriously expresses the belief that the comic page is a new art form that deserves respect merely for breaking free of the written word.

As in any other group, the people who think they're princes and queens among men probably aren't. Anyone who has to drop names to join a conversation ("Oh, I was just talking to Alan Moore's wife's cousin the other day, and she said he's definitely doing the Swamp Thing/Watchmen crossover") instead of graciously mentioning the work of up and coming writers or artists in the hopes of passing along good fortune, scares him. He tries not to visualize a cocktail party devoted to measuring the size and integrity of lightsaber packaging. Their toys come in cellophane and, occasionally and shamelessly, kids' meals.

Ben can't actually remember consciously deciding to attend, or even actually paying at the front door.

Five or six volunteers in bright orange VOLUNTEER shirts and name tags rush to clear a path through the halls for shuffling zombie Alec Guinness. He loses fingertips with alarming frequency. The volunteers plant highway barricades in front of doors to the closed main auditorium in clear violation of fire codes, and just then a renegade band of Klingons picks a fight with the spiky haired cleaned-for-American-kids'-cable anime fans of the fighting genre—the ones where they spend most of a season trading one or two punches per episode.

A queen bee volunteer squeals. She's slightly pudgy, thirty-something, and very short with a cute, motherly face and a dark, short ponytail. Her embossed R2-D2 earrings catch the light and really bring out her eyes as she pulls Alec Guinness out of the way. In his desert wanderer robes now you can almost see that he's a minute away from Dying the Tragic Death of the Mentor. Two Klingons leap at the underprepared spike-heads. It's a distraction tactic; the other Klingons throw down a table full of amateur showcase art for cover. Figurines and maquettes of gravity-proof 19 year old women apparently capable of juggling swords and guns while performing trapeze acts go flying. Twenty percent wear racoon costumes.

Most spike-heads manage to escape, but the stupider among them squat and grunt and try to evolve into stronger forms. That doesn't work against the incoming threat of four-hundred pounds of enraged Klingons. Hairgel bleeds sadly down walls, tables, and too-shocked-to-move onlookers.

The amateur artists of the hijacked table stalk off to pen angry notes which the Comic Journal will ignore in favor of another screed either from or about Dave Sim.

The Klingons fire wildly but hold their position; there's a lot of WWII trench warfare strategy, possibly left over from a vigorous Axis and Allies tournament earlier. The blooper session pours out and several anti-Trekkie fans milling in the hallways take ricochet damage. The crowd divides: TV sci-fi fans who hate Klingons, assorted Discordians and Technopagans who love a good brawl, and anime fans. The latter are reinforcements; some of them have swords that turn into guns, or at least sharp, oversized cricket wickets that turn into guns.

A handful of orange-shirts march toward the Klingons wielding giant silver serving platters for shields. Unfortunately, they don't hold up against projectile, not energy, weapons. A pile of red-shirts and broken shards of coffee mugs grows.

All of this noise attracts the LARPers who decide that the proper response is to fan themselves with kerchiefs stowed in their sleeves. Vampires affected with self-loathing have little tolerance for violence. One yells "Get a life!" a lá William Shatner on Saturday Night Live. There are nervous titters.

Two or three spike-heads break their concentration by sprouting defensive tentacles. This gives them the rally they need to mount a reliable defense. They stop losing ground as they lob their lighter casualties into Klingon space like so many pineapple-headed human-sized spears. Lavender blood seeps through the carpet. Ben can't tell whether someone doped prune juice with stomachache medicine or some Klingon went way overboard with the makeup. Something strikes the wall above him and he looks up; he's behind a huge Bender-the-robot cutout holding a petition to bring back Futurama, which he signed willingly.

Conference security peeks his head around the same corner as a stray shot tears the last word off of poor Bender's speech bubble. Ben watches him mouth the phrase "Renew my shiny metal..." and walk away. Eight dollars an hour isn't enough to care.

The Klingons now have a two-front war. Anti-Trek pins them in on one side. The anime fans demonstrate a now-credible style by evolving greater and greater hairstyles; some have gone from blue to yellow to purple via pure concentration. Yet the Klingons have a secret weapon: their queen bee.

Take an average-looking woman, remove her makeup, and put her in an unflattering outfit apparently built around an armored corset. Layers help—think leggings, multiple slips, petticoats, and skirts, and an undershirt. A male tank top is best. Add a long-sleeved shirt, even if the sleeves don't reach to the wrists, a vest, and a jacket where again, sleeve length doesn't matter. Each layer can date from a different decade, or at least a different geologic period of fashion history. It also helps to wear as many buttons, pins, and VIP passes from as many cons as possible. A sash is optional.

She can be pretty or not; it's best to be just on either side. The important thing is that she is one of the only women around and, more importantly, is willing to put up with the kind of attention she will receive.

Most of the women he's seen so far are just honest fans—pleasant and reasonable people. However, the lure of being a queen bee is too much for a certain type of woman to resist. If she can't do it elsewhere, perhaps a law office or a junior high school, here must do.

The queen bee rules wherever she can find willing subjects. There's no shortage here. Ben blames all parties. Anyone willing to give into the illusion that the woman holding court over a table of rapt fans is the most important or attractive or interesting or beautiful woman in the world really deserves the results, Ben thinks, in the same way that people in democracies deserve their leaders. Failing to show proper deference here, though, is a whipping offense.

Strange few of the professional actresses suffer this; they've survived long enough in the business to fake politeness and realize that science fiction or fantasy television isn't exactly the Boardwalk of the entertainment world's real estate listings. Male actors are less cognizant.

The real genius of the Klingon tactic is that a queen bee commands immediate respect. It doesn't hurt that their queen bees show more than enough well-tanned-one-way-or-another cleavage, but it comes primarily from her unwavering belief that she deserves immediate respect. The hive of followers helps. Though the entire attendance as a group preaches distrust of authority (mostly from having authority come down on it so hard or at least failing to protect it from peer groups who don't secretly cry when the sensitive types compose angry poems vaguely about them or understand the allusions of the artistic types and their visually similar supervillains), it generally falls in line at the shrill whistle of "do as I say".

The gentlemanly zombie Alec Guinness shambles in to petition for peace. The remaining volunteers, and a harried con organizer with a clipboard and five years' less hair than when he started the real work six months ago, watch him from around a different corner. He's also capable of commanding authority. The 5'9" actor (an inch shorter four years after his passing) has no chance against the 5'2" Klingon warriorette, who's admittedly 5'6" in heels with an impressive bosom not out of place at a Renaissance Faire, which Ben calculates would require less makeup—and not just on the face—but just as much whalebone. Of her dozen Klingons, eight still offer serious suppressive fire, two are clearly casualties, and three or four huddle and whisper plans to sneak Romulan Ale into the Grand Ball later. Ben had some once. It's just three-dollar wine with four dollars worth of blue food coloring added. She brushes past the actor, then jinks to avoid gun-sword fire and accidentally knocks him into a wall. He crumples.

Anime fans tend to be a little younger than the Klingons—high schoolers rather than college kids and disgruntled record store employees. Most of a cubic meter of actual factual real female bosom is a major distraction. That's it for the spike-heads. A half-hearted anti-Trek/Klingon skirmish continues, but it has mostly degenerated into self-described "hilarious" Shatner impressions and toupee jokes that weren't funny the first time, ten cons ago.

Ben takes another bite of the chocolate and peanut butter granola bar he didn't know he had out of the backpack he doesn't remember carrying. He hums as a preemptive measure to block out the parley.

"What are y'all doin' to ma boys?" she screeches. "Y'all need to sho' some respec' before I throw you on outta here! This is ma con! This is our room!" She launches a string of unimaginative profanities that even these guys outgrew in junior high school.

Randy will love hearing about this later, though Ben hopes it's from another friend secondhand. He cringes trying to imagine how he could possibly explain why a Klingon has a Georgian accent. He suspects that she's used the words "huggles" and "LOLLERS!" in actual face-to-face conversations.

The whole scene is a lot less funny in person, with the orange-shirts unable to master conference rule number one (don't kill your guests, even if they're already dead) and six (no actual fireable gunswords or working phasers with costumes) of conference organizing, the Klingons unable to use the elements of surprise, organization, and arguably superior firepower to overcome their foes, or the fact that the spike-heads, having put up a credible defense in the end, look ready to cry after a lecture delivered in Internet chat room format from a housewife and mother of two who probably can't inspire the same discipline in her children, husband, dogs, or even lawn.

By gum, she has it here, Ben reflects. The anti-Trek fans start singing and reenacting a Leonard Nimoy music video about hobbits. The severed head of zombie Alec Guinness comes to a rest at his feet.

o o o

Being Awake Again

There's a crack in Ben's world. That's how sunlight spills through a thumb-sized gap on either side of the window blinds. If he were more awake he'd call them legally-blinds. This is okay in the spring and not so bad in the fall when the sun rises over the mountain at a humane time, but the middle of summer is awful and the waning of fall allows the solar system's largest and least reliable alarm-clock to hit its own snooze button and sleep in for a while. Without that, Ben has no hope of waking on time.

There's a dry, gluey taste in his mouth, as if he'd slept with it open all night. His blanket is half off of the bed, all sideways, and the top sheet has twisted around his legs, pushing his pajamas up to his knees and leaving ropey marks on his calves. He doesn't remember sleeping on his belly, as he can only ever fall asleep on his back, and wonders why he feels as if he's landed ungracefully from an airplane without aid of parachute, brushing through a few soft pine trees on the way down.

He wants to watch "The Bridge on the River Kwai" again.

It's almost 7:30. He can make it to work by 8:30 if he rushes, assuming twenty minutes to shave and to shower, fifteen minutes for breakfast, and twenty minutes of driving. It takes forty by bus, but there's a special lane, a dedicated schedule, and he can usually find a quiet seat and read for most of the trip. It feels like less of a waste that way, though he's lately started to go through Randy's bookshelf of genre fiction. He's never envied the other techies—or worse, MBAs—who compulsively read and write e-mail on various unreadable and unworkable PDA screens and keyboards. Paper, to him, feels tangible, besides the fact that even the roughest paper and worst mass-market printing has quality of details perhaps six and maybe ten times that of a really good and detailed screen. Maybe it's the organic connection to the earth; he appreciates finding an incompletely pulped page, with words marching across an embedded chip of a tree. The smell of the binding glue also reminds him of that terrible, horrible gum that used to come with collecting cards during the early '80s, the kind so bad it would have been better to eat the cards and throw away the gum.

He feels guilty now that he's never seen "Lawrence of Arabia" and doesn't really know much about the history of the peninsula. Maybe he'll watch it this weekend, after blocking out three and a half hours of seriously devoted couch-sitting, if he can stake a claim to the big TV downstairs before Randy discovers a Supergirl marathon.

Now it's 7:40 and he definitely won't make it to work by 8:30 unless he foregoes shaving. Maybe it's time to grow a beard. He also will have to rush through the shower, and even so he'll need to run into an Omega Man situation with regard to traffic today, though in that case the point of going to work vanishes. He can arrive as late as just before 10, as he's on salary. Also, his boss has worked whatever necessary magic so that the programmers on this project at least can leave early if they've done all of their work at sufficient quality. About half of them work from 10 'til 7 pm, when they rush out in packs for a quick meal before converging on some interchangeable club to see one of a dozen indistinguishable bands. The other developers leave around 4:30 pm to avoid traffic. His latest estimation puts the quiet hour between 8:30 and 9:30 am as worth almost three or four hours of core-hours productivity.

Ben pushes himself up onto his elbows and massages his eyebrows with his lower palms. Partially, he knows, at least when he's more awake, that his refusal to set the alarm clock, instead relying on both his internal timer and his body's desire to regulate its own schedule, is counterproductive. He has a vague and growing sense that his dreams are exhausting, in the same sense as the original Star Trek movie—overlong, overdramatic, and full of symbols and images that never make up for the lack of an interesting and coherent plot. He worries most when they bleed over into his conscious mind for the day.

Now it's 7:47. Subvocal biological imperatives sing a wordless reveille, not just the obvious of one particular internal organ feeling really really full, but also another important organ feeling really really empty. His head has stopped pounding, but his feet are cold from exposure to the air.

He sits up to untangle himself from the sheets, not regretting the motion as much as he does the fact that he's wasted twenty minutes thinking about old films for no good reason when he could be eating breakfast now. He swings his legs over the side of the bed, flinching as his knees crack for no good reason and pads stiffly to the dresser for a pair of socks and fresh underwear. His bathrobe rests on a hook on the back of the door. He grabs it and throws it on, holding it closed while he ducks down the hallway into the master bathroom.

Time flies with hot water involved, though he saves two minutes by opting for the beginning of a goatee. He invests thirty minutes in showering, dressing, and making his bed. As he staggers down the stairs, hair still dripping, for breakfast, he sees Randy Randy with his latest cereal monstrosity.

"Hey there stranger. Working long hours yesterday? I didn't hear you come in last night."

Ben shrugs. "Normal day."

Randy pantomimes a double-take at the lateness of the time and rushes up the stairs. It's his normal morning routine. Ben munches cereal and grabs the paper for something to read. Wednesday, November 16.

Only when leaving the house does he see today's paper on the step. It's Thursday's paper, November 17. Then he remembers what Randy said and why a little voice urged him to argue. He *did* talk to Randy when he came home. Then he went straight to bed. That was Tuesday night.

Unless this is an elaborate prank where Randy cooked up an entire newspaper—comics, classifieds, and ads—to convince Ben that it's Thursday, Ben's lost a day somewhere. It's 8:33 am and he's almost a day late for work.

o o o

Work

Ben parks in the subsidized lot a block away from his company's building. He sneaks in through a side door, lest he meet anyone who noticed his apparent absence. Either even public radio is in on the prank or he really did lose a day somewhere. He finds listening to NPR while commuting so boring it's soothing. Also, he tends to speed to loud music, so he rarely gives himself the chance. The poor choice of radio stations in the city helps, with the huge corporate conglomerate with a deejay in San Francisco pretending to be a local deejay in several West Coast markets, the same playlist on at least three local stations on a two-second delay across them, and an awful choice of music based more on which acts and songs the labels want to promote than musicality, originality, or quality. At least, that's his current argument for pretending to care about the fate of kumquat farmers in Belize. Sometimes he parrots back the BBC World News announcer's accent.

Ben's company takes up three floors of a nine-story office building downtown. Most of the programmers stay on the sixth floor, with sales, marketing, and support on the fifth and management and various meeting rooms on the seventh. The idea of trying to be sneaky doesn't seem fully rational yet, but his best guess is that people will leave him alone if they think he's working and will forget any oddness as the day wears down. He scurries to the underused elevator on the east side of the building.

He's lucky; the security guard downstairs doesn't care and he meets no one he knows. Ben flips on his light switch and pulls out his chair when a greeting too cheery for a programmer at 9 am makes him jump.

"Hey, Ben! Running late, huh?"

It's Andrew, the politest New Yorker at least in the city and possibly in the world. Ben has the recurring image of Andy smiling and waving to a cabby who's nearly run him over. They probably kicked him out for being kind to tourists. Ben once found himself in agreement about New York City with a Texan, which alternately frightened and inspired him.

Andrew wears a baby blue dress shirt with shockingly white and starchy collars and cuffs with gray trousers and milk chocolate-brown shoes. The office only hints at a dress code, at least since the managers took over another floor and acknowledged that the programmers would thus rarely have meetings with customers who might entertain the silly idea that the quality of software correlates to the discomfort of the programmer. In practice, it does: inversely.

Ben unconsciously checks that his black polo shirt remains tucked into the cleanest pair of blue jeans he could find. He checked it in the elevator, too. His ubiquitous hiking boots are on the high end of the informal policy which regards footwear as an allowed accessory. He's divided most of the programmers by age and experience and graphed that against the average level of formality of their clothes.

For example, a new recruit, Danny, interviewed, even with the programmers, in a full suit and tie. In under two weeks he had set a new schedule for wandering into the office near the crack of 10 am in grungy athletic socks and old concert t-shirts, like most of the rest of the twenty-somethings. Almost everyone over thirty-five has an affinity for shirts with buttons.

Outliers occupy space on both sides of the Oxford shirt-gap. This includes the twenty-two year old Andrew as well as Eric, a grizzled fifty-something Unix programmer whose entire wardrobe, as far as anyone can tell, consists of t-shirts from motorcycle gatherings. No one else could pull off that look, not without a graying-blonde Santa Claus beard or the jolly spare keg.

With today's wardrobe data collection well under the way, Ben feels sufficiently composed to reply. "Oh, hi Andrew. Yep, a bit late today."

Andrew shakes his 16-ounce steel thermal coffee mug. "Need caffeine!" It's a common programmer joke, which means both that it has never been funny and that at least half of them make that joke at least once a day.

Ben auto-responds, "You know it!", raising his own "Code Monkey" mug in response. Andrew's only being friendly on his way back from the coffee room. He doesn't know anything; he's already moved on to laugh and brighten someone else's morning, regardless of any practical effects he could have. Ben slumps back into his chair and breathes. The real test will be to see his inbox.

His near-obsession with keeping his e-mail clean has reached the point of monitoring a hierarchy of folders to store messages related to various projects and to and from a dozen someday-useful mailing lists. His real discipline comes in a twice-daily Sherman's-march to the sea, once just after he arrives and once just before he leaves to cut a swath through everything with the intent of demoralizing any potential resistance and preventing new growth in the near future.

Throughout his day he pokes and prods at things while avoiding a particularly onerous task or waiting for his mental gears to shift, but he always practices restraint, knowing full well that responding to the wrong person or list at the wrong time will fill up his inbox faster than he can deal with it.

He's a programmer. It happens anyway.

Today's light. Besides the usual midweek mailing list traffic, one company-wide message about a meeting on the benefits program stares back at him alongside two spams that have escaped the company filter and a status report from a junior programmer Ben recently agreed to mentor on the current project. That's it. He has no new tickets assigned, no bugs, no feature requests, and nothing awaiting his review. The only visible artifact of his missing day so far is the fact that he has three messages in his inbox, whereas normally he'd have maybe twenty-five or thirty, and that strikes him as backwards.

He thinks about leaving his office immediately for hot tea, as he still holds his mug, but then tells himself that it will be his reward for filing his new mail. The benefits program message goes away. The other message makes him regret his promise. His partner on the project wants to know how the persistence layer works. He thinks he's found a bug.

The persistence layer is the hairiest part of the code. Ben sometimes uses the word "hirsute" as a synonym, in part to avoid the cliche and in part because he amuses himself by mentally mispronouncing it as "hair suit". He sighs and leans back in his chair to chase down his thoughts.

How can he explain the system? He's tried, many times, when people ask "So Ben, what do you do?" or "How's work?" or "What's new?" Some day, he swears, he'll refine his explanation into perfection, so that his conversational partner will smile and nod with new understanding.

The complexity comes from what thoughtful programmers call an impedance mismatch. Unthoughtful programmers don't think of impedance mismatches, but it's not a good term anyway. He won't use it. Programmers actually mean that there is a conceptual mismatch. Ben doesn't have the electrical engineering background necessary to explain exactly what an impedance mismatch is in technical terms: the part of math that explains imaginary numbers of opposite signs never really comes up in philosophy classes. Though they do often talk about imaginary things, they avoid strenuously any appearance of even wanting to add or subtract to or from them, let alone compare them. He made *that* mistake while talking to his sister-in-law, who actually is an electrical engineer.

Right. An impedance mismatch leads to wasted power and increased noise in a system, which is a decent enough metaphor. His post-breakfast and inter-commute lull has started to fade.

Okay, it's a conceptual mismatch. That's simple. He can explain that. The two main parts of the system jeer at each other across a deep chasm of misunderstanding: the database and the code. It's the difference between a filing cabinet full of records and a room full of self-motivated workers, or at least worker robots who respond to simple commands. They're robots; the unifying image Ben's group has chosen for this project is of an automated assembly line. The financial reporting application will, when finished, allow businesses to track expenses and receipts and analyze all of that information in various ways which, while not actually interesting to accountants, are fundamental to their work.

Emily *hated* the robot analogy. "Robots? Is that all men think about? Robots, sports, cars, explosions?" He tried to explain the idea of modern factory automation. She gave him the look.

He himself can't entirely accept the notion of an assembly line as it fits the generally accepted practices of accounting, but it's only for the benefit of the programmers. When Andrew or Eric talks about the conveyor belt, everyone else ought to know that they mean the part of the program that runs data through various financial manipulation routines.

The database is basically a high-powered filing system. That part seems to stick with everyone. His parents mostly understand. Emily picked it up right away. Randy either absorbed it or let it bounce off his head.

He almost has his script memorized by now. Imagine a room full of filing cabinets. This is our database. There's a librarian with a gun standing at the entrance. I'll take questions later. His job is to help you find what you're looking for and to prevent you from doing any damage while you're in there. Every filing cabinet has records, but each drawer has only one type of record. We could have a filing cabinet representing people in the military, with names, ranks, and serial numbers, so the cabinet will have three drawers and one piece of paper in each drawer for each military person it knows about, and each paper has a simple word or phrase or scrap of data on it. If you want to know everything about a military person, the librarian grabs the three pieces of paper for that person and makes a copy for you.

His father Daniel particularly liked the military images. "Semper Fi!", he mock-saluted.

This is good. The librarian knows how to do this because it has a kind of map of all of the records in all of the cabinets in the room, and it has some amazing mind tricks so that it can flip through all of the pieces of paper in a cabinet very quickly.

Ben leans back in his chair and rests just the tips of his boot heels on the desk between his keyboard and a thin yellow legal pad full of doodles from this week's meetings. Maybe an interactive presentation will be clearer. It could be a puzzle, or a riddle.

"Why are there multiple drawers in each cabinet?" he asks, Socrates-style. It's the same reason that every record has a piece of paper in each drawer. You might not want to know every piece of data about a subject at any one time, especially as things grow more complicated. Imagine if you stored every possible interesting piece of data about a person: hair color, eye color, favorite flavor of ice cream, shoe size, number and placement of freckles, average preferred water temperature in the shower, and so on. If you want to know your friend's birthday and asked the librarian, you wouldn't want to receive a six-foot tall stack of facts! That means good database users have the habit of asking for exactly what they want—and only that—instead of going through all of the work, at least metaphor-wise, of carting back handtrucks full of records. Ben underlines the word "good" twice to emphasize its moral component.

Randy helped him with the list of bizarre attributes. Ben always proceeds over "and so on" very carefully so as to leave out the less palatable possibilities that never stray far from his conscious mind during that sentence.

Another thing you have to remember, he lectures silently, is that while you're looking up data in the room, so are other people, and they might be adding new files and update old ones. Good librari-ans will prevent you from bumping into other people. Really good librarians make sure that all of the data in the room is correct, as far as they can tell by knowing more or less how the data should look if not what it signifies. It's supremely important that people receive the most accurate and up to date information possible but only as soon as someone updating it has actually finished filing the new data in every drawer necessary, so only one person can change a thing at a time.

That's why the librarians have guns; they have a lot of power because they have a lot of responsibility.

He's happy to have sneaked a Spider-man reference past Emily for once.

There are other complications, such as when you realize that you can simplify the room by making another cabinet that holds only addresses and you can take all of the information about a military person's address and a normal person's address and store it instead of in each separate cabinet only in the address cabinet. The librarian knows to look in both cabinets and combine the information when you ask about a Marine, for example, but that stretches the image, at least more than the idea of pistol-packing librarians, records stored vertically in filing cabinets, and filing cabinets with potentially hundreds of drawers and nearly unlimited depth do.

"Son, you don't *ask* about a Marine. He'll either tell you or you will deal with it."

The important point is that an entry in a database is a lot like a file from a filing cabinet; it's a bunch of labeled data. His mother compared it to filling out paperwork at a doctor's office. "Good point, but not so much busywork," he admitted.

Ben leans forward in his chair over his desk to adjust the blinds. He has his desk pushed almost against the window to minimize the glare on the screen. The morning light pleases him, especially as it falls on the plant he's never quite researched enough to remember the type. As darkness starts to take itself seriously in winter nights, he closes the blinds; its blackness bothers him as if it were the pupil of a giant eyeball pressed against his window.

He sighs. The databases explanation is solid. Everyone in the past few conversations stayed with him to that point. Objects are more difficult, but Ben really likes them. When he feels especially perverse to everyone who asks "Why do you have a degree in Philosophy?" he describes objects in terms of Platonic ideals and types, not "the building blocks of modern software."

The goal of creating and using objects is to minimize all of the potential connections and the complexity of those connections between pieces of your code. His job is basically to produce a simulation of the real world. The part he likes is writing a sort of blueprint for the object. You know what's important about the robots in your factory and as far as the objects care, that's their inherent robotness. As long as you treat all of the robots appropriately, keeping in mind that ideal, it doesn't matter whether the robot is tall or short or has a friendly face or goes into a murderous rage and kills tourists, as long as it has that inherent robotness that you and it both respect.

Randy made a list of suggestions for ways to kill tourists. Ben used "washing puppies" for his mother Ellen and his sister-in-law Mary. Puppies are cute.

Ben argues that this is the difference between telling someone "Go make your favorite sandwich" and telling someone to open the fridge, take out the peanut butter and jelly, and go fetch a butter knife first, but don't forget to open the jar, yes both jars, and so on. At some point you have to have something that knows how to make a sandwich, but by dividing the world into objects and sending messages between them, you let those people that really like peanut butter and jelly know how to make their favorite sandwiches and those people who prefer egg salad to know how to make that kind and you, the bossy person reminding everyone to eat lunch, only have to know how to tell everyone how to make their sandwiches. You remain free of any idea of how long you have to boil the eggs—three minutes, same as usual. You don't even have to know which mustard to use. The right answer, of course, is brown mustard, because the yellow stuff is technically pabulum and usually more just pablum, in the cereal sense. Likewise, strawberry is better than grape jelly. Jam is better still.

"So an object is like a recipe?" his mother wondered.

"It's more like the way a cake has frosting and the cake itself and a message written on top and that fantastic raspberry filling. It has separate pieces that are unique to the type of cake. Do we have any cake left?"

All of this is background to the real problem which is that a filing cabinet in the database room represents one slice of information and probably not all of the information an object needs to know. A person has an address and a favorite sandwich and a name, maybe a rank, and possibly a serial number, as well as a shoe-size, et cetera. If you just want to tell someone to make a sandwich, how much information does that person really need to know about himself? Does shoe-size have a correlation to preferred sandwich? Does rank? What if you don't even need to know that you're dealing with someone in the military? Do you need the librarian to hand you a file with all of the military-specific information?

At this point, he's lost almost everyone already. Even his own tummy growls.

The odd part is how this well-intentioned monologue never stops people from first, asking "What kind of work do you do?" and second, asking for advice about their own computers. At least his immediate family has stopped asking. It's difficult to explain the poetic beauty of well-designed software with clear boundaries between entities and accurate ideas of what each part should do while you're up to your arms in badly-designed and insecure software randomly eating your precious data and vomiting error messages.

He considers his coworkers, who really do understand this stuff. Some of them are die-hard gamers, who in decades past might have spent their precious non-work daylight hours rebuilding carburetors and tuning fuel mixtures to tease ever-decreasing amounts of performance out of cars. Now their hobby drives them to swap various computer parts in and out of multiple machines.

Commoditization means that this works; just as you can install one hideous yellow monster windshield wiper on your car to, in theory, decrease wind resistance, so too can you also purchase various and mostly ugly cases and huge squat fans to improve air flow through a computer. The premise is that this will allow you to do more and more impressive things, as faster and powerful both almost always bring a big bag full of heat to the party. Heat is pretty much the natural enemy of computers. Ben wonders right now if the reason so many programmers go barefoot is to improve their own temperatures.

That doesn't explain the preference for facial hair, however, which would seem to hold heat in.

He never gets much done before the daily meeting at 10. Just about everyone else arrives at the crack of 9:45 to make a pilgrimage to the great coffee shrine. Some also detour through the wilds of their inboxes before slouching in to grab a comfortable spot on the wall, possibly sharing a harrowing tale of the expedition with a fellow mendicant. The gamers have daily tales of adventure without actually having to live through anything.

Ben still has his left hand curled around his mug when his two minute meeting warning chimes. Somehow the good half-hour of spare time he sneaked out today has flown away. The code monkey looks thirsty. It's meeting time.

o o o

Just Standin' Around

Just about every programmer Ben knows claims productivity as his great motivator, using it to avoid meetings, to walk away from boring conversations absentmindedly, or, in extreme cases, not to shower or shave or change clothes. This claim is sometimes true. Other times it's an excuse to waste time on other things.

He can't tell the difference. Programming is a creative work. The goal is to solve a problem once, elegantly, then move on to new problems. If you find the same problem again, re-use the solution. Maybe reinventing a solution is interesting when studying programming or when experimenting with a different technique or programming language, but any external pressure not to reuse code will cause what passes for revolution among prideful coders.

He's seen developers try self-organization themselves. It always devolves into respectful anarchy. The best programmers often like leading other people the least. Any order imposed from outside either has to carry the weight of paycheck authority and endure the general disrespect that in any group with more motivation to actual action might signify genuine rebellion, or make a compelling case in language that developers might deign to understand. They're not all Missourians; it just seems that way.

Ben considers his perspective enlightened; his philosophy degree must be worth something more than fast-food vocational training. Assembly-line workers, of course, respect more those plant bosses who roll up their sleeves and put together a few widgets himself now and then to save their employees from mandatory overtime for a tight deadline. Above some brass ceiling, you absolutely have to play golf and the meritocracy ends. Then you become management and stop coding forever.

He holds his breath and tries to hold a single thought in his head instead of counting the steps from his office to the meeting room. He did only once, for a lark, and now alternates between trying to find the shortest path and recounting to verify the number.

The daily meeting is a compromise between management and developers. It's a block of time in which no developer writes any code. It also saves potentially dozens of smaller, spontaneous conversations throughout the day, when they actually *might* write code instead of picking at their mail and wishing it were lunchtime.

Ben this week is the amanuensis. Like administrative assistants everywhere, he objects to the alternate term, though he regrets not having robes to wear during his week with the pad. Everyone else must stand. In theory, this means that physical discomfort will keep the meeting short. It often even works.

Jerry calls the meeting to order. He's the head of the department, a half-programmer and half-manager. Ben's mnemonic for his name is "Garcia", more for his outlook on the world than style of dress, living, or musicality. While other people can translate between the two dialects spoken on the two floors, Jerry apparently enjoys it.

The remaining twenty programmers mark the edges of the room. The department has two teams with fluid numbers and smaller sub-teams of various configurations depending on the current project. Right now, the financial reporting system is big enough to claim all of Ben's team for at least the next couple of months. Yet they all meet together, every day.

A twenty-person meeting quickly grows unwieldy. Ben's rough margin math estimates a minute per person maximum to summarize the results of yesterday's work and the goal of today's work. In practice, fifteen or twenty seconds usually suffices for almost everyone. That leaves more time for anyone who has learned something interesting or who faces something really tricky. He stopped writing everyone's name down two days into his first term; everything moves too fast. Now he concentrates on drawbacks and conquered challenges.

Today is predictably dull. Work continues. Carlann found a tricky spot in figuring out the appropriate workflow for auditing signoffs for Sarbanes-Oxley compliance and wants someone to work with her this afternoon. Ben notes this dutifully in blissful routine, and then it's his turn for the penultimate report.

He hides his brief panic behind pen scratchings until he finds his ten-second lie. "I have another day or so shaking out the bugs in the SQL statement optimizer."

People nod. It's complicated code: a program that writes programs. Ben loads a toy clay mold with varicolored non-toxic clay, pushes a lever, and squeezes out a circle, star, triangle, or square-shaped lump of goo. This robot-to-librarian translator has to run quickly, producing very precise language and transferring across meanings so nuanced that the librarian can find the optimal path between various filing cabinets.

The meeting ends at just under twelve minutes. Everyone files back to their offices in little clumps of twos and threes.

As Ben tears off today's notes to post on the corkboard, Jerry speaks.

"Nice to have you back today, Ben. I've always admired your penmanship." He may be the only person who could sound sincere saying that. "Productive meetings yesterday?"

He only needs to evade for a couple of seconds. "It's hard to say what'll happen. You know."

"True. I'm glad it wasn't me for a change. Maybe they'll listen to you. Hey, let me hang those up for you." He stabs a bright red pushpin through the paper. It pivots, then hangs straight.

Only during the seventh dip of his apple-cinnamon teabag in the hot water does Ben finally decide that, whatever happened, he didn't go to any meetings yesterday.

o o o

The Grind

It takes twenty minutes to immerse himself in code. There's a sweet spot from 11 to 12:30 when, if he closes his door, ignores his e-mail, and turns on the classical music station, he can write about a day's worth of code. It's not the code of the typical twenty-year-old caffeine-fueled monkey either, with misspellings, strange bugs, and a disorganized stream-of-consciousness flow that either needs an editor of the literary sense, or the programmer equivalent of German shepherds coaxing an anxious and skittish mob into neatly organized lines. In the five years he's programmed professionally, he's developed some discipline.

Ben has several rules.

First, he never codes while tired. If he's having an unproductive day and isn't making any progress, he'll go for a walk, work on something else, or, if it's close enough to 4:30, call it a day. It's a good rule, when he actually notices himself getting too tired to code. Still, it's a good rule.

Second, he never keeps dirty code. It's as distasteful in his mind as eating at a diner where the old waitress who calls everyone "Hon" wears no hairnet and chain-smokes while relaying plates from the kitchen. Maybe the results will have character, but there's a good chance of picking up something really weird and unpleasant and hard to shake. He never told his father about the entire day he spent trying to find the perfect name for a file, though.

Third, he works in very small steps. He can keep a lot of strange details in his head, but if something goes wrong, he'd rather rely on the computer's notes than his faulty memory. He's noticed that all programmers are optimists, at least regarding everything but their own lives, believing that things should just work without any evidence that they actually do.

Finally, he almost always goes for the simplest approach, invoking the subtractive spirit of Antoine de Saint-Exupery. It's part pragmatism and part elegance. He has tried to articulate this simple and ephemeral beauty only once, on a late-night call with an out-of-town Emily. It's not a painting of, for example, a blue square on a white background, but the idea that that painting is effective at what it is.

Emily's response was itself effectively simple. Where's the art in code?

Ben once spent twenty minutes pulling knots out of the shoelaces out of a pair of old sneakers headed for the trash. He allows himself to feel the same sense of relief, as if he had made the world a little cleaner. She appreciated that argument better. They spent the next weekend discussing the similarities of law and code. He's since intended to write an article encouraging programmers to increase their knowledge of and activity around legal issues of shared importance.

Without her to proofread it he's never worked up the motivation.

His current code resembles tangled tendrils of spaghetti more than shoelaces. Writing a translation layer is always tricky. It's an apt metaphor: both the objects and the librarian have their own dialects and idioms that cross language boundaries badly. He pantomimes conducting a huge, complicated business transaction in single-syllable words and rhyming sentences of only six words apiece, without even gestures. Then he re-checks that his office door remains closed.

In certain circumstances he doesn't yet understand, the translator goes crazy and instead of asking for directions to the nearest museum in perfect conversational phrases, it asks perfectly for the ingredients of a pizza. If it were gibberish, the librarian would rightly refuse the request and kick the requester robot out of the library. The robot can handle this, dutifully reporting that circumstance up its chain of command until a supervisor rings up someone who can look into the problem. Usually and hopefully that someone is someone like Ben, who can fix things before an actual user discovers a false cognate problem. The real problem is that both the requester robot and the librarian give and receive what seem to be logical responses and requests, at least when the robot has to try to make some sort of sense of an answer given to a question unrelated to the question actually asked.

Sometimes Ben himself answers an either/or question with only yes or no. He spent a whole weekend in the doghouse once not so much for saying "no" to "Would you like to watch a movie or go out dancing?" but for asserting that his was a reasonable and logical answer.

Rule number four sometimes fails with people.

Bughunters are one part detective, one part janitor, and one part historian. He wonders how he'd look in a fedora. There's often a twisted path of clues and misdirection. There's usually a mess to clean. The most important part of the process is recreating a situation and understanding why it happened—and then fixing it in the smallest, least intrusive way possible. Sometimes that works.

In general, the closer he adheres to his sense of good taste in code, the easier it is to find and to fix bugs. From this he derived rules two through four. It reminds him at other times of reading poor translations of Hegel and Nietzsche. The longer the sentence, the more abstract the words and concepts, the easier it is to lose yourself on a sea of ideas, far from your destination and dry land, instead adrift in exceptions and preconditions to land in places unknown and unexpected and misunderstood. Kant too.

The right approach is rarely "See Spot run" simplicity, but it's often that vague and unwieldy expressions hide the real issues—by design. They instead stand up and yell that the author didn't really understand; who knows what he's done amidst flourishes, cantilevers, and cornices? Ben's joy is the expression of clarity, the elegance of simplicity, and the pragmatic beauty of efficacy.

A bug is ugly. It's not the beautiful bilateral symmetry of nature under a powerful microscope. It's not the diversity of life to a biologist. A meatball tumbles off of a paper plate onto a white shirt and khaki pants, to roll under the buffet table where it sulks, lonely and forgotten and unfulfilled.

Ben recalls the onion bagels someone left in the break room. He likes cream cheese with pineapple. Breakfast has worn off; he's punchy.

Debugging is another battle in the never-ending war against entropy. He staves off the impending heat-death of the universe by a few seconds by bringing more order into the world, making his own corner of it more perfect. As a sub-Creator, only he can build something original, something never before seen, right now.

He catches himself watching his thoughts march away and invokes Corollary B to Rule One. Never work past a meal.

Ben has narrowed the problem down to one section of code. The robot always tells the translator exactly what it needs from the library. The librarian always looks up exactly the right thing, every time. Yet somewhere in one particular type of request involving records of depreciable values, the request changes subtly in the translator's mind between hearing and repeating in another language, turning from depreciation into the addresses of accounts payable.

No one has shuffled the location of the filing cabinets without telling the librarians. Everything still follows the Dewey Decimal System. Still, the translator's effectively performing non-deterministic light-speed linguistic drift. Ben's an American soldier turning back the Vichy from raiding L'Académie française and...he's doing it again.

The nice little sandwich shop downstairs makes a marvelous turkey, Swiss, and tomato sandwich with guacamole spread on Wednesdays. A cup of vegetable soup fills out the meal. Once, they even floated radish rosettes inside.

His elevator has just passed the third floor when he realizes again that it's Thursday.

o o o

The Unexpected Boot

Post-BLT, Ben sees Jerry smoking outside the door and typing on a little PDA. He didn't know Jerry smoked. Ben nods and pulls open the door, but Jerry touches his arm.

"Ben, it didn't work. I'm sorry. We're having an all-hands meeting in fifteen minutes. Can you make sure everybody's there?" His hands tremble and he suddenly ages ten years.

Ben nods again. "Conference room?"

"That's right. Thanks." Jerry returns to his PDA.

Fifteen minutes later, there aren't enough chairs for everyone around the table, so half of the team is standing. Jerry walks in behind the VP of development and the quiet murmur hushes. Jerry looks sick, just like Ben felt the first time he went to a bar: half nervous and half nauseated from cigarette smoke and humanity's underlying quiet desperation.

A shuffling, scraping noise upstairs ends with a thump. Sometimes the sales guys close a big deal and jump around like wildmen.

Jerry croaks several meaningless mumbled syllables, then pulls it together. "Thanks for being here everyone. I'm sorry about the short notice. You all know Ned, the head of our department. Ned?"

Ned's out of place on this floor. The fact that he owns any suit, let alone a well-matched and obviously tailored suit, is sufficient evidence. He looks out over the developers unblinkingly. "Thanks, Jerry." It's a throwaway. "I just came down to tell you all how proud we are of you. Without you, we'd have nothing. You're the backbone of the company and I know you can handle any challenge we face.

"As you know, we've bid on some big conversions lately. We've just won our largest project yet."

There's a murmur. This is great news. It's hard work, and dealing with legacy systems is painful, but this is the big goal. They're a serious company now. They do multi-year projects for huge customers.

"The deadline is three months. Effective immediately we're suspending all leave, temporarily."

Ben watches John turn a peculiar shade of reddish green. He's a week away from his wedding and a two-week European honeymoon.

"I know you'll make it. We're all pulling for you. I don't have to tell you how important this is to us. If we make this, we're swimming with the big dogs."

Fish. Running. Ben reassembles that sentence to make it make sense. He hopes it's the key to understanding the whole speech. Sometimes he diagrams sentences as if they were three dimensional puzzle pieces. Ned's in non-Euclidean space.

"That's it. We're counting on you. Thanks, guys!"

Ned's MBA shark-scurry takes him back to the safety of the elevator while the mob is in shock, not lynch, mode. The sacrificial Jerry throws Ben another look again and all Ben can think of is how they've already spent six months on the current project, and it's all new development. It's not a legacy system at all.

o o o

Firsts

Lunch

IT's taken two weeks of scheduling to meet again. First Ben had to cash in his promise to visit high school friends with Randy in Vancouver one weekend. Then Emily had midterms. Instead they passed the time with lingering phone calls, just learning how it felt to talk to each other.

This solved Ben's problems wonderfully, offering all of the joy of conversation and banter with none of the nervousness he felt in person. Certainly there were occasional flutters in his stomach when he answered the phone and heard her voice and he still sometimes found himself short of breath when dialing her number, hoping that she couldn't tell, worrying that it sounded as if he'd bounded up three flights of stairs and done a victory lap around his bedroom before calling. As far as he could tell, she didn't; she just seemed so happy to talk.

When a free afternoon appeared on both their schedules, they agreed to meet for lunch on Saturday. Ben arrives three before two.

His hand is on the door handle when he suddenly decides to turn; she's a block away down the crosstreet.

She looks adorable, with her hair back away from her face, black pants, cute little black sneakers, a puffy black coat, and a powder-blue knit cap. It's not quite cold enough that he can see his breath, but it is chilly; maybe March will end well this year. She scans the buildings on her side of the road, stores and restaurants on the ground floor and apartments above. She's walked a few blocks, at least. The tip of her nose and her cheeks are the slightest bit red, a very pale rose, from the cold and she has her hands in her pockets.

Emily's smile starts very small when she sees Ben: a pursing of the lips widens into a full grin, showing dimples and teeth and all. "Brr," she shivers, still smiling. "It's chilly today."

"Hi, Emily," he says, opening the door. "It's great to see you."

Once inside, once the door has closed behind them, she gives him a ferocious hug. When she stands up straight, her head comes up just about under his chin, but she's a little shorter now leaning forward. "It's great to see you too." Her arms clutch almost enough to make him gasp.

Then she leads him upstairs. He obeys, tingling inside when he notices the way she trails her left hand slightly behind her.

The restaurant is part of a local chain famous for eclecticism in menu and decor. Each location adheres to a minimal design scheme: a bar along one wall, great massive wooden beams, hanging wine-glasses six deep, a polished Lucite-over-oak bar itself, and several tall, padded stools with a scuffed brass pole footrest beneath. The Saturday lunchtime rush has left and the place is empty.

The rest of the room has variously-sized tables strewn about in an attempt to maximize for seating as well as walkability for waiters and patrons. A heavenly bodies motif peppers the walls with posters of suns, moons, and stars, as well as other objects of art that match somehow. A lovely wire acoustic guitar sculpture along the far wall has a sun as its rosette. The placement pattern seems both precise and random.

"Seat yourself!" advises a wooden sign at the top of the stairs. Emily looks back and up at Ben for guidance. He smiles back and chooses a small table in the corner with seats opposite. From there, they can look out the window onto the street he took. There's a general low bustle of activity; it's more worth watching in summer afternoons and evenings.

The waitress interrupts a conversation with the cook to deliver a basket of sliced bread and two glasses of water. There are already small tri-fold menus on the table.

"Coffee?", she asks.

Ben looks at Emily. "No, thank you." She studies the menu.

"None for me either," he replies, catching the waitress's eyes. "We'll be a few minutes deciding." She nods and heads back toward the kitchen. The cook holds a wooden spoon and leans against a countertop. There must be fresh soup. The last time he ate here, or at least, at another location several miles west, he'd had a cup of fantastic artichoke and cheese soup. That restaurant had more impressive decorations, from the old world roadsigns (mostly German towns, judging by the length of words and low but not unpronounceable vowel to consonant ratios) to the amazing men's restroom fixtures: a tangle of pipes, valves, and gauges, culminating in flashing lights whenever someone flushed the urinal. It's the kind of entertainment that could cause men to leave the dinner table in groups.

Ben sips water cautiously as Emily scours the print off of the menu with her eyes. Her lashes flutter and she shivers and looks up. "Oh, wow, sorry. I'm absolutely starving. I missed breakfast today." She puts down the menu and folds her hands on top of it, leaning far forward with hands clasped. "How are you?"

He feels impressed, yes, and a little flattered. She noticed something that bothered him even before he figured it out. Now he's the one with an uncontrollable smile, perhaps a little smaller than hers. Perhaps it's a little more reserved, but it is no less genuine.

"I'm great. Did you have any trouble finding the place?" He'd suggested the restaurant tentatively; it's a late lunch, in the middle of the afternoon, as far downtown as possible without crossing the river to the west and plenty of other people around. It's as unthreatening as he could make it within her walking range.

"No, not at all. I convinced Shelly to drop me off at the mall." Emily's roommate also seems young, cute, and sweet, at least from the times she's answered the phone.

"Good. Great." Then a beat. "So..."

"So," she challenges back with a pout subverted by her twinkling eye.

Ben throws up his hands. "Alright, you caught me. I have no idea what to talk about. It just amazes me that we're finally here. Sitting. Talking. You know."

Her cheeks blush red, beneath. It distracts Ben from counting the remains of last summer's freckles on her tiny nose as a rush of blood to the cheek darkens under the gentle curve of her ears. She covers it with a quick drink of ice water, but smiles around the glass. "I've never been here before. What do you recommend?"

He's a carnivore, though he keeps his elbows off the table and respects the magic of heat applied to meat. "Good burgers. The one with the fried egg is good." She sticks out a perfect little pink triangle of tongue and crosses her eyes. "No? The mushroom and Swiss is also delicious. Otherwise, good soups, though they have different ones every day. Oh, you have to try the waffle fries."

His hinder brain, the one that notices how other people react to him, suggests that she finds him amusing in the same way that an archaeologist appreciates a particularly beautiful and rare piece of pottery or how ornithologists jabber on and on about the sighting of a bird previously thought extinct. Something else makes him straighten in his chair, relaxing his back and making him feel taller and bigger and stronger and a fierce and fearsome protector of home and hearth.

"I think they also do a fruit cup, if you don't feel like fries or soup."

She stops making faces long enough to giggle. "I've never had a man offer me a fruit cup on a first date."

This could be serious. "Hypothetically, would it give the man a sense of charm?"

When she's completely honest, the playfulness disappears. There's no telltale crinkling of the corner of her eyes or twitching corners of her mouth. This time, there's not even a tilting of the head. "I think he's doing okay." Ben regrets not pulling out her chair for her.

"I'm glad," he concludes, and immediately regrets the tone of the cadence, but she's already returned to her menu again and he pushes away the thought. Ben decides he can't resist the Reuben sandwich, as he'll likely forget to buy both corned beef and cabbage before St. Patrick's Day, with the cheddar artichoke soup. Emily picks the classic cheeseburger after all—no egg, no mushrooms, and good old-fashioned cheddar cheese—with waffle fries. She also orders a diet soda. When the waitress pushes, Ben nearly orders a cider, but sticks with water. The chain has its own brewpubs, a fact that it uses to great effect, at least to people who understand the difference between average and excellent beers.

The waitress leaves, taking away the last barrier between Ben's nervousness and a real live actual female who seems to like him. He hasn't yet found a thread of conversation that seems likely to last through the twenty minutes it might take before the food arrives. He chuckles at the awkwardness. It refuses to take the hint. His eyes flick to the wall decorations but keep returning to Emily, no matter how he tells himself that he can't just sit and stare at her.

She runs both hands through her hair to pull it back from her face, making tiny ponytails with her fists below her ears. "I am so glad that midterms are over. Chemistry just won't stick in my head. I study and study and keep it there long enough to pass the test, but two hours later I can't tell you the difference between a benzene ring and...uh.... See? I can't think of *anything* right now."

He's heard this one before. "Cubic zirconia."

"Cubic zirconia?"

"One is a very stable relationship and the other lasts only until the other person finds out."

She looks up.

"Uh, don't ask me why. I heard it somewhere."

Emily shakes her head. "Very cute. More cute than funny."

"I know another one about electrons, but that's the limit of my chemistry memories. How were your other tests?"

"That one was the monster. It rules out hard sciences as my major anyway. I feel more and more like pre-law these days. Give me something to research and build on, or a theory to develop and a chance to argue it. That's what I want."

This is new; she'd disseminated a few times on the phone, but determination adds steel to her voice now. "How many of your current credits transfer?"

"I'm not sure. I have an appointment with my advisor Tuesday morning to figure it all out. He'll be happy that I've finally made any decision." A thumping, shuffling noise comes from under the table.

Emily pushes herself back in her chair with her hands grasping the edge of the table and elbows almost locked. She glances underneath and suddenly lets down her chair with a bump and a distracted shrug. "Sorry, my shoe fell off. I wiggle my feet when I'm excited."

"This whole epiphany came out of your midterm?"

She looks through him and even through the wall to the adjacent apartments. "I *think* so. I mean, I won't graduate next semester, but I think this is what I want to do."

This is all he can do. "It's better to have a plan that takes time than to rush headlong into the unknown. I've always regretted not doing that, anyway."

Her cute little head-tilt returns and she meets his eye again. "I like that, when you tell me I'm doing the right thing."

Honesty knocks on the door of his mind. "Only when I think you're doing the right thing." He'd never say it, at least not right away, but he thinks she's so much happier even only considering this plan that he can barely stop himself from offering to drive her to her appointment right now, three days early, just to make sure she goes through with it.

She grins. "I also like how easy it is to wind you up sometimes."

"I...yeah."

"You're so serious. It makes a girl wonder what she has to do to convince you to lighten up." He recalls the last couplet of an Ambrose Bierce poem about the devilish heart of women. By the look on her face right now, she not only stays in touch with her mischievous side, they have each other on speed dial.

When Ben really introspects, he sees himself as arguing twins. Strangely, the various parts of his mind or soul or whatever that all contribute to his decision-making sometimes switche tasks. For example, right now the intellectual part of his brain has tacked into a curious wind and really wants to ask her what she meant. His endocrine system delicately votes for that option. His heart wonders if she's teasing him, and his common sense shouts stage directions of "Change the subject!" and "Say something sweet!" His higher mental facilities have turned the idea itself into a puzzle to solve instead of the far better challenge to discover exactly what to say to extricate himself from this potentially hazardous mess without hurting her feelings, having ice water thrown in his face, or feeling completely foolish.

Also, he's not sure if he really wants to know what she means... but then, maybe he does.

Sometimes his mouth, which these debates leave ungoverned, takes over. "Whatever you're doing now, it's working."

Horror and pride rush join the words as they bounce off of flat surfaces back into his brain. She raises one eyebrow, but can't keep it up with a flat expression, and then they both laugh together, she trying to say "Touché" and he feeling relieved and, yes, a little lighter.

Then he realizes that it's still his turn to talk. She holds her mouth slightly open and her big green eyes wide; she's almost paused. He'd contentedly sit and watch her, whether watching him or looking out the window. If he catches the light just right, he can even see his reflection in her pupils, a tall man, maybe a little stocky, with hair unkempt from a stray breeze outside, cut maybe too short to stay in place, a nose he's always appreciated for being straight but perhaps a bit longer and wider than necessary, and a dazed expression on his face. "Sorry, I found myself lost in your eyes" won't work here; he's never had the right tone of voice to say such a thing without having to pretend that it's the obvious kind of joke.

He can't stop himself. "Emily, I have to be honest." Her eyes widen and the cute little lip pout disappears. "Men in general have a difficult time making honest conversation with pretty girls. Women. Beautiful. Beautiful women."

Her grin tickles a primeval panther warning. "You started that sentence so well, too! Ben. . . I'm not a scary, exotic monster. I'm just a person. You're cute and you're funny. When you're not tripping over yourself trying to impress me by being someone you're not, I really like you."

There's another lightening, but he still fights to quiet the pounding in his chest. "Now you tell me. I even wore pants for this?"

"You don't normally. . . ?"

Oops. "It's something Randy says, some sort of fratboy motto or something. 'Pants are optional.'"

She shakes her head. "That's terrible. Is he some pasty geek who runs around in what, a toga, claiming that anything otherwise would violate his sense of personhood?"

"Close. If we're lucky it was togas, and it was more a theory than a practice."

"And you live with him?"

"Everyone has bad habits. I know his. They're easy to see; they're on the surface. In some ways, he's more genuine than anyone else I know. Sometimes he's crass and rude but," Ben shrugs, "I'm a guy. I don't notice half of it."

"The blind live with the blind. You'd better have good table manners!"

He reaches for his water glass with one hand and tries to sneak his napkin off of the table and into his lap with the other. "Too late!" she giggles. "I grew up with a younger brother, so as long as you don't expect to dig into roast wildebeest carcass with tooth and nail in the middle of a fancy dinner party, you'll be fine. He'd probably be a brother of no pants, too."

He breathes deeply, eyes half-closed. It's better. "That's okay. I don't even like wildebeest."

"Mm-hmm. Tastes like chicken?"

"I would think pork, but your guess is as good as mine."

The waitress approaches with their drinks and Ben's soup. The soup smell tempts him, warm and hearty cheese with a tart vegetably touch of artichoke. Instead, he pushes it to the side and wills the cheeseburger to arrive very soon.

"Oh, please go ahead."

"Are you sure?"

Emily waves her hand, palm up and outward. "I don't mind."

Ben blows on a spoonful. Aromatic wisps of steam tickle his nose as he eases the soup into his mouth. "Mmm, it's just like I remembered. Would you like a taste?"

He gauges the position of his spoon and the so-far-uncontaminated part of the soup before pushing the bowl toward her. She fingers her spoon idly, then digs in with a merry "Why not?", then "Oh, that is good. Artichoke soup? What could possibly have convinced you to try this the first time? It seems so unlike you. You can have it back now, thank you."

Ben shrugs. "It sounded good at the time."

"Good or weird?" she counters.

"Deliciously weird. I do weird things every now and then to shake up my life. It keeps the world interesting." He speaks around bites, stirring from the bottom up so that it cools evenly.

"Weird or daring?"

"Sometimes there's no difference. Sometimes I force myself to do new things I wouldn't normally do just to prove that I can. I even cook and eat broccoli now. Don't tell my mother!"

There's a silence. She looks away. Her expression is maybe wistful, in a way, but there's a little water at the edge of one eye. Her smile hesitates. He can't decide if she's waiting for something, or someone, or just him.

"What is it?" he starts.

"Sometimes I forget you're a lot older than I am. Every time you say something adorable, I forget again."

Being adorable hasn't appealed to him since the third grade; in general it evokes the idea of aging aunts doting over nieces and nephews before supper at interminable family reunions. A different connotation tickles his psyche when Emily says it. His eyes caress her face.

The change is quick and profound. With two blinks, the water has disappeared, the smile has widened, and a dimple on her right cheek betrays her. "Does this daring include flirting with every cute barrista that crosses your path?"

"Uh, no. In your case the daringness was flirting back."

"What was so daring about that?"

One option is to tell the truth as he sees it, that he's never understood how to talk to women with the kind of verbal sophistication that makes them melt. Thinking of that situation still causes his heart to race and his palms to itch with a pre-sweaty nervousness. The other is to say the first clever thing that pops out of his mouth and let his brain figure out what he actually said later, when there's time to analyze it for wit, creativity, efficacy, and whether it might ever work again.

"I had no idea what to think—a pretty girl, uh woman, starting a conversation with a customer. It doesn't happen to me very often. I didn't know what to say. You surprised me." Only a supreme exercise of will prevents this admission from becoming an apology. It's an effort strengthened by not allowing his mouth to express some of Randy's funnier non-sequiturs during conversations with his mother and other older female relatives. A near-miss at Thanksgiving one year caused the whole room to fall silent as supposedly virgin ears pretended that they couldn't believe themselves and most of his male relatives either took profound amusement in how he tried to backpedal or leaned back with the profound relief that they weren't the ones afflicted.

"Good," she says. Before he can probe the idea—almost before he thinks he might try, the waitress has set his sandwich and Emily's burger on the table in front of them. Emily asks for a bottle of ketchup, and, while waiting for the waitress to fetch a fresh one, attacks a huge dill pickle with obvious relish.

There's not much else to say for a while. Her burger rapidly disappears, and he's polite enough not to interrupt. He keeps trying different conversational gambits in his head, but nothing sticks. "Good fries," she says between bites, for example, and he nods, mouth full of perfectly salted corned beef, beautifully melted cheese, and puckeringly delicious sauerkraut. He has happy memories of his mother grilling Reuben sandwiches on lazy Sunday afternoons for him and his father. He'd cook them himself if he remembered to buy the ingredients and to ask his mother how to make the sauce.

Suddenly Ben hopes Emily's cute head-tilting doesn't presage a pointed question, maybe "What are you thinking?" He doesn't look forward to pondering aloud the ingredients of sandwich sauce or explaining why he's thinking of that while sitting with such a pretty girl. He can't keep his eyes away. For the most part, she seems absorbed in her food. Though even now she still looks so dainty and delicate, she takes her meal seriously; he's already cataloged her subtle routine: a small bite, chewed thoroughly, a quick napkin lip-dab, and alternating sips of her drink and two fries at a time.

Firsts

There's so much he wants to ask her, though every question slides away before he can grip and voice it. Where did she grow up? What is her family like? Does she want children? What does she think of him so far? What is the one thing he and only he could say that would make her fall in love with him? When can they meet again?

He's sidled into a few of those ideas before, but his memories of phone calls fade away compared to how real everything now seems. Normally he can replay conversations in his head, recalling tone of voice and body language, but the phone ruins all of that—it's dark and audio only, his eleven year-old self with the blankets over his head listening to old-time science fiction radio plays with invading aliens and wishes that suddenly go awry with cruel twists at the end. Those had left snippets of dialog popping into his head inopportunely and vague impressions of their stories, rough enough that he can only recall plot details when watching modern shows that have recycled the ideas, usually badly. In his mind, every phone call they'll ever share will take place visually and spatially while he lies on his bed in the dark, no matter the actual hour or place.

Ben stops mid-chew and looks up. That's it. He's always wondered why he hates to talk on the phone in cars; he loses his sense of place. He can't associate the conversation with anything because the moving visuals distract him. Interesting! Emily glances at him and he shrugs. "Tasty!" he says. She smiles.

He's timed his water to last just to the end of his sandwich, but still ends up with mostly ice and three bites left. Emily beams over the crumbs of her burger and offers to share the remaining fries, while chattering about schoolwork. He obliges and wills himself to salivate. He has no particular insight to share, but she's relaxed enough to let him escape with a few "Please do go on" and "Had you had that professor before?" type phrases.

When the waitress finally reappears, she offers dessert perfunctorily and nods at the decline, then presents Ben with the bill.

"Dutch?" Emily wonders.

"My treat."

"I'm a liberated woman." She reaches for a purse he hadn't noticed.

"I'm a gentleman."

"I'm a poor college student. You win." She smiles as if somehow she'd won too, or instead.

Ben flicks his eyes up and right to calculate the tip. Even though Emily hasn't seen the final total, he bumps it well past fifteen percent; waitressing is hard work. Ahhh, now he can stretch, first his legs and then his arms. Aside from drink refills, nothing keeps them here. What next?

"Can I ask what time is it?"

He wears an analog watch without numerals, though he always has to count to figure out the hour. "Hmm, almost three-thirty. Am I keeping you from your studies?"

"Oh, no. I promised to meet Shelly by four though. We need to visit the library before it closes today and probably tomorrow too."

"Short hours on the weekends?"

Emily rolls her eyes. "Noon to six on Saturdays and one to four on Sundays. It's crazy."

Ben pushes back his chair and stands. "I hate to keep you," he halfway lies. "Shall we?"

As they walk toward the stairs and exit, Ben nods to the waitress. He pauses to let Emily pass him on the stairs, so he can guide her with his hand. The brief brush against the small of her back feels so incredibly *right*; she smaller but not weak and he strong and gentle.

Bye

They stand at the foot of the stairs, in the restaurant's lobby. A ubiquitous metal-and-glass retail door stands between them and outside. Beyond that threshold, the date will end and the future may begin. Ben looks for words.

Emily starts. "Ben, I'm so glad we did this. You were right about the waffle fries, but I remain dubious about egg on a hamburger." The shift there in the middle from genuine sincerity to a bit of mocking, a bit of teasing, is gentle, like the curve of her neck as she pulls her hair up and under the little blue hat. He wants to protect her from the weather, but instead flexes the fingers of his right hand and balls it up inside his pocket.

He's spent. . . three hours, total, in her presence. Why does he want to bundle her up against the cold? What compels him to walk her to her car, just in case he can catch any airplanes that fall out of the sky at her? It's not that she's dainty and delicate; he has the unshakeable impression that she'd happily punch him in the stomach for saying something incredibly stupid. Something about being around her makes him feel strong, maybe, or protective, as if he really could catch a falling jet engine to keep her from harm.

It also seems that every time he starts chasing down those thoughts, she can hear it. He watches her watch him, as if she keeps a mental catalog of his actions and body language and expressions, to flip through her notes late at night and dictate conclusions and observations into a mini-cassette recorder. Perhaps she's actually performing anthropological field research on abnormal social patterns of single men in their late twenties.

Then she switches again, to concern. "Ben, I like the strong and silent thing sometimes, but this is the part of the date where we banter and delay saying goodbye. I haven't left yet, hon."

He can't pretend he wasn't lost in daydreams. Fortunately, his echoic memory has a five-sentence capacity. "Uh, the egg really is good. Someday I hope you can see that." He cringes, but hangs on the idea that she handed him an excuse.

"That's the spirit! Now I really do have to go before Shelly fills up my seat with shopping bags." Properly prepared for chilly weather, she stands, hands at sides, and shrugs a small happy sigh.

He holds out his arms. "May I have a hug?" At least his voice stopped cracking some ten years earlier.

They meet in the middle. Ben doesn't know where to put his arms, there being so many interesting places his hands might end up, and settles for crossing them at the wrists between her shoulder blades. She responds, pulling in to tuck her head on his right arm for just a moment. Then she pulls back and lifts up on her toes to peck his lips, very lightly. By the time he realizes this, she has slid her left hand down his arm to his hand.

Emily mouths the word "Bye" as she pushes open the door and bounces, turning, out into the cold. The light has just changed in her favor and she rushes across the street toward the mall's parking garage.

Ben watches the little blue cap until it disappears. It's the one spot of color in an industrial gray neighborhood under overcast skies on a Saturday in early March in the city. Then he leaves the restaurant himself, turning down the side street to his car. The powerful feeling has returned. His mind flashes, and he sees himself clad in animal skins and a huge, horned metal helmet, with powerful arms raising a double-sided axe over cowering foes. Emily, nearby, beams.

o o o

Urbanities

Ben calls Emily the next afternoon. It feels odd—his Midwestern upbringing frowns even on shopping on Sundays, though apparently going out for a late lunch is one small step lower than a Commandment. He rationalizes that not only does she definitely have no family visiting—as might be the case if they lived in, perhaps, Ohio—she's probably doing homework and might welcome a brief interruption.

The pleasantly bland, blandly pleasant yet asexual voicemail operator recording answers. "Um, hi Emily, this-is-Ben-and I had a ...good time yesterday and hope-to-do-something similar soon.... I guess you're at the library. Well, sorry to have, uh, missed you and give me a call when you have a chance, maybe all-tonight-I'll-be here. Bye." Click.

Two little inside voices immediately babble. First, why didn't he see if the system offered the chance to erase that message and try again with something coherent? Second, at least his voice didn't crack.

Practicality answers the first. It *was* easier this way. He had to fight off no awkward inclinations to ask "How did I do?" or "What do you think of me now?" He had to search for no dull conversational starters such as "What did you do after we left yesterday?" and "How was your homework?" How much can two people do in twenty-four hours, especially when one is an overloaded college student switching majors and the other doesn't own any exotic pets or even have any interesting piercings?

Ben brings down his neighborhood's weighted funkiness average. Randy made a chart one night to demonstrate that filling the yard with inflatable Halloween decorations in mid-February would meet or exceed the expectations of the covenant agreement, if there were such a thing. Ben doesn't own a motorcycle. He doesn't go rock-climbing. He's never felt the urge to eat carefully prepared blowfish, to jump out of a well-behaved airplane, or to strip to the waist in a dank basement to hit another disaffected twenty-something male. As far as he's thought this through, his best way to compete is gentlemanliness.

In practice, this has even extended to opening car doors for dates, though the logistics of that often require creative planning. It does give a good way to gauge the helpfulness of the young lady in question, though: if, after properly seated, she unlocked his door for him, she was definitely a keeper. Then he bought a new truck with keyless entry and had to concentrate on other, less obvious signs. Does she like her mother? Does she expect him to lead all of the time? Does she pick fights over meaningless decisions? Does she like his friends?

In olden times, he'd probably would have had to practice his penmanship before writing her father a letter to ask for permission to walk her around town on Sundays after church, in full view of everyone. She'd have little chance to lean over for a quick kiss. He can still feel the tattoo of her lips, hers warm and gentle, parted slightly in a smile, with his surprised and stoic. She'd pulled herself up, her hands on his sleeves, and turned her head the way she did while considering a question. He'd blinked from surprise at something approaching his head, so he couldn't see whether she'd closed her eyes or kept them open to see the surprise on his face.

If he closes his eyes again, he can almost summon the entire moment. There's a sense of cool air ahead and to the left. That's the glass door, retail common and effective at blocking only the most egregious weather. The warmth directly ahead is Emily, post-hug. Then, there's a tug on his sleeves, a sense of leaning forward and electricity. His nervous system catches fire gently, an invisible blue glow. Drops of blue food coloring fall into a champagne flute of filtered water. Swirling clouds move through his body as powerful currents carry it to all corners in seconds. Its intensity diminishes as it goes but the pleasantness lingers. He feels it again now, a tingling energy in his fingers. A lightness in his upper back makes him roll his shoulders back and forth in new-felt freedom.

He leans way back in his chair, one ensocked foot on the wall and the other swinging back and forth at the knee. With a dazed grin on his face, he dangles the phone by its antenna from his right hand and runs the fingers of his left through the fibers of the carpet.

Randy knocks on his open door. "Cordless phone in here?"

Ben swings around as subtly as possible without falling over. Once, a plastic lawn chair committed slow suicide underneath him and he rolled away in a neat ball. His friends actually applauded his grace.

"Ahh, talking to a girl." Randy can't really raise one eyebrow at a time physically, but he has the inflections right. "Who's the little chickadee, Ben?"

He tried to evade this subject once before. Though Randy never found out the real truth, his wrongness was close enough that it felt creepy to dance around the issue. "Emily. We went out for lunch yesterday."

"Emily, sweet sweet Eh-mah-lee.... There's a lot of cute in girls named Emily. Where'd you meet her? Don't say work. You'll hurt my head."

"Coffee shop, a couple of weeks ago."

"Mr. Ben! He is the master of the scene! Look at you go. Here I thought you stayed in your cave all day, but you were out prowling. She cute?"

"Pretty little blonde girl. You'd like her. She'd hate you." This is the only policy that works.

"Aww, hey. I'm just playing—but how did it go?"

The tingle returns and his blood flow diverts in interesting directions with both anticipation and memory. Ben holds out the phone. "It was nice. I'd like to see her again."

○ ○ ○

Unpleasantries

It had started so well.

After meeting randomly during working hours, eating lunch together on a Saturday, and walking in the park after a shift at the coffeeshop, Ben had finally suggested going on a real date like real people do.

That meant, to him, dinner and a movie on a Friday or Saturday night. They had agreed on everything except the movie. Now his phone relays her irritation without passion or comment.

"A superhero movie? This is what you consider entertainment? Men in tights and impossibly-bosomed women heaving around in adolescent fantasies, solving all of their problems with muscles and impeccably-timed plot coincidences?"

He wants to say that her choice of movie, something about the relationship between a mother and her daughters, sounds dessicating, but he can't fit any words in between hers. It wouldn't help to compare deeply moving emotional dramas to playing a three-on-three basketball tournament on the blacktop in Death Valley having eaten three huge pretzels beforehand and wearing a parka. Worse, he can't figure out how she's parroted nearly the exact phrase he used to explain his distrust of comic books to Randy before.

"How do you respect someone stuck in his own imaginary world, wishing for magic powers so he doesn't have to get up and take action to solve his own problems themselves? Do you want to continue that passivity by supporting those movies?"

If only Studio Ghibli had better stateside distribution. She'd have loved Totoro, for example, but if she's in full-rant mode about comics, he doubts that she'll appreciate the distinction between a fairy tale and complete fantasy. A quote from George MacDonald or C. S. Lewis appears, then vanishes uncaught.

"Well? Say something!"

"It sounded interesting. It's not high art; it's entertainment. I didn't realize you felt this strongly."

"You didn't think about what I wanted. You didn't even ask. You just made a chart of possibilities based on the," she switches to a professorial mock-baritone, "proximity of the theater, most convenient opening time, attractiveness of the female lead, and highest concentration of explosions per minute."

"No, that's, uh, no on the female lead and explosions. Does it help if the graph was only in my head?" A little humor might defuse the situation.

There's a moment and silence. "Don't patronize me, Ben." Then there's dead-air silence.

He calls back. "I think we lost our connection." Her silence chills his bedroom. "Emily, I want to find something we can enjoy together. This isn't it. Let's move...."

"That's not the point!" His experience with women is that it often starts as the point, but then the point becomes something more like how dare he speak (if he's said anything) because he can't say anything that could possibly make up for his mistake or why doesn't he say anything (if he hasn't) because silence only makes it worse. He rolls back his eyes and tries to think of a recent experience where he tried to evade responsibility for some transgression, when he learned of it, but can't. Perhaps there is some gesture or note of contrition he's never quite mastered or struck that would salve these misunderstandings.

"...and I don't appreciate that assumption. I don't think you can go an hour without planning something out. Can't you live? Can't you breathe? Can't you let something happen, maybe live in the moment for once?"

He pushes away the movie listings, hoping she can't hear the newsprint rustle.

"It's like you're a robot or something or you're programming yourself, or I don't know. Just...leave me alone."

There's another click and dead air again. He calls back once, but the line is busy. He sighs.

Ben's insight rarely flashes like lightning strikes, with ominous clouds and warning thunder, and electricity in the air raising his arm hairs and the whole world holding *his* breath before a great flash, a great power hurling him into the air, and a clap of darkness both aural and visual before newly-epiphanated consciousness rushes back in to fill the vacuum. Usually it only sneaks up on him, mouse-like, and he only realizes it after hearing scurrying and scratching in the walls.

She answers again, with a weary "Yeah?"

"Emily?"

"What, Ben?" It's far off and a little breathy and slow.

"What are you afraid of?"

"What?"

"What do you fear?"

"Don't change the subject. That's not going to work."

"It doesn't have to be this way. We'll figure something out."

He can hear her breathe now. The deep intake has ragged edges. "Because you have a plan? Because you have six rules on how to have an argument? Four ways to defuse a situation? How does it have to be, Ben? How many times, how many ways do I have to give in to someone I like, admire, before he'll acknowledge that I have feelings too?"

"What if we switched? This time we see a movie of your choice and next time we see one of mine?"

"I'm not going to a stupid superhero movie."

"There'd be a veto system." He tries to keep the cringe out of his voice.

There is a very long pause. Ben looks at the phone, expecting that she's hung up, when Emily laughs. "That's completely stupid. It's clearly a ploy to take me to two movies with you."

Usually saying the first thing that pops into his head leads to trouble, or at least people looking at him oddly, as if he had a sign around his neck warning everyone else about non-sequiturs. "Would you believe I hadn't thought of that?"

A post-tears sniffle sneaks out of the earpiece. "Yes, I would. For all your faults, you really are a sweet man sometimes."

"I just want to be fair. I really do like you."

"You should. It's only fair."

A weight lifts, though it leaves his muscles dull and tired, as if he'd carried his own body up several flights of stairs only to find the door locked and no elevator, slide, or parachute to carry him down again. Still, it's a sense of relief.

"That was our first fight, huh?"

"Yes," she says. "It wasn't so bad."

o o o

Five Ways To Panic

Disbelief

BEN reclassifies the people in his office. The general reaction to Ned's announcement is shock. There are light murmurs of stunned thoughts, such as "I can't believe it" and "This isn't happening". A handful of coworkers finds courage only as Ned leaves the floor. They take the idea as a challenge, considering management as a polite and manicured substitute for the democratic process, and call on their colleagues to rise up and vote down the idea.

Three people, quiet and thoughtful types, have blank expressions. Eric and Mark have had this experience before, Eric having programmed for longer than many of the rest of the group had been alive and Mark having fled the shiny-until-you-do-it world of game development after cramming five man-years into two calendar years.

Jerry has the foresight and, perhaps, political capital to send everyone back to finish their work in the next 30 minutes and then leave for the day, recommending a good night's sleep and a fresh start in the morning. Clumps of employees wander back to their offices, leaning against walls and doorways to talk things over until precisely 40 minutes later when Jerry marches through and actually sends everyone home.

Ben eats a bowl of ice cream, a bowl of potato chips, and some yogurt-covered pretzels while playing video games from two to six.

After burning his afternoon, Ben has a quiet night out of a sense of duty more than rational thought. He cooks pork chops and adds applesauce, green beans, and a small salad which Randy refuses to eat as they're out of Bleu Cheese dressing, half-watches part of an episode of some old syndicated sci-fi/horror show with giant mutated Sky Oxen destroying Beijing, and falls into bed at 10. He can't remember any details of his dreams beyond the sense of walking past row after row of post office boxes, their dull bronze faces revealing nothing about their contents, somehow both walking and watching himself recede into the distance. It still seems familiar and strange. He wakes with a vague sense of dread unalleviated by the dubious glee of Friday morning.

It's 9:28 on Friday morning. Ben leans back in his chair. Weak sunlight lightens the cityscape's wintertime palette of grays. He gives the internal developers-only mailing list another ten minutes before it explodes in a clown-car frenzy of message following message in a shower, first of impressive numbers and then soon a numb appreciation of "Hey, didn't I see that one before?" until the joke has lost its humor.

Jerry's greatest insight was forestalling that flood; they're all supermen behind keyboards.

Today someone will have the unenviable task of building a plan presumably doomed to failure on the level of the Hindenburg Historical Recreation Society—not just a bad idea but the sort of idea where you almost hope for failure just to prove, underline, exclamation point, and cackling skulls-and-bones the point. At least, that's how Ben's notes read. Someone else will have to tell the current customers that they have to wait three months for any progress. That's three months if and only if things go according to a plan that not only has never survived contact with the enemy but would only have a chance of defeating the enemy if a subtle network of spies sneaked it into enemy headquarters with a crate of fine alcohol to provoke a night of merry-making culminating in the public reading of the plan and fits of choking laughter that crippled the army head-first.

The hallways are silent. It's nearly 9:30, but no one else seems to have arrived. Even the coffee machine stands abandoned.

Ben pulls up the bug database to search for the nastiest, hairiest, longest-lasting, and most-legged bug so he can wrestle it into submission before mounting it over his door as a trophy. He wonders if a plaque would make a good motivator for best bug-squasher of the year. A moth would be appropriate, but he prefers *Anoplophora Glabripennis*, a mean looking long-horned beetle native to China.

He hasn't decided on his strategy yet. This has the fingerprints of a new executive's exuberance and willingness to work himself half-dead for a couple of years just to take a chance at joining upper management, which actually rewards unwork in a way that honest people never comprehend. Ben doesn't play golf but remains convinced that there's something fundamentally insincere about not carrying your own clubs.

The best plan Ben has is also the only plan that managed to stay in his head. He refused even to mention the situation to Randy, who would have loved the opportunity to debate the merits of a system in which the managers of capital run over the skilled workers of production. Every time it starts to walk on stage, he pushes it away. Assuming that someone sweet-talks the current customers into delaying the current projects, assuming that it's possible to deliver the most important parts of the conversion as soon as possible, (not all at once, and certainly not the whole project at once, right on the dot of three months), and assuming that the seventh floor listens to and understands the technical objections of the sixth floor....

There are more scraping sounds from upstairs. The last time Ben heard that, he was on the fourth floor to review technical marketing documents while the facilities department rearranged his office to his liking.

... but making assumptions that big means he might as well predict that the whole situation is a practical joke pulled four and a half months too early. He ponders and weaves the ifs and maybes into a rich tapestry, but he remains Parcival, denied his life's goal a few moments from completion only to watch some beautiful Galahad sneak in ahead to make everything look easy.

The floor is still silent. Maybe there won't be a flood of angry messages to skim and, eventually delete unread before the morning meeting. Maybe they'll have combined meetings now, or maybe they'll continue in two wieldier groups of twenty. Forty people is at least forty minutes of meeting apiece; he theorizes a super-linear relationship between the size of the group and the amount of time it takes to work around the room.

The upstairs banging continues, but this time it sounds like the placing and filling of dozens of chairs: the light four-legged thump, a mild shuffle, a softer but meatier whump, and the scrape-scrape of adjustments.

The longest-lived, most often duplicated, and highest-priority bug in the database is a close relative of the one he fought in the translator code. Instead of mangling the results the librarian hands to the robot, this one turns questions from the robot to the librarian into commands for the librarian to tidy up the filing cabinets, in the sense that a cabinet with fewer file folders looks cleaner than a cabinet full of file folders. There's no real pattern, but it's happened four times now under similar circumstances.

He sighs and taps a pencil on the desk and finally agrees to track that down after fixing the translation, provided that no one interferes by giving him advice—he resolves to cease to call it management, preferring instead to believe at this moment that the noises upstairs come from the installation of a game show studio that straps half-naked Japanese men to a giant wheel and spins them one at a time until they cry, and then the wheel stops with its arrow on whatever piece of advice is the new management directive.

He's not sure where the giant scorpions fit in, but they do.

It's 9:45. Even after poking his head out the door, Ben can't see lights in Jerry's office. He risks sneaking out the door, down the hall, and around the corner to confirm his suspicion. Jerry's phone message light blinks four times. That's a night's worth of voice mail. He hasn't come in this morning.

His heart pounds. Is there a chance that today is Saturday? It'd be the perfect capper on the week. He retraces his steps to look for any evidence. His computer calendar claims that it is, indeed, Friday. It synchronizes to an atomic clock hidden in a mountain somewhere in Wyoming perhaps, twice a day, so any conspiracy must have roots far deeper than someone with Randy's attention span could summon.

He gasps with a second suspicion. Walking to the main elevator, he pushes the button and slides in as the door opens. Everyone else who didn't try to sneak in unseen has already seen the scribbled note taped above the buttons.

"Developers, meet on seventh floor."

o o o

Rage

He's already late, but there are still bangings and scufflings from upstairs, so there's time to fill the thirsty monkey mug with hot water. The teabag choosings are slim: mostly fruitlike flavors that don't sound delicious at all—strawberry? blueberry? Ben settles for lemon ginger as a pick-me-up and leisurely waits for the elevator to return.

In seconds, he's on another planet. The sixth floor is pleasant; neutral colors and minimal decorations speak of silent and bland productivity. The company's creativity and rebellion tend to burst out of developer offices, most often during plastic toy fights. The seventh floor brags corporate hipness with metallic blues and grays and odd oblate glass and black metal tables in reception. Floor-to-ceiling windows afford a view mostly of traffic but occasionally and from just the right angle, the river. That's it for personality. The front receptionist once set out a tiny vase of yellow rosettes to add color, but they disappeared the evening the CFO complained. Ben's never found an appropriate synonym for "humorless" to fit that abbreviation. Fusty isn't quite right.

A foosball table and three aging pinball machines could find a good roomy home here, but they won't.

The walls close in past the reception area, forcing into a narrow hallway with conference rooms on either side guarding access to actual offices. In case of a programmer invasion, MBAs barricade themselves inside and poke spears through the walls in an effort to protect the top executives. The largest of the four rooms is Lewis. The others are Clark, Sacagawea, and Charbonneau. Lewis holds the angry mob he'd heard downstairs. The receptionist rolls her eyes and tilts her head to move him along. He nods back and shrugs. It's not her fault.

A double handful of other developers have dragged in whatever chairs they could find—except the perfectly shaped and uncomfortably comfortable two-piece foam monsters from the reception area— mostly from the other conference rooms. Fortunately, the naming theme doesn't apply to the furnishings, lest two rooms play at American Colonial and the other two a strange mixture of French or, worse...Ben's never decided what particular type of awful he could imagine in the Sacagawea room, mostly because there are so many ways it could be offensive and tacky.

He feels the energy. It's the sound of someone far away plucking a string about to snap, fibers tightening and straining and crying out. Jerry's not here. Ned's not here. Instead they have Ned's boss, the VP of development. Ben can't ever remember his name. Steve? Eddie? Four or five people try to talk to him over each other. A few words escape the meaningless stream, but the tone enough tells its own stories.

Ben slips into an empty chair in the corner of the room near the door to lean against the glass pane and steep his tea. The VP sits at the head of the conference table and *listens*. The flanking chairs are empty. Not even his mustache twitches; he has all of the movability of Mount Rushmore. Wouldn't those four be better choices for the conference rooms, if the west coast could show patriotism without irony?

He hates the sound of conflict; he should have left when he realized what would happen. Usually he can type for hours and hours every day on a decent keyboard while ensconced in his own chair without ill effect, but in the minute he's been here, he's soaked up a month's worth of unpleasantness and frustration. A sharp pain draws his awareness to the first knuckle of his left thumb and a dull ache precedes numbness in his fourth and fifth fingers. Wincing and shifting his mug to the other hand, he rolls his shoulders backward to stretch the muscles between the blades. There's a slight popping feel—muscle, not vertebra—and then a raw, tired feeling on the left. The thumb feels slightly better.

He realizes he's deliberately ignored the content of the meeting, merely appearing because he had no idea what else to do. The VP (Paul? Brad?) speaks, giving the same hobbling explanation Ned offered just before his flight—did he come in this morning? It's strange that he wouldn't be here. Evidently this has been the morning's pattern. Even Andrew looks dubious. Ben tries to recall the dates he chose in the betting pool for the kid's eventual disillusionment.

Five or six sentences of non-explanation allow the agitators to sink back further into those chairs that allow it and catch their breaths, except for Carlann, who's folded her arms so tightly across her chest that she's turning purple. Someone anonymous in the back makes a snide accusation and everyone shuffles nervously, some looking around for the speaker, some finding their shoes fascinating, and others nodding with vaguely sick expressions on their faces, torn between the lure of authority and confidence and the desire not to follow a stupid idea to its inevitable fiery conclusion.

The VP (Frank? Steve? No, that's a repeat.) seems to infuriate half the room by existing. His lack of reaction seems deliberate; he maintains a perfect "I hear what you say" expression, radiating an air of mild and amused disbelief through all of the accusations. He probably sweats aftershave. If he were to lean back in his chair to put his hands behind his head, his blue-tinted shirt would look as fresh and clean as it did when it came from the cleaners. The undersides of his wrists probably have tans, too. He's too smart to give things away there, as he lacks even a smile. His only notable expression is the sympathetic "Isn't this fun?" eye-gleam.

Ben's eyes focus and unfocus. He sips bitter-strong lemon tea. Yick. It's so noisy in here that he forgot how long it steeped, and there's no good place to put the used teabag.

Suddenly, three people around the table stand up. At first they're timid, but they gain confidence in their solidarity as they storm out of the room. He thinks he sees the VP's aura deflate a bit, not that he actually sees auras of course, but he somehow to Ben seems more vulnerable even while he continues to avoid answering a question without pity. Maybe it's that everyone else wonders if anyone else finds him unconvincing.

Then the VP mentions "Jeremiah" and Ben's conscious attention finally connects that to "Jerry". No one who knows him uses his full name, including his mother, or so goes the rumor. He rewinds and plays back the previous sentences. "Excuse me," he hears himself ask. "Did you say that Jerry's on leave?"

"We thought it best to give him some time out of the office to revise the plan."

That doesn't make sense. "He's working from home today?"

"I'm sure that Jeremiah," the name escapes with more precision that it needs, "will explain more details when he has them."

Ben doesn't buy it, but he can't foresee coaxing out any more details about a probable layoff. He forgets and sips again, grimacing at excessive lemon and wishing for honey or even a sugar-substitute packet. Eric catches his eye from across the room and makes a throat-slashing motion while keeping his hand from his knee and follows with a dead-man's protruding tongue and closed-eyes gesture. Ben nods.

With part of his mind invested now in conscious listening, it latches on to a few more phrases before retreating again to more peaceful contemplation of the tea's aftertaste. Then something else sticks and he hears himself asking again, "What was that about hours?"

"We know it's the holiday season soon and many of you have families, so we don't expect married employees—or parents, of course—to put in weekend time." Now the VP allows a smile.

"By implication, the single and childless have nothing better to do with our lives and would waste our time anyway?"

"I prefer to think of it as having the opportunity to do good deeds for your coworkers. It's the holidays."

It's also a challenge. Ben takes a deep breath and sets his mug down inside the legs of the chair. He watches himself walk to the close end of the conference table. The two developers seated there clear the way.

Ben leans over the table and rests on his hands to put his face as far forward as possible. He's quiet and precise. "I don't care for your implication. I don't care for the way you present it. My life is my own life. You pay me for the time I'm here and I give you honest work. You don't own what I do outside of work. You don't put a value on it and expect me to agree with whatever you throw my way. You don't," and he slaps his right hand on the table hard enough to make the room ring, "rate one man's life above another."

Ben pauses for breath and for once, the VP doesn't respond right away. His eyes have even widened.

He can't go back now. He checks his current position, hoping that it was all just a fantasy, but he's still on his feet. Why not? "I think this project is a mistake, but I will work to see it succeed. I will not give up my life for that work, though. Be clear on this."

As he waits for the elevator, he realizes that sneaking back in to retrieve his mug would ruin his exit.

o o o

Deals

After an hour of paging several coworkers to find someone to retrieve the thirsty monkey mug, Ben moves up to hot chocolate, but it doesn't speed his progress on either bug. A surge of unhappy footsteps a few minutes ago marked the meeting's end, but a stream of developers had trickled out after his explosion. He figures it's the end-of-a-party syndrome, where everyone secretly feels ready to go but no one wants to be the first to leave.

The floor's hush is not the usual quiet of concentration and flow, but the hush of "Hey, someone's pet did something unpleasant on the floor and oh, I see, the first person who mentions it has just adopted a new problem". Poisoned air seethes in and out of the open doors, billowing and collecting like smoke in the closed offices. He can't see whether the plumes are fatal black or seething red or blue-green, angry-eyed reluctant acceptance.

He knows his mood. It's a fury to code so fiercely, to turn out multitudinous lines of the program with determined velocity and something to prove. If they tell him to die on this hill, he'll fight his way up one side and down the other until he's outlived everyone else, just to show them that he can do it.

He identifies that feeling as stupid, too.

The red curtain lifts from behind his eyes and he weighs his options. The only tactical objective that makes sense is to continue his normal work until told otherwise. That is, he keeps his normal working hours, his normal working pace, and his normal schedule through the dragging new conversion. The world refuses to acknowledge his reasonableness, but it'll grind with friction for a while, then slip into place. He'll be the fulcrum if he can stay strong and keep his feet's solid ground-grip.

Fixing these two bugs today will prove it. He'll reward himself with a nice, relaxing weekend of not thinking about it at all because he's a good programmer and can handle anything. If he sets his mind to it, he'll stop doodling on the notepad, stop flipping back and forth through mailing lists, shut the door, and spend two solid hours devoting his entire attention to his work. He'll clear the toys off of his desk, close his web browser, and close the blinds so he can't stare out the window. He will.

If he starts now, he has an hour and a half before he absolutely must eat lunch. If he concentrates, he can write fifty lines of really good, well-tested code. Both bugs are likely small, probably fewer than five lines of offending code apiece, so if that's ten lines to write, he has 36 minutes to write and test the bug fixes, leaving most of an hour to find the bugs. That's half an hour per bug. He's chased down the translation bug for a while, but he's never put his whole mind into it. If he really buckles down, surely it can't take half an hour, leaving more time for the other bug.

Then he'll have lunch, somewhere. A small contingent with fluid membership leaves on most days between 11:45 and noon. Another leaves around 12:30. Several decent restaurants within walking distance serve lunch quickly enough, even for a party of seven or eight, that lunch rarely stretches past an hour and a quarter. Ben always feels vaguely guilty at the fifty-minute mark, wishing the server would hurry up with the check and walking back faster than the average slow post-lunch mosey of his coworkers. If he fixes even the first bug, he can easily go with the second group. Otherwise, he'll eat lunch at his desk, though he'll stop programming while he eats, allowing his subconscious and unconscious to fit the pieces together while his consciousness rests. His mind clears.

A knock disturbs his math. Dewang and Eddie, two junior programmers, both bear the weight of the world in their shirt pockets as they stand outside his door. His eyes flick to the clock in the corner of his screen, beneath the untouched code window. "What's up?"

Dewang shifts between feet in the hallway before ducking in, head first, as if crossing under a short gate. "Ben, we have an idea." Eddie follows and wheels in an extra chair. His head bounces with encouragement.

"I do not want to work overtime every night on a project that will stretch for many months. We will offer to Mr. Gill to rotate on four teams of ten that each have the option to work overtime one week out of each month."

Eddie interrupts, "But we don't force it; it's only if we miss our weekly targets, you see?"

"Weekly targets?"

"Every part of the conversion has a step and a place in the ordering. We must make a list of each step and its place and give each one to a week."

"What we do now, except on a longer term."

Eddie hops in his chair. "That's right, it's just normal. We make a schedule, we cut out the fat, we stick to it, and we succeed."

Ben counts the holes in the corner of a ceiling tile. Thirty-seven. "How do you know the steps are equal? How do you know that Team A won't have all of the really tough weeks, the ones that should have been two weeks—or more?"

There's silence. Yep, thirty-seven. Then Dewang suggests, "If the step goes longer then Team B will take over the overtime and it will remain fair."

"Every step will fit into a week?"

This time, Ben breaks the silence. "We have a schedule. Three months. We don't know what all of the work will entail. Things'll slip, and they'll figure out important things that no one remembered until they break." His knees ache with the possibility that the project will grind on and on, bones on bones. He promises himself that the fear will go away if he ignores it.

Eddie's voice cracks. "What do we do, Ben? This is impossible." Dewang still looks thoughtful, though his eyes are still wide, white completely surrounding the iris.

Ben leans back in his chair, left thumb tucked under his belt buckle and right arm alongside his head, cradling his crown in his elbow's crook. "We do what we always do. We do what they pay us to do—write good code, keep sane hours, and produce what we can produce. That's the deal we agreed to. They don't change the rules now."

Dewang still wears a thoughtful expression, though he narrows his eyes and nods gently. Eddie's even more nervous; Ben wants to offer him a little paper bag, but he doesn't have one and prefers to point him toward the restroom instead.

○ ○ ○

Numb

Ben finds the strange data-loss bug while slowly going mad with the translation bug. As usual, it's a stupid assumption made by two or three people in different times and places. Judging by the flood of angry energy in his clenched fists and his jutting jaw, he has a Tech Tip for the next meeting.

He rubs his eyes and leans back in his chair with a stretch and yawn, then looks at his watch, expecting maybe 12:15 or 12:30, with plenty of time to catch the second coterie, but it's nearly 2. Whatever he can grab will barely be nuncheon, let alone lunch.

One of the best technical interview questions he's ever heard is, "Devise a general mechanism to recognize customer names." A well-loved programmer game is to devise algorithms and traps to weed out the fifty percent of programmers who consider themselves above average but really only exist to make the five percent of really great programmers between one and two magnitudes better than average.

Average programmers rely on capitalization alone.

Decent programmers allow for more than a single first and last name.

Good programmers acknowledge apostrophes and hyphens.

Great programmers, programmers with experience, and programmers with worldviews far beyond gathered suburban yuppies, take your pick, allow for accents, symbols, and other one-in-a-thousand instances unless you have customers outside, say, Peoria and its suburbs.

Ben works with several good programmers who learn from the great ones. Their system transfers knowledge and experience. However, there are still a few inconsistencies. Most of the names the current system handles are simple enough for the average programmer's rules to catch. They're *decent* rules, but even a system that makes one mistake in a thousand tries makes plenty of mistakes when it handles a thousand records a second.

Because it's so easy to create solutions that work almost every time, a couple of programmers have optimized for that case. It's not deliberate—the system allows for accents and breath marks and even symbols from non-phonetic languages. However, the code doesn't respect the implications.

The human eye can identify and recognize several different symbols; whatever pattern recognition schemes it uses requires very little extra data to differentiate, for example, between ö and ©. Computers are different. At their heart they recognize no patterns except by conventions where a pattern of changes of voltage from high to low in this particular configuration signifies one thing and a different pattern of changes signifies something else.

It's important where you start counting and how far you count.

Plain English with no accents or decorations or symbols is always fine. However, there's only so much information you can store in any system. If you want more characters, you have to tell the computer to use a larger alphabet, and you both must agree on where that alphabet starts and stops and how large each pattern of changes is.

Ben's mother smiles and nods at this explanation. "Like a code," she says. He promises himself again to call her for real after work.

When, for example, the robot asks the librarian to retrieve information about Jörgen Nilsson, the librarian has to ponder the request. It has four options. It could add new information, fetch existing information, change existing information, or remove information. It actually goes through that list, in order, when deciding what to do.

The problem is that it uses the wrong pattern, one which doesn't match an alphabet that can handle poor Jörgen's name. That alphabet change affects the description of the request. When it compares the patterns it understands to the request, it doesn't match. The alphabets are too different. The request to retrieve information doesn't look like a request to retrieve information.

"That's funny," he repeats. The code, as written, always makes the librarian throw up its hands and delete something unless the robot explicitly says, "Fetch a file" or "Update a file!" or "Add a file!". "Have a nice day!" or "How's the weather?" cause deletes too.

"Just like Chico Marx!" Randy exclaims. Those movies ought to come out on DVD soon.

The fix takes two parts. First, he changes the librarian's patterns to match regardless of the alphabet used. Second, he permits the librarian to throw a fit if it receives a request it doesn't understand instead of performing random and probably very wrong actions.

He watches three or four people each make a compounding mistake without thinking things through. It only takes ten minutes to write a test case that shows the bug in the appropriate spot and fix it in a simple way that ought to work. The real fix is more subtle and requires the kind of thought and foresight and clarity that he thought the great programmers had begun to spoon out to the rest of the department.

He ponders mailing his report to the entire department, but deletes the first and last lines, which seem vaguely insulting in their use of the phrase "Unicode-unaware morons". Perhaps it's less cute than it is inflammatory. The pains in his stomach aren't helping him think.

By the time he returns from lunch, even the bare-minimum thirty minutes, it'll be 2:30 or later. That leaves two full clock hours before he goes home, counting at least one ten-minute break he will allow himself. He's already worked through at least one. It's almost not worth eating now.

Slipping off schedule starts as a fuzzy feeling in the back of his head. Someone packs it with the gritty cotton fluff found in over the counter pill bottles, half desiccant and half padding. A dry sensation tickles his upper nose and his mouth has made its own glue. The thirsty monkey holds only a grainy brownish ring.

Ben stands and flicks open the window blinds. Everything seems far away; he watches the world from the small end of a telescope situated six inches behind his eyeballs. The low and southerly west sun barely crests the hills. Strangely for winter in the city, there are no clouds blocking the view, and the orange glow in the sky sets fluffy jet contrails aflame to bring out highlights in the bricks of the building across the way, almost a Roset.

The snack machine in the break room has always intimidated him; besides offering tired-looking apples and oranges, it has reasonably cheap but frightening microwaveable mealettes: beef stew, salty noodles that resemble soup when reconstituted with hot water, and even individually cellophaned hamburgers. The approximate nutritional value of the entire machine tends towards that of salt and sugar licks thrown into a nearly-ripe rice paddy, but it's close and convenient and will keep his Krebs Cycle fueled.

The single-serving beef stew would fit in the thirsty monkey mug and might barely cover the bottom of a stew bowl at home but it only costs seventy-five cents and two minutes to heat. Ten seconds into eating at his desk, he realizes that the clenching of his stomach has more in common with the pain in the middle of his back, between the shoulder blades, and his irrational desire to knock over the hapless vending machine when it switched products too slowly. He resists it, as he's already given in to that itch today to find and fix a bug—any bug.

He hears shuffling again from upstairs and gives silent thanks for having no weapon sharper than a dull plastic spoon. He observes himself taking the elevator upstairs calmly, nodding pleasantly to the receptionist for the second time today, and kicking a rolling chair through a window, despite the laws of physics, before announcing in a low, quiet voice that this noise and exuberance for closing a big sale is deleterious when considering the people actually doing the work.

He catches his daydream between trying to recall the approximate position of fire extinguishers between here and there and then to calculate the closest equal-temperament pitch to the collision of nearly-full fire extinguisher with nearly empty management cranium. He substitutes instead a brisk walk outside. Besides, the stew is way too salty, especially the potatoes.

Ben hates that.

o o o

Resignation

On overcast December days in the city, the sky darkens early into a grayish glow that lends life an airy unreality. Clear nights grow truly dark, the color of blue velvet at midnight, but low clouds weave tightly together and streetlights and headlights and traffic lights scatter gently their diffuse beams. Everything moves more slowly, or maybe there's less in the background to notice and process.

Ben remembers arguing with his mother at age seven about going to bed in the summer. "It's still early," he cried. "It's still light! It's not night; it's day!" The varying length of a day, sunup to sundown, still confuses him. He continues half-hearted coding and runs through a dozen discarded plans halfway, but somewhere his head tickles and pushes him to shut down for the day, grab his coat, and go, to make the most of the few minutes of daylight he has remaining. It's nearly 4 pm.

The floor still has a hush, almost that of the single last-minute long weekend they'd spent a couple of years ago, yet without spontaneous games of hackey sack or soda can pyramid contests or the brief-but-fierce artillery wars of lobbing foam balls over walls and around corners at each other that broke out every forty-five minutes. There's a sense of waiting, anticipation, maybe high noon in Arizona circa 1873 in front of the saloon, where everyone knows something will happen, someday, eventually.

He'd feel better, he thinks, if Jerry were here. Jerry's not perfect; he tends to delay major decisions in favor of a group consensus to absolve him of sometimes risky responsibilities, but he's led well for almost four years, replacing a predecessor who cared less about results than hard-to-measure but impressively-graphed short-term statistics. At some point in the mid-'90s, PowerPoint became the first refuge of the incompetent.

Ben pushes away his keyboard and folds his arms on his desk, right hand over left bicep and left hand under right bicep above the elbow. He closes his eyes, and he rests his forehead on his forearms before pushing back in his chair to stretch his back. There's a weary tension in the muscles under his shoulder blades as if he'd clenched them all day and they prefer now to lie around the house moaning and asking for tea and crackers and maybe some soup if he feels up to it, if that wouldn't be a bother.

He breathes deeply and lets his mind wander, free-association style, for a moment. He tries to avoid this at work and cannot prevent it before he sleeps, but his dreams have been restless lately.

A calendar appears with rows and columns of unlabeled marching squares. They leap off of the flipping pages and rush at his point of view. Black wire-frames with white backgrounds overlap and recede into the horizon, month after month. Some days break, revealing their tight edges as wires under tremendous tension. Sick musical snapping sounds ricochet; strings become springs: wire and wood. Squares snap together into blocks, gaining an extra dimension to complement one, two, and four. They pile up in front of broken-day scribbles. They're smooth and heavy salt licks, or business-safe Swedish furniture, boring in its utilitarian design, the ideal of a flat surface expressing its only attribute in the only way possible: flat.

It's a house, a tower, a ziggurat. It's a monument to hubris, a cell that threatens to lock him away. It's days and days and blocks and blocks, blank-faced, huge multi-ton sandstone piles in the desert at the river delta's edge. All there is is the slow march of calendar leavings making patterns of their own—they must make patterns, they've overwhelmed anyone who could possibly bring them to order. They won't stop. He can't tell when his perspective shifts from watching with his own eyes, but his own tiny self dodges falling blocks, red shirt and blue pants and a smear of light-brown hair. He's a cartoon character in a game, a caricature dreading the inevitable slip and misstep that stops the action with a series of sad bloops and a close-up of a greasy smear on the side of one block.

He shrinks or the blocks grows and the view from space flashes, with the Great Wall of China on one side and the next several months of his life on the other. The heartbreaking day-breaking sounds continue; their multi-frequency screams and gasps echo in an empty, egg-shaped chamber. The blocks crash into each other, now heavy and solid, maybe bowling balls or billiards. Immovable objects bounce and jostle by design, neither fitting together gently nor giving way to find an ideal arrangement as might a shaken can of mixed nuts. Each fights for its original place, a local maxima of position, frequency, and prestige. They're still bland, but they have such angry and demanding personalities that he can start to distinguish a few.

114

That one there, twenty-nine for sure, falls at him as if gravity were an act of its malicious will.

He runs, but blocks in front of him, blocks beside him, and blocks behind him stop him. He climbs, but hard and cold and chakily dull sides are too smooth to gain purchase. He cuts his hand on the corner of one block, drawing back his hand before its partner can smash and trap his fingers. Blocks beneath his feet fit together without seam and only the barest hint of a difference between days to mark their passing. The sense of magnitude and view of the universe as a whole evaporates. Twenty-nine swoops ever lower, ever faster aiming straight for him. Everything holds its breath. With a dramatic pause, the block stops briefly to gather its strength and then slams down on Ben.

A rushing wind sound fills his head. Distant twangs and snaps die sadly off, like the last few lonely microwave popcorn kernels, and everything fades to white. He feels only a squeezing in his chest, as if something presses him flat from the bottom up, forcing everything through ever-smaller arteries and capillaries. Then it reaches its breaking point and holds there and then pops with a flushing, swallowing sound and feeling he hears and feels. It's such an ache as if there's nothing left but a hole there and then he doesn't even feel that at all anymore.

Ben raises his head. His lower right lip and that side of his chin feel hotly sticky and his mouth is dry. He rubs his face and checks his watch. It's 5:30; the other offices are dark. The traffic sounds outside have increased, though they're still distant under the sky cover. He realigns his keyboard to check his e-mail one last time before fighting the bug again, but instead somehow locks his screen for whatever reason he can't explain.

A moment later, coat in hand, he presses the elevator button. Thoughts of cubes and cables swoop in from somewhere he can't describe with shadows of dark, winged creatures. He chooses the stairs instead. A far off sound of tension and release echoes.

Oddly, the little voice that usually feels guilty for leaving a piece of work undone has absolutely nothing to say.

○   ○   ○

Couples

Equinox

R ANDY marks the changing of the seasons with a discipline notable in its presence, if not its subject. Most of his friends figure that it's an excuse for him to follow through on an idea at most once every three months, though the winter solstice tends to merge in with someone else's holiday party. Only the summer and fall receive any real attention, and that as barbecues.

March turned out surprisingly pleasant, so he'd suggested to Ben and Emily the idea of a picnic. They and Randy and Libby would retreat to a local mountaintop park with plenty of parking or easy access via public transportation, and a spectacularly appropriate view of hills and budding greenery, and of course sandwich fixings or fried chicken and definitely some forms of macaroni salad, coleslaw, cold drinks, potato chips, and gelatinous dessert if not also cookies, to welcome glorious springtime.

Ben rolled his eyes when the presentation turned florid and pretended interest in a television commercial. Emily, watching Randy and not Ben, admitted to no small curiosity about finally meeting Libby. Ben hid a snicker.

After promising that Libby would appear and consulting a calendar, Randy proclaimed that the afternoon of Saturday the 22nd at 1:30 pm should be warm enough and, hopefully, dry. Emily scrunched down her left eyebrow and turned to look at Ben, who claimed that he had merely coughed, and agreed that, yes, Randy's plan sounded fine.

It's actually sunny and, with a sweatshirt, remarkably pleasant, though the wet grass makes Ben glad to have remembered a thick blanket. He and Emily are early; he buffered plenty of time to walk to the train from her house and ride across the river, through downtown, and halfway through the mountain with ever-increasing hunger from the swirling scent of fried chicken. Emily had made two batches of chocolate chip cookies, and Ben has already sneaked two, wiping away crumbs with well-timed expertise. As a distraction, he wondered aloud what Randy will bring. He cannot imagine a picnic without picnic-type fruits—grapes and watermelons, as March is a month not known for bountiful crops, at least in North America.

The sun bleaches white a few clouds out of reach of a caressing breeze. At the top of a trail, a clearing slopes down a larger hill, bound by trees on the west and south sides and the trail and smaller undergrowth on the north and west sides. Emily spreads a blanket and sits. Past the ridge of trees at the western edge of the hill, the entire city sprawls in its two-river valley. Skyscrapers slope down to one river. The industrial center on the other side pokes upward with revitalization and renewal. Bridges span north-south and east-west. Ben stares. He always feels small here. It strikes harder at night when every light in house, office, and car represents a single person, and the collective glow plays out millions of stories every day. He'll touch but a few, ever.

Emily has said little today. He looks back at her as the breeze teases and tangles the ends of her hair. She sits on the side of her left thigh with her knees bent to the right in tan pants, white tennis shoes, and a navy blue fleece. She savors a cookie with contentment on her face—bird songs, fresh air, butter fat, sugar, and chocolate. If she stayed there, she could join the scenery as a beautiful bronze and concrete monument to man's place in nature. He has an urge to kneel down before—no, beside her–hand on her shoulder, to join the overflowing moment, to absorb her appreciation, but fears that he'd interfere, as if trying to measure her rapture would change it, that his unconscious appreciation is as close as he can come to understanding what she finds so beautiful.

She finishes the cookie and stretches unselfconsciously, legs straight and in front of her and arms pointed up. One hand pulls on the other wrist, and then she switches. She drinks deeply of a water bottle from her backpack. When he blinks, he can see her eyelashes flutter as she closes her eyes, face to the sun and the breeze. He was too far away for that detail, but he can *see* them in his memory.

Laughter precedes the rest of the party up the path. Ben recognizes Randy's sound; it would be cruelty from anyone else. He jokes to demonstrate inconsistency or injustice or ridiculousness, rarely to berate or belittle, as Ben often must explain. The world would go wrong if anyone took half of those ideas seriously.

Everyone meets at the top of the trail. Emily stands and smiles to introduce herself. Randy and Libby finish another private joke, foreheads together, and turn to face her. "Hi Em; this is Libby."

Emily offers her hand. "I've heard many wonderful things about you." They clasp and squeeze with alert feline grace, though neither relaxes into an easy posture.

Libby twists her mouth and raises an eyebrow. "Randy likes to tell stories." He feigns the start of a hug, but then pouts, puppy-eyed and droopy lower-lipped, and she attacks his hip with a tickle and he drops the plastic shopping bags. It tips, and a bottle falls out with a shuffle-clink.

Emily glances sideways at Ben. He's never known how to handle this either, but jumps in front of the bullet anyway. "I like the red hair. It looks nice on you." He almost convinces himself.

Libby breaks the tangle to turn hungry eyes his way. "Thanks." She pulls a handful of hair into view to ponder. "It was time for a change. Blonde just wasn't me anymore."

Randy jumps in. "People take her seriously now too. . . you should see it. Ow, hey!" She withdraws the stomach pinch and sets her jaw under a wicked grin as if daring him to swing, with one foot forward and both fists up. She throws a slow punch at his face. He slaps it away gently, to grab her hand and twist her arm until he has her in a slow hug from behind. Then he leans around and kisses her on the cheek until she slams her hip into his and they break apart, laughing.

Emily looks lost. Ben grinds the base of his palm into his forehead; he had only warned her to avoid calling Libby anything until she offered her preferred proper noun, without explaining that that's as much as he's ever understood. Ben kneels to rummage through the backpack for paper plates and silverware, figuring that he's hungry and food has at least a chance of keeping Libby quieter for fifteen minutes. He holds out a plate to Emily and asks Randy, "What'd you figure out there?"

"Glad you asked. It's a salad day—macaroni salad, potato salad, Jell-O salad," he sing-songs, stacattoed and rhythmic. "Also, two, yes, two bottles of sparkling grape juice. The fruits of the vine as you might say."

Ben waits for the orphan at the end of the sentence. It doesn't arrive. ". . . And cups?"

"Zee vine, ve drink it straight from zee bottle, oui?" Randy waggles his eyebrows and twiddles a fake cigar, like a triumphant half-French, half-Russian Groucho Marx handing one bottle to Ben.

"Uh, thanks." He mouths the word "water" at Emily and she reaches for her backpack. They're not yet to Paris, evidently. Ben hands out the other plates and silverware as Randy and Libby stake out their blanket corner. Besides the chicken and cookies, Ben threw together a fruit salad from canned ingredients, rinsing the pineapple chunks to make them feel fresher and packing the coconut in a separate bag, having once lost an argument he hadn't actually participated in about how it was an abomination in shredded form, not daring to ask what people expected from a German Chocolate Cake. He closes his eyes to enjoy the idea, then reminds himself to bake, borrow, or steal one soon.

They eat in polite silence. Randy makes an occasional chewing noise, and he and Ben pass containers back and forth for seconds. A surprising wind threatens to shuffle everything several yards southeast, at least until they rearrange their meal from heavy to light vertically, stowing papers and chicken bones and wrappers under corners of containers and backpacks. Randy and Libby exchange significant looks throughout the meal, he with his legs out in front of him, bent slightly at the knees to create a diamond for his plate and one bottle of juice and she, cross-legged, leaning back slightly on his right shoulder and stealing drinks when everyone's looking.

Ben loads up on macaroni and Jell-O, with a double serving of fruit salad. Chicken-wise, he started with a medium-sized thigh, having grown up in the potluck world where meat runs out first to leave tables of green beans and other casseroles for the adventurous or the poor souls too hungry to wait for seventeen different types of lemon bars. He still likes those. Carbohydrate satiation makes the protein smell more delicious, so he floats the idea and, with assent, helps himself to a couple of drumsticks, sighing about the finger-greasening inadequacies of the plastic fork and knife.

Emily shows little of the gusto she'd demonstrated in the restaurant, seeming content with small samples of everything. She returns to her sideways posture, halfway between and an arm's length from both Ben and Libby. Her eyes flick between them. "When I was little, my dad would always take me to the park. We'd walk around the pond and then sit on the bench and feed the ducks popcorn. It would be so nice to have some popcorn."

Randy grins. "White cheese, perhaps?"

"I don't think ducks like cheese," Emily shrugs. "It was just regular popcorn."

"No, I'm just saying that that's the one true flavor. White cheese."

Libby jumps in. "You are a fool and the paragon of bad taste. It's caramel corn or nothing."

Randy leans forward. "Caramel corn? With those nasty little Spanish peanuts that chip your teeth and that goo that makes unpopped kernels even harder than tensor calculus? Disgusting."

Emily pushes away her plate, food half-untouched.

"I suppose the delicate play of the contrasts of color, tastes, and textures is too complicated for someone whose main goal for snacks is that they turn his fingers day-glo orange. That's a flavor you want to put in your body?"

"They invented caramel corn to cover burned popcorn. You know it. Don't hide it. Also, it's white, not orange. Don't let your smugness hurt your vision, dear."

Randy and Libby have blocked out everything else. Their volume gradually increases to a level that might have been a normal conversational tone in a motorcycle racing pit. She leans away from him to prop herself up with her right hand and use her left hand for accusatory and emphatic punctuational gestures. Randy wears a tight smile and his eyes flash. He leans back on both hands and stifles a yawn.

Ben has shifted his concentration to chew bits of meat from the thick end of the first drumstick when Emily taps his calf with the back of her wrist. He blinks. She mouths something sideways at him, eyes still on the argument. He shrugs and returns to the meal before she throws a shorter, half-profile glance, and raises her eyebrows in a "help?" gesture. He finishes his bite and makes a show of wiping his lips and, by now, seriously greasy fingers on a napkin. Emily draws her knees to her chest.

The aural level has stabilized enough and the pool of near and easily flung witticisms has dwindled such that Ben can slide in and draw out one word much louder than he'd like but not far enough that any other group can hear, he hopes. "Well, *I*...wish we had some popcorn too."

That ends it. Neither Randy nor Libby makes it halfway through the first sentence before trailing off, she throwing doubts about his command of self-evident facts related to culinary truths and he attacking her understanding of his excellent cognitive and insightful perceptual skills. The grove rings with silence. Then Libby starts again.

"That's the dumbest thing you've said yet, Ben."

He shrugs. "I like popcorn. Take me out of your will."

Randy digs through the bags. "That reminds me. If we're all done eating, how about a little frisbee?" Libby is on her feet in a second, and she grabs the disc and runs into the clearing.

Ben holds up his remaining drumstick. "I'll be there in a minute."

Randy looks at Emily, who shakes her head and offers to cover the food. Then he has the frisbee aimed at his head with near malevolent, if wobbly, force. As he leaps away in a full-body throw, Emily unlocks her interwoven fingers and sighs through puffed cheeks. "Does that happen often?"

"Libby trying to kill Randy? Once or twice a day, in my experience."

"The general pattern, I mean. The arguing and violence."

"I don't take her seriously. I've only seen *him* take one or two women seriously, and that was very different. That's just how they communicate; they found an honesty that makes everyone else nervous. I had a great-aunt and uncle like that once. At family reunions they'd gang up on whoever was unfortunate enough to sit across from them at dinner and try to hold two simultaneous conversations with the poor kid, apparently ignorant of the verbal presence of the other. They'd interrupt only to argue over passing the rolls or the jam or whatever."

Emily stretches her legs, rotating her toe in a small circle. "That doesn't sound so healthy."

"I actually prefer this to another girl Randy knew once. She was all over him every time she thought no one was looking. That may have been the last time I actually saw him uncomfortable—poor guy kept wiping lipstick off of his face and ear and neck."

"That bothered him?"

"He brought it up once, obliquely, in the context of a nature show about how queen bees mark all of their workers with their own scents, or something."

"Insightful."

"It really wasn't. The actual phrase was, 'I call the fat one Debra.'" Emily tilts her head. "The queen."

She laughs, despite herself, hand to mouth with quiet torso shakes. "That's terrible. That's awful!"

Ben grins and sets down the bone. "I almost fell out of my chair. I had no idea what to say, and left the room as fast as I could, just in case I'd really hurt his feelings laughing."

"You can do that?"

"I laughed so hard I had to blow my nose and wash away the tears. Then I figured out that he probably said it as much to provoke a reaction as to express any deep-seated emotional trauma. He's never really carried any, not that I've known."

"That doesn't sound right."

"I couldn't do it, but in some ways he's the healthiest person I know. Maybe he's the sneakiest. I don't think he has any malice in him. Every time I play a trick on him, I feel like I've just pretended to throw a ball for the puppy who then puts on reading glasses and climbs in a leather chair by the fire to read the financial pages and say, 'Mmmm yes, very droll, yes.'"

Emily pauses her leftover packing, and turns to watch Randy. His arms are wild as he throws the frisbee as hard as he can at Libby, who has discarded her heeled sandals and wiggles her hands near her knees in a classic women's softball shortstop pose, ready to dive for the disc. "Maybe I've underestimated him."

"Everybody does. He prefers that, really. Once in a while he'll do something flat-out brilliant and genius and surprise everyone and then go right back to being unremarkable except for how unboringly normal he really is."

"Do you admire him?" She has an honest expression. She leans in close; her face is open with...less curiosity than genuine wonder.

"I could never be him, but in some ways he's more human than anyone else I could ever know."

Now Emily stares at Ben. He meets her wide eyes.

"You really mean that."

"I do. I don't think anything's ever knocked him down. It's as if he's incapable of feeling regret or holding a grudge."

"That's not human."

"That's not really it. Maybe he just doesn't act on them, or maybe he's a sneak."

Emily shakes her head. "I can't understand that. If someone hurts you, how do you not react?"

"The happy hobo mentality."

"The what?"

"This character I made up to tell stories when I was little. He was a hobo with no job, no home, and nothing besides the clothes on his back. He kept falling into one adventure after another trying to make money, but he'd always lose everything and end up in the same situation as before. The thing is, he always walked away at the end whistling and thinking, 'Hey, always tomorrow!'"

"Like Charlie Chaplain?"

Ben slaps his forehead. "Well, yeah. I'd never realized where he came from."

She smiles. "Good that you stole from the classics, though. It's better than learning opera from watching Looney Tunes, right?"

He rolls his eyes, "That's a separate conversation altogether. The point is that there's an archetype somewhere here. It's not the Greek tragic hero who fails because of his hubris, but maybe the luckless vagabond—the lovable scamp—who never succeeds but never gives up because he has nothing to lose and everything to gain."

"A ho...bo with a heart of gold?"

There's a pause. "That's awful enough to have come from an English major. Are you secretly going into law to sneak puns into contracts and briefs?"

A wink and a devilish smile flash across her face before she mumbles something about the judicial system being the second greatest source of dirty jokes in Latin after the medical profession. Suddenly he loves her a little more.

In the distance, Libby runs away with the frisbee, trying to keep one step ahead of Randy, who exaggerates a cartoonish gait. She yells threats. He happily ignores them.

Ben shakes his head. "We'd better join them before they fall off of a cliff or something." He stands. She pulls herself up with the hand he hadn't really offered. No matter how many napkins he uses, he still can't get it clean.

"Only if you promise never to chase me off of a cliff," she warns.

"I promise," he starts, stopping just before finishing the thought out loud. She turns, waiting. "That's it. I promise." He smiles and she accepts that, bounding off into the clearing.

He sighs and tries to silence whichever perverse deviltry gave him the rest of the sentence. "I promise only if you promise never to lead me off of a cliff."

o   o   o

Train

Randy had forgotten to mention that he had the pager that weekend, whether out of the belief that ignorance would make it go away or from experience that it rarely went off. At least, that's what Ben reads on Randy's face when he suddenly drops the frisbee mid-swing, clasping his hand to his back pocket and frowning at the little display.

He yells to Ben, "Get Libby home!", scoops up his backpack, and disappears down the trail.

Ben had only seen this happen twice since Randy had volunteered for the bimonthly weekend rotation. A strange disease swept across the customers of his information services department in which middle managers, weak from playing Solitaire all morning Friday before departing for long lunches around 11 am and never really making it back into the office, panicked at not being able to check their work e-mail at 2 or 3 am on Sunday and were willing to pay the IT department triple the normal hourly rate with a guaranteed four-hour minimum for a help desk monkey to discover that the screaming, crying, or threatening manager had, despite all protestations, entered his password incorrectly.

The second time, Randy disabled their Caps Lock keys remotely.

The interruption takes the fun out of the party. Randy had been a buffer, soaking up the tension—Ben and Libby chilly toward each other and Emily just nervous—by not really ignoring it but maybe denying it, as if by will he could make people feel comfortable.

Fortunately, Emily had nearly finished packing, and within fifteen minutes they sit on the train heading east. Ben finally decides that Randy doesn't really care if people feel uncomfortable, as he'll have a good time anyway. Even Emily had loosened up around Libby enough to play frisbee for a while.

The train is surprisingly busy for a Saturday afternoon, with a few scattered empty seats as it whistles out of the long tunnel and rumbles into downtown. Ben and Emily have seats together with Libby alone in the row ahead. There's little conversation; Ben wonders if he can convince Emily to come along while taking Libby home so as not to spend time alone with her. If he's lucky, it will be a very short trip.

In the handful of stops, the train finally fills. A young motherly-looking woman takes the last open seat, right next to Libby. Libby makes a face and turns around to face Emily.

"I can't believe Randy had to go into work. Can you? He just left me there, and now it'll take hours to go home."

Emily shrugs. "Hopefully he'll be back soon." She looks at Ben, but he pretends to find the poetry along the top of the car more interesting. It is, in the sense that it's replaced poorly designed ads for health insurance. He has two different possible routes to where he thinks Libby lives, but he can't decide which might be faster. It's a gamble; if the freeway is busy, traffic won't drive any faster than the maximum speed on the surface streets, but there are no traffic lights. Then again, the ability of drivers to merge or to allow merging traffic to merge seems to have decreased in recent years; he contrariwise expected greater experience with on-ramps to have improved the situation.

The next stop is the first of several where pedestrians ride for free. The aisles fill. Libby continues her monologue, and when Ben stands up to offer his seat to an older woman carrying two small plastic bags of groceries, Libby slides next to Emily.

Ben holds the chrome pole behind the seats and leans his head against the scratched plastic window.

"... and I don't really mind, so much, but the least they could do is tell him when they're going to call. It's simple courtesy. I hate how rude people are these days. We had plans and they can't leave him alone for two hours? Some people have no patience."

He likes watching streams of people spill out of the train and head in their own directions. He's had this idea in his head since junior high school of tagging everyone in one spot and then watching little red dots diffuse throughout the city on a satellite map. As an undergraduate, late one night he imagined it making patterns like dyes joining a water solution. Where do they go? Do they eventually merge again?

"It's always crowded on the train downtown and if there weren't so many people it would be so much faster. Don't even talk to me about buying tickets; the train always shows up just then and there's never enough time to buy a ticket. They should have a ticket machine on the train, so you can just board the train and buy your ticket there without having to rush. Wouldn't that be so much easier?"

A loose squad of bored teenagers ambles aboard. One guy wears his pants halfway to his knees and a filthy and fading sweatshirt covers up an old rock concert T-shirt probably stolen from his father. A tiny blonde girl hangs off of his arm. Her chubby brunette friend giggles on a phone. The brunette has a tiny vinyl pink purse. The boy has terrible posture, and the blonde staggers as the train wobbles while she tries to run her hands across his chest. Ben probably has fifty pounds on the boy, but notices himself sliding closer to Emily, just in case.

"Then the second time I broke my toe, I had to wait in the emergency room for almost two hours before even an intern could look at me. They wouldn't even give me an ice pack after the first one melted! Then the best thing they could do was tell me to keep off of it for two days until I could go to an orthopedic clinic? I was furious. It was so rude."

The boy has messy hair in the same vein as too-cool-to-comb-it pop star or overslept-for-a-lecture grad student. The girl stretches to kiss him. He submits to it, looking elsewhere. She giggles at the passion of his boredom.

"No, I really can tell when it's going to rain. It swells up. Look, I'll show you." Libby fidgets to pull her right foot up onto her left thigh and slip off her sandal. "It's because," she continues, "they didn't set it the first time and I knew it'd be trouble. Then they wanted to break it again, as if I hadn't had enough pain. I don't know what they teach doctors these days."

There's cross-traffic at the next stop: cars lined up at a stoplight dedicated to the train. The boy shoves his hands in his pockets and slouches off of the train. The blonde pulls her friend, who protests something into the phone with loud slogans of mock anguish teenage disbelief. As the train accelerates, the boy manages to stay just ahead of the girls despite his hitching up his pants every two steps and their running, arms linked, in little tiny strides more suitable for kimonos than flared jeans.

"...and I didn't talk to my father for a week after that. He learned his lesson, though. I'm his little princess. He could never stay mad at me. Why would he? Now my mother, I don't know what she was thinking sometimes. She couldn't ever have been a teenager, she had no idea what it was like. It was always about making sure I never had any of the fun she missed out on."

Ben counts to eleven twice on the route map just above his head. Eleven stops and he's still only halfway to being rid of Libby. He rests his head against the window again and puts his left hand on Emily's left shoulder. After a moment, she rests hers on his.

○ ○ ○

Friday Night Somewhere

Ben isn't sure what to expect from Emily's Friday night plans. It's, as she put it, "a little party, not very big at all, just some friends from school we met as freshmen. I think there are a couple of philosophy and English majors, so you won't feel out of place. If you want to come, you'll have fun."

He feels silly entertaining visions in which he stands with his left arm on the brick mantle of a fireplace and a large brandy snifter in his right hand, to lead a debate between fresh-faced sophomores over the elevation of historical inevitability in German thought starting with Hegel and vulgarized in Marx, promoting a dialectical view of the world as the primary driver of social, philosophical, theological, moral, and eventually economic development. Just when he forced that out of his head, its sibling suggested that he warm up the crowd from the local Catholic-run university with the idea that the Protestant Reformation was actually just another outbreak of the Platonist and Aristotelean conflict—a defensible position when appealing to the rigid post-Roman philosophical system that had produced Augustine and Aquinas as well as feudalism, though it requires ignoring most of the Republic. As the debate wore down, he'd gently steer the conversation toward the other topic, though admittedly going from "Plato versus Aristotle through a millennium of history", a subject of ongoing interest, to, effectively, "did Marx say anything interesting or at least new?" is a letdown, there being little real debate for anyone besides the true believers who'd just muddled their way through *Das Kapital* or, worse, *Atlas Shrugged*.

Brandy always makes him cough though.

Ben's always believed that that particular intellectual flirtation should start and finish by the second week of the spring freshman semester, if at all, leaving a spring break unmarred by muddy thinking. He hadn't attended many parties as an undergrad. As a philosophy major who lived off of campus at a small private Midwest school, he wasn't even in the Popular National Guard, as Randy put it; people rarely called him up for duty. Even if he'd gone, the kinds of parties where people wanted him around might have barely risen to the excitement level of his anticipation anyway. The first and last time he played a trivia game as an adult, he'd lost the game at a question that asked the name of the opera set partially in Japan that ends with the suicide of the titular character. That was the highlight of the party.

Ben works his way through the intersection of a tired street in the northern part of the city where he rarely drives. He arrived at Emily's house around 7 pm to drive her and Shelly to the party by a comfortably late 7:45. He sat on a castoff college couch and tried not to blush when he overheard Shelly whisper, "He's cute!" from the other room.

Emily sits in the front to navigate, and Shelly arranges herself good-naturedly in the fold-down seat on the passenger's side. She is much taller than Ben had anticipated, perhaps 5'9", and otherwise completely unlike his phone-inspired image. In fact, she's a pretty brunette with curly hair, perpetually pursed lips that pucker out in front and turn up kindly on the sides, and perhaps a few more pounds than average, carried very pleasantly.

Rather than faux-California-chic strip malls placed as punctuation every few blocks, or even '70s era cedar-shingled strip malls and shopping centers, the scenery mainly consists of mom-and-pop grocery and convenience stores, grubby ethnic restaurants, squat little houses with no side yards, peeling paint, and bars on the lower windows, and a coating of grime in the corners of everything that even benevolent soapy hurricane forces could never dislodge.

The sight of a fabric store on the corner, originally painted bright sky blue but now unevenly faded, with bare yellow bulbs ringing the edge of a large plastic sign proclaiming F BRIC proudly to the sky, touches him in a way both profound and sad, as if watching someone's half-realized second-chance dream slowly wither. He says nothing; the hour's half-hearted sunlight always washes everything in bleak halftones.

He wonders why he feels so out of place, like the financier walking onto a construction site in $200 shoes and a well-pressed shirt and tie; it feels industrial, somehow, perhaps the plumbing of the city, moving food and goods in and out and he doesn't belong, shouldn't see the plumbing. Cranes rise without shame above docks in the river to load and unload grain and other raw materials barged down to the ocean and perhaps even a few shallower ships that swim sixty miles from the sea.

Emily guides him across a two-lane bridge over an old railway shipping yard which must surely leach irons back through the soil downhill to the river. A squat water tower stands guard; its unappealing brownish color is almost completely unlike tree bark. This is the land of the chain-link fence. These suburbs couldn't escape the encircling, engulfing city.

Emily points. "I think that's your next turn there, on the right." The street is darker than it should be for the evening hour. It's foreign. It's not the suburbs where he grew up. It's a place of hand-me-down furniture, liberated from the neighbor's curb on trash day.

Ben snickers. Emily looks up. "What? What is it?"

He glances at her. "I was just thinking. I have a college couch too. I inherited it from friends after we graduated."

"You're weird."

He promises himself to think about that.

The house itself is near the end of the street, with appropriately ragged lawncare and furnishings. A half-height chain link fence surrounds a forlorn concrete slab overgrown with weeds and holding an empty birdbath. The cars of college students who care more about having transportation than its state fill both sides of the street. He feels a sense of relief in that he won't be out of place among students who played water polo and lettered in crew in their prep schools, though he admits a small thrill when he considers the possibility of debating philosophy with them as an actual productive member of working society.

He eases into a parking spot just around the corner and helps Emily slide the seat forward for Shelly to decamp. The cute little "Thank you" he receives is maybe the third and fourth word she's ever said to him in person. He reminds himself to stop counting.

Another group arrives at the house just ahead of them. It's people neither girl recognizes, but they all slip in together. The inside reminds Ben of his home, sort of, as the decor has no overriding theme, not even modern eclectic. The dominant feature of the front room is a home theater system with rat-tangled cords and toppling piles of CDs and DVDs. Two couches along adjacent walls host rumpled students who chatter excitedly. A small dining room, maybe a nook, he's not sure, leads to the kitchen to the right. The narrow hall between the kitchen and living room must lead to bedrooms. A door on the wall opposite the kitchen wall looks outsidey.

There might be fifteen people here. A few suspend their conversations long enough to nod and smile toward Emily and Shelly. No one offers to take their coats. Ben sidesteps into the dining room, which he now considers little more than a convenient location for a card table, and drops his coat on a pile on a chair. Shelly aims for the kitchen to find a drink, dragging Emily behind.

That leaves Ben just past the doorway, feeling a little lost and hoping it doesn't show. He turns to a cold rectangular window to survey the street from the inside. Weeks-old newspapers, blown to the side of the road by passing cars, rest against rows of weeds with nowhere better to go. Even so, a family planted here might bloom. A path traces the edge of the world, where he can all but see the archetypical perfect yuppie couple, he in a sweatshirt and short, balding hair hidden under a baseball cap and she a tiny blonde with a ponytail and sunglasses. Both sip frothy coffee drinks as they push a yellow covered stroller with an adorable kid-and-a-half inside. Half of the time they have a dog, either a small dachshund, poodle, or Scottie, or a large Lab. This neighborhood would also allow mutts of indeterminate origin.

He tries not to breathe in a quiet desperation that cannot shift from unfamiliarity to hominess as he considers lead-paint and asbestos insulation through the metal-framed, single-paned window. He knows, deeply, that families make their homes here, but he can't understand their warmth. Is his doubt so strong that he could never recognize it? How do they do it? How do they find their peace in imperfect circumstances?

"I'm Ted. Which of those two cuties is yours?" Someone has come out of the kitchen. Ben spins and a very tall, very thin man in a silk shirt tucked into khakis catches his eye by some accident. He shifts a dark beverage in a big red plastic cup to his left hand to hold out the other.

Shaking hands back is an instinct at this point. Responding isn't. Ben opens his mouth, then closes it. He hears a click.

Ted laughs. "Don't worry. Shelly and I go way back. I'm just teasing. Come on in. Want a drink?"

Ben makes a show of wiping his forehead and whistling. "I'm glad you explained." He winces further inside for leaning in closer and mock-whispering, "If Emily'd heard me answer that question, I'd have to go home alone." He stayed up all night playing a video game once, then instinctively tried to reload a save when he spilled spaghetti on a dress shirt the next day. He almost gave up on gaming right then. He pushes the image of the reload button out of his head.

Ted blinks.

"Oh, right. Uh, ice water would be okay for now."

"Huh. Driving soon?" There's a pause. "Ah, I'm just teasing. You're all right. I'll be back in a sec."

Ben gives the room another look. It's cleaner than he expected, with no swimsuit posters on the walls and no clothes piled in corners—either this is a coed house or someone exerted a lot of effort making this room presentable. Tiny torn paper pieces and, apparently, rose petals dot the corners. Any vacuuming happened in a hurry.

The available light comes from a chandelier fan in the dining area. White blades surround white-painted glass sconces with decorative

golden floral designs that almost match a pair of lamps his grandmother owns. A halogen light in the corner of the living room spills
its glow across the plaster ceiling. It's homey. The baseboard heaters
are on, under the windows. Inoffensive dance music thumps beneath
the low hum of conversation. No one dances.

Ted returns with ice water and Emily, who has her own cup full
of something Ben can't identify. She sips. Her eyes remain on Ted
as he nears the punchline of a story involving an English professor
and a pop quiz.

"So we convinced her to put it off until the next class, which
was okay, she had two Freshman English, and then the next class we
convinced her that she'd already given us the quiz and it was the
other class she put off. When she figured it out, it was too late."

Ben takes his water and hides a grimace beneath a sip. He'd
helped to hide a professor's gradebook one semester and then prompt-
ly forgot where it went. Six weeks later, it reappeared where he was
sure it had never been.

"No way! She believed it?" Emily, eyes on Ted, hands Ben her
cup. She shrugs out of her coat.

"What could she do? I would have loved to see the other class,
though, with her handing out the same quiz as before."

Emily laughs and drops her coat in the corner. "Thanks, Ben.
That's terrible. I wish we'd thought of that."

Ben smiles politely. No one notices.

"Oh, sorry. This is Ted. He's in Poly Sci."

"Yeah. We met a few minutes ago."

Ted divides the full force of his attention between Ben and Emily
now. It's very egalitarian. Ben dismisses it as the mark of a man

trying to impress his audience. "Where did you two meet? You're not in school, are you?"

Emily gleefully starts in on the story. "I picked him up at the coffee shop. I thought to myself, 'Self, that quiet guy in the corner needs a little attention.' It turns out I was right." She hugs his arm and tilts her head onto his shoulder. "I was right, wasn't I?"

Ben smiles politely again. Ted shows the tips of his teeth. They're white and, except for his incisors, tiny. "I can't complain."

Emily squeezes Ben's hand and lets go. "That's what a girl likes to hear."

Someone knocks on the door. Ted's eyes jerk involuntarily toward the noise. To his credit, he keeps his smile, such as it is. When he looks at Ben again, he leans in imperceptibly closer and whispers. His right hand slices a flat plane parallel to the floor. "I have to play host again. I'll catch up to you two later." He opens the door and Ben shuffles further into the nook.

Emily walks around Ted and the open door into the living room. Ben sips again. From what he overhears, the soccer team has now arrived and Emily's met an old friend she hasn't seen since the library earlier that afternoon. Shelly's still in the kitchen.

It's nearly 8 pm. Yawn. Ted, the only person here with whom he's actually shared more than a sentence besides Emily, makes his shoulder blades itch in anticipation of receiving a knife engraved, "It's only business." Ben takes another drink and considers the window again for a moment. Instead, he heads to the corner of the room nearest the stereo, where he can look through the CD cases and maybe discuss the dismal state of modern radio—but even Plato would have shrugged at that.

o o o

A System of Weights

Catchup

THE fear of the thing, Ben decides, can be worse than the thing itself.

He wonders if there's a relationship between fearful and eager anticipation. He spent the night of his first sleepover away from home in grade school playing with the coolest toy ever. He pestered his parents to buy it for weeks until, impressed at such singular concentration from an eight year old boy, they gave in. He can't even remember the toy now; his enjoyment lasted less than half as long as his desire.

The horrible, terrible, no-good schedule that management foisted upon development presents interesting technical challenges, when he analyzes it through pure intellect. The entire project—as nebulously outlined by sales to customer, hinted at by sales to management, and rationed out in stingy asides in the hallway by management to development—is far too large and complicated to finish in the allocated time. However, his curiosity always pokes him to compare what the customer might actually need versus what the sales department has convinced the customer to buy versus the actual request and specifications the developers eventually receive.

It took two weeks to prepare to start the project out of the sixteen originally allocated, time enough, as Ben and Eric figure, to have actually given the customer a product that does something.

Despite the feeling of impending doom and the frustration of doom delayed, the actual work is tolerable. It's tedious in spots, but the challenge of identifying and scheduling the project presents interesting tradeoffs. There is a rough order to the steps, and there are enough steps to sketch out the program in rough strokes, painting the picture's foundation in the large before adding tiny details. It's almost like making a mural, where someone masks off individual sections and every painter concentrates on a square foot of space. You must step back to see the gestalt.

That almost makes up for the nearly negligent lack of direction. With no access to the customer and little in the plan besides a detailed description of the inputs and outputs of the old system, determining the meaning and implications of the new system, or even customer preferences, requires a level of accuracy exceeding that of television weather reporters and palm readers. Carlann jokes about bringing in FBI-retained psychics to improve the specifications; her punchline is that even "He's wearing ... blue!" is more information than they have.

The entire project is tragic in its routine. Almost everything their customers consider worth paying for has had an unrealistic deadline. There's always some component of reality somewhere, though nothing so far has come so untethered from basic physical laws. Their schedules always slip gradually. No one mentions it early, but panic inexorably strikes when sales fields increasingly desperate calls from the customer and management directs them to rephrase the excuses from development into something a little less honest and a lot more palatable. There was one exception: a large customer possessing the enviable problem of more money than actual problems. They happily spent man-month after man-month on a poorly-envisioned project with no real goal.

Ben visualizes Sisyphus but cannot identify; perhaps the condemned Greek would be more sympathetic with an audience giving contradictory advice on different rolling styles. He loses his taste for mountain climbing.

If he ignores the deadline and wills away a malevolent tumble of calendar blocks, his life remains unchanged. They divide the work into developer-week-sized chunks, plan the next week on Friday afternoons, and do what they can when they can. Jerry reappears to stonewall all questions, explaining only that they'd continue their normal work otherwise. They do.

Despite his best mind-over-matter mantras, Ben notices the stress while sitting alone. His left leg bounces seemingly beyond conscious control. The first time he notices, his head aches from trying to track his monitor as it rocks back and forth gently and he wonders who is rolling heavy equipment up and down the hall. Then he notices his calf's tired ache. He drinks ever more, sometimes leaving his office every thirty minutes to demonstrate various stages of the water cycle.

His dreams run from his recall. They disappear into vague and shadowy fogbanks that burn away after sunrise, leaving loss and despair. The worst part is feeling as though part of his life vanishes during wakefulness. One morning, half-asleep, he speculates that, if what he thinks is real were actually a dream, that he could only remember his actual life as if it were dreams. He jumps out of the shower, shampoo still in place, to convince himself of the reality of his bathroom mirror.

Over breakfast, Randy suggests dreaming himself a better job and a jet ski. Ben considers Randy sufficient evidence that he really does exist.

The fourth week strikes in mid-December. Days shrink and night-time expands until the solstice. Skies pregnant with cloudy rain block even the modest southernly sun. When Ben awakens and stumbles into the bathroom, the lights hurt his eyes; he prefers gentle awakening sunbeams to climb into his window and enlighten his dreams. When he drives to work, headlights cast beams. Shadows huddle together in corners before slithering back into the streets. When he returns home, the yellow streetlight at the corner glows dully through the skeletal hands of naked tree branches hiding it from view. He tries to keep his normal Tuesday night routine at Wild Thoughts, but by the second week he feels so exhausted that all he can do is cook supper and eat in front of the TV before falling asleep at 9. He probes at the idea that he misses it, somehow, but every time another worry pushes it aside. Busyness alone remains, neither progress nor action toward a goal, but the dubious comfort of filling every working moment with thought and movement and squeezing every waking moment for ever more productivity.

Unfortunately, that preoccupation only increases.

Ben sits in the living room on a Friday night watching his roommate berate *Star Trek* reruns. Randy has lately declared himself "single on purpose" to "learn to enjoy [his] own company", staying home more often and dressing up less frequently. Ben suspects that Randy is on the cusp of declaring that he won't date another woman who expects him to wear a tie more than once every couple of months. That's the only behavioral change Ben notices, unless there's some unmentioned deep archaeolopsychological excavation occurring.

Apparently this particular episode has gone to the plotline well for a bucket again tainted with time-travel. "The real problem, of course, is that there's no drama. There's no real danger. Everyone will escape with their exquisitely form-fitting uniforms mostly intact by the last five minutes, no worse for facing impending space-time shattering peril than last week. After saving the galaxy twenty-two episodes per year times a low estimate of even five years plus at least three movies, I'd be a wreck."

Ben shrugs. "It's entertainment. It doesn't have to make sense."

"I reject the idea that people expect half-hearted plots and unrealistic characterizations. They have an entire universe built up and they're afraid to tell a complex story? They can't? They spent their entire budget on that huge space battle two weeks ago and have to throw in clips from previous episodes strung together on the thinnest of threads?"

"Maybe you expect too much."

"I'll put an hour-long science fiction show made on a shoestring budget by people who really care about what they're doing, people who know what good writing and characterization is...are...against a high-gloss mass market product made by nine-to-fivers who count their years until retirement. There must be thousands of people dying to create something like this compared to, what, a couple of hundred who do this every week, who rarely rise above the bare minimum?"

Ben grimaces Randy's way. "How do I take this 'One man with a vision can change the world!' speech from someone who takes his job as casually as you do. Do you even wear shoes there anymore?"

Randy's sardonic laugh bubbles as involuntary chuckle-coughs. "Don't mistake a job for a calling—especially if you've turned off the ringer."

The characters exchange several significant lingering serious glances as a dramatic note sounds and they come to realize that, at the exact time as last week, something strange has definitely started. Commercials blare. Randy mutes the sound. "My point is that there's an art in work somewhere, and you can tell when it's not there. Someone didn't wake up one day believing that the world needs another story about a subspace anomaly bending spacetime so that only this week's imaginary subatomic particle can fix it. Maybe someone tried to tell a story, but other people painted over his drafts by the numbers, throwing in whatever tested well with this week's hottest target demographic. The result is this mess."

"Yet you're watching."

When Randy doesn't laugh, it's a little scary until Ben recognizes and interprets the mock-sinister lean-in poker face. Then it's hilarious. "I steal television; I ignore commercials."

"People watch though."

"Some people say that everyone else is stupid, and pull their opinions from TV and newspapers and the radio and whatever famous person fad started this week. I disagree. People like to be comfortable. Sure, they like the familiar, but we're all so busy trying to convince each other that everyone else is stupid that we make ourselves believe it, despite all contrary evidence."

"Your solution is that people should leave any job that feels like work to pursue their passions?"

Randy rolls his eyes. "No, my solution is to recognize people who pursue their passions and do them well. I don't need another lousy episode of *Star Trek* to find fulfillment. If it disappeared forever tomorrow, I could...."

"...look up reams of bad fanfic on the Internet," Ben interrupts.

"I want things done well. Just because something exists, it has to continue? When it's over, when it's no longer useful or fun but is only tedious, why continue? What benefit is there? Move on."

Ben folds his arms and slouches himself down the couch to stretch his legs. "If it's not fun, don't do it? If it's mere work one day, even if it's a great adventure the next day, you pack it up and find something else?" He knows he's pushing, but this conversation bubbles inside in the place that fell during Ned's announcement.

"No, no no! Listen. It's simple. If you're not willing to put yourself into something, it's not worth your time—and it's definitely not worth ours. Let it go. Go worry about something you're willing to do well. Don't delude yourself. Don't lie to us. Don't hang on to something dead trying to will it back to life by pretending it'll get back to its best years one of these years."

"Walk away from a commitment when it's too hard to stay." Now the bubbling feeling sinks.

"If you're not willing to do your best, you've already walked away. Be honest about it." Randy unmutes the TV then nearly drops the remote when one character mentions the heightened levels of mystery particles and begins a bulk astrophysics brainstorming session. Several major characters from various departments apparently took the same theoretical physics class at Starfleet Academy and read multiple prominent scientific journals between missions. They're also accomplished jazz musicians.

At least, that's the gist of what makes it into Ben's head as he stomps into the pantry for a broom and dustpan; the kitchen floor is filthy.

o   o   o

Disturbing

Ben sifts his ideas. It would be easy to dismiss Randy's notion as anti-corporate ranting, but it's not accurate. No one finds it surprising that the desire for money and the aversion to risk turn what could have been art into bland and derivative Product. He stretches his legs. His toes pull on the sheets at the foot of his freshly made bed.

145

Nothing intrinsic to art for its own sake makes it better than art designed toward commercial purposes, either. It's too easy to counterprove by mentioning movie directors who've already achieved commercial success but pursue interesting yet disastrous side projects.

The idea that scarcity leads to better results than abundance tempts him. He's proud of what he's earned and the life he's built. Apart from parental assistance his first two years of college, Ben considers himself self-made. He pursues his own dreams and chases down his own opportunities.

He sees himself young, perhaps nine or ten. His mother drops him off in the Sunday School class where he first hears the word "serendipity". She's a harmless pink-and-purple dragon. Her goofy children's personal flotational device grin pops up and she calculates the ratio of those opportunities he truly deserved to those happy accidents that serendipitously dropped into his lap. Ben's big toenail catches against the sheets and the tip folds back; he'll trim it in the morning.

If he can't credit success to the purifying crucible of uncomplained hard work, which he now recognizes as the grim Puritanism he'd prided himself on leaving behind when resolving to consider work as only a part of a normal, healthy life, what does that imply about suffering for art? Yet he can't discard the idea of devotion to a goal. How many would-be Michelangelos blanch at the idea of coaxing their own Pietas out of car-sized blocks of marble? The goal doesn't have to be externally spectacular, either. How many would-be parents consider mountains of diapers, years of interrupted sleep, and the constant punishments, rewards, worries, costs, terrible fears and monumentally small joys of eighteen years before the real fun begins, and choose otherwise, thinking themselves incapable of that huge amount of work?

He pulls himself closer to the head of the bed, to give his feet more room; he prefers not to feel any mattress edges as he sleeps.

He hasn't awakened on the floor in years, in part or in full, with a dull ache somewhere and no recollection of what happened nor when.

Then again, devotion itself is no guarantee of success. He's evaluated and re-evaluated Emily, for example, trying to find any impurity in his motives or his execution of the plan. Ben considers himself patient and open to compromise. How could the depth of his desire to make things work, the amount of will and energy he considered himself capable of providing, been insufficient. Wasn't wanting enough? Can't good intentions smooth away every minor misunderstanding?

Lying on his back isn't working, so he switches to his side, bending his left leg so his calf and thigh almost touch and sliding his right arm under the pillow to clutch it to his head. A thin sliver of yellowish light from the streetlight on the corner pokes through the string holes in his blinds. Diffuse circles overlap on the wall. During a flirtation with astronomy in high school he considered painting actual constellations on his ceiling in luminescent paint, though he stopped before choosing the actual type of sky projection required to translate the position of stars from an unbounded spherical section to a bounded plane, let alone how to encode their relative magnitude armed with a small supply of paintbrushes, dropcloths, and a stepladder.

Another thought forms as his breathing deepens and slows. What if success isn't the goal? What if it's something less measurable? Ben tiptoes to a gilded rulebook exhibiting a bookishness against which all other books simultaneously pale and fulfill and explaining the optimal result of any circumstance in easily-digested tables and figures.

He stops. *Randy never defined success.* His argument focused on quality, defining it in terms of something people recognize when it is present and miss when it is absent. Is that an excuse more immune to criticism than "I don't like it but don't know why"? It can't be that simple. Ben shares that dissatisfaction in movies when he cringes and the rest of the audience cheers at consequence-free, grammar-school simple, cartoon vengeance meted out by wise-cracking adolescent heroes. He grumbles at the magician who promises to make the moon disappear, then cries his way through a heart-wrenching tale about a cancerous little boy receiving a puppy for Christmas and leaves the stage to a standing ovation after never actually performing any magic tricks. It's eating the cheap, satisfying meal of a bag of cheddar-flavored potato chips every night despite having access to honey-grilled chicken, garlic mashed potatoes, and a fruit salad with fresh watermelon, cantaloupe, grapes, pineapple, dried cranberries, feta cheese, and slivered almonds.

It's 12:34 am now and he plans to get up by 8:15 to make waffles before shuffling into the office by 9:30 to finish this week's task and leave by noon, while saving some of his precious Saturday. Bone knocks against bone and he hates the feeling of his bare ankles rubbing together. This time he sends his feet to separate corners.

He hears the thought approach but fails to reach the deadbolt before it kicks down the door. What if it doesn't really mean anything? What if the only metric of quality the universe will hold against him while stretching his life against a cosmic doorframe is the scoring mechanism he devises himself? He stands in a doorway in space. Cartoon planets and comets and stars spiral drunkenly in the background. A severe nebula holds a measuring tape and a pencil. Ben's grows shorter and the austere nebula clicks disapprovingly as it retracts the tape, tick by tick. He doesn't live up to "Graduate-level Degree". He's a few inches short of "Millionaire by 35". The doorway's too short to mark how far he is from "Happily Married" or even "In a Stable Long-Term Relationship". Even "Writing the Great American Novel" is closer, in that he's *read* one this year. The two ticks that stick, "Buying a House" and "Holding a Real Job", are sufficiently low to the ground that the teenaged high school graduate two doors over almost crests them by rearranging his feet and improving his posture.

Ben's back twinges painlessly as if his current posture has twisted his spine. He swivels to straighten his hips.

Seeing himself suspended in the empty vacuum of deep space gives him no vertigo. Watching a measuring tape slip through anthropomorphic fingers of a stellar body does. He realizes how far he hasn't come and how much time he doesn't have. How many lives does the universe measure and find wanting? How many opportunities has he missed? Is his destiny to live a quiet, desperate life, waiting to hear another knock on another door with a doorframe more amenable to his measure? Will he have to account for every wasted moment?

His best explanation sounds hollow: "I didn't know what else to do!". His heart pounds involuntarily and he hears-feels his jugular veins echo. The heat in his head pulses and expels out other thoughts. His intestines feel watery and cold and cramped; icy hands massage them with evil intent. He hesitates to open his eyes, fearing some malicious beast with passionate, fiery eyes perched on the foot of his bed, just watching, wings curved in to embrace him unescapingly.

He's awake now. Fuzzy yellow dots spot one wall. Electric red lights declare 1:12 for everything in the room to see.

o o o

Distraction

The office is quiet again, though not the quiet of an empty morning. It's the hush of empty cathedrals or mortuaries: respect and more than a little fear. Everyone is uncomfortable because no one knows what to expect. The regulars, mostly cleaning crews and a minimal security detail downstairs, treat the newcomers with a respect more polite than genuine. The quiet is familiar, hardly an occasion for veneration, though they recognize the recent uncertainties.

Ben relives staying home from elementary school to realize both that his mother actually had plenty of work to do around the house and that his favorite television shows continued to air without him to watch. The day ground on; the unfamiliar failed to fit into his routines.

He stands outside the break room to listen to the office breathe. Most offices are dark. His gaze echoes through the claustrophobic emptiness. The only light comes from the windows at the edges of the building. Selfish December clouds tax sunlight away from the helpless residents of the earth below. He moves in dreams, slow-motion trances—not his near-wakeful anticipation on early weekdays, but the feeling of unrestful, fitful sleeping late on Sunday while walking through his plans for Monday.

He sips green tea and imagines the thirsty monkey bounding between bamboo stalks and shoji screens on three sides to reach a hidden desk. The finely polished wood of the desk is single-carving smooth, belying tight grains and invisible joints. Ben suspects its creator is a master craftsman who measures thrice before cutting once, soaking the joints in water and letting them expand together to avoid glue, nails, or staples. The monkey shows off immaculate posture by perching atop an ergonomic chair, then stretches his fingers twice to fly through code.

More impressive to Ben than that the monkey can program at all is that it uses a plain text editor, not one of the myriad development environments that attempt to make programming easier by requiring a mouse to manipulate graphics and select menu items. The monkey is hardcore; he works precisely and perfectly without mechanical prompting. He fires off test compiles to prove that his last few minutes of typing never upset the computer out of discipline, not necessity. Everything always works.

A fat bumblebee buzzes around Ben's mug before lighting on the break-room clock, which clicks as it notches ahead the hour hand. He really has to stop daydreaming.

A new chart on the wall outside Jerry's office graphs their current progress against their deadline. They settled on simplicity. Every developer writes his weekly goal on an index card and tacks it up. Every developer who completes a task marks a giant X through the card. The completed cards in the appropriate week show immediately the state of the project. It's a reverse-standard growth rate graph so far, with earlier weeks mostly finished and the current week mostly unfinished. Yet there's too little wall to handle three months of project, not with forty developers per week making two columns of 3x5 cards around five feet tall and one foot wide, not counting axis labels on either side, let alone how long the project will actually take.

Now the chart flips and tips to represent not elevation above the ground but distance beneath ground, where they begin at the level of the Dead Sea and climb the blasted rocky wastebowl walls to sea level. Some—most—weeks they tumble back down again, only to climb faster and further to make up for the imperfect anti-progress of previous weeks.

Ben's seen home movies of the path the Israeli army took through the Sinai peninsula during the Six Day War and understands both why they swept through with such speed and why they returned it with such comparative ease. Remains of the war machines rust ignored at the banks of the Suez Canal, as if in thirty-five years no one had the will to clean up such blatant reminders of risk that could happen again. WWII bombs still appear in Europe and Oregon sometimes.

He's marked off three of his four cards. If he can make it to his desk today, he may complete the fourth in time for the next meeting's Ceremony of Completion. That new motivational solace weighs oddly; is doing the expected worth backpats from coworkers who wear pins that read, "Be nice to me! I did my job today!"?

From this angle at the center of the floor, the great pillars grasping the bedrock far below even the sub-basement hold up the entire building to the sky as an offering to man's dominance of gravity and, perhaps, capitalism. They form a perspective study in their stoic wall-to-wall march. If he ever designs a skyscraper, he'll trade generically square, beige posts for something with more style, perhaps Corinthian columns. He prefers the Ionic capitals, but the Corinthians fit better with flat ceilings. Doric isn't even an option because he disbelieves the effectiveness of entases in an enclosed area where "far" and "away" really aren't.

The monkey trades the immaculate hand-crafted desk and paper doors for a marble drafting table beside a small bubbling pool. It's a luxury bathroom with no exposed plumbing, not an Olympian lounge. He dons an olive wreath and sips ambrosia instead of salty noodle soup, wielding a quill pen in each hand to scribe Greek letters on a vellum keyboard. This technique is even faster than his typing in feudal Japan.

A rough wind blows wispy clouds away from the horizon to reveal a soundstage and fog machine. Ben looks up. The overhead heating unit rattles and coughs warmer air into the room. He's out of tea now. Viscous honey oozes from the tilted mug.

Three steps back return him to the break room for more hot water. He meditates on his promise to walk straight to his office as a mantra as he re-estimates the number of steps, then counts backwards to reach negative fourteen at the doorway. Is his average stride length relevant? He debates whether the small shuffle-steps he needed to round the desk and pull out the chair should count or if "steps" connoted "strides" as a fixed unit of measurement.

The monkey grins and rides a rocket ship, something between a cartoon firework and a '50s-style "Will You Live on the Moon in the Year 2000?" creation. Light from exploding stars glints off of its exposed teeth. Rounded fins bolted to the fat metal cigar taper to sharp points. It has somehow fitted a top hat and a bow tie in the fishbowl it wears on its head. There's no visible oxygen tank and no sign of being worse for the wear with everything else exposed to absolute zero and solar radiation. It holds a ruler marked in meters and Roman pace in one hand and a rheostat in the other. The ruler is exactly one passus long. The monkey twists the knob to the right and the rocket's flame lengthens, turning bluer and bluer until the center disappears. Instead of moving, the ruler shrinks to under a meter. The monkey waves it as it holds fast somewhere around a pes. If anything, the monkey's grin increases with the rocket's velocity.

Ben starts his apologia; he's obviously viewing the monkey from a frame of reference with a vector appropriate to the rocket, so he should see nothing abnormal, or the monkey should appear to shrink too, as if he could even focus on something moving so fast that at least part of it would appear one-fifth of its normal size, but that argument careens into deep space as the monkey rides wild loops and shines dual flashlights and somehow overtakes and passes the beams frozen in place. Simian skywriting produces an offensive phrase and Ben lands heavily in his chair.

It's nearly noon. He wanted to leave by one. The monkey mug is thirsty again.

o o o

Indelible Youth

Ben flees at 12:15. His hallucination stops as he leaves the building. The giant foam sea cucumber melts back into the security guard at the front desk and the hula music becomes regular traffic noise again.

He squeezes his fists and sucks in his stomach and he very consciously avoids thinking about anything, not the pounding in his head nor the sidewalk's wobbling and waving, and definitely not the implications of going irrevocably crazy just before his thirtieth birthday. He stuffs his fists in his pockets and turns the walk into a near-jog, moving as quickly as he can without attracting attention. He doesn't

153

know where he's headed. He only wants to move; his pulse demands exertion to justify its pace.

His car is east. He heads west, down the slope to the river, before turning south for the slight incline. It's chilly but not cold. He has his leather jacket but no hat or scarf, and sees his breath but feels the wind bite tentatively the tips of his ears and his cheekbones. This neighborhood is bridges and freeway; elevated arterials push several blocks further inland from the river.

Images swirl again. His coworkers scurry, heads down. The monkey doubles his size, clutching a swollen hairy belly and laughing uproariously. Emily on the last night he ever saw her turns toward the passenger window, streetlights illuminating her cheek, a blank look on her face and eyes wet with emotion. Every few steps, an involuntary contraction of his diaphragm and a catch in his throat make him choke down another breath. His feet are heavy and his hands burn. He clenches and unclenches his fists.

Occasionally Ben feels creativity bubble up inside, special revelations emanating. It burns, barely waiting for him to put pen to paper as merely the catalyst in a consuming reaction. His muscles hum and his fingers twitch and he is too flawed to work fast enough or to capture inspiration before it leaves him. He gives himself over to the watching muse while its attention lasts.

Now he wants to escape that unblinking eye.

He perches on a precarious plank atop a thirty-pound fulcrum. He's edged slowly past the middle and now any step will trade his potential energy for actual energy before a long, lonely descent.

Ben rarely visits this part of town, the warehouse district. It's less than a mile from his office, but it appears rarely on tourist maps. A long-neglected rail line bisects streets within view of the river front. Occasionally unmanned trains rumble through, shipping unknown raw materials to warehouses and machine shops under the bridges. He's never seen one, but he hears two-toned horns blow sometimes while working late. Weeds form a barrier a healthy distance from the tracks.

Ben slows. It's a different world, a foreign land. He's never unloaded freight from a cargo train. He's never loaded a truck in the rain. Only during one summer installing sprinkler systems with an uncle did he discover the simple joy of taking a ten-minute break to gulp water and sit silently, boots off, in shade.

There are people who find this familiar; their lives revolve around freight and containers and manifests. He fails to build a life around moving shipping pallets, counting down two hours until a coffee break, two hours until lunch, two hours until another break, and two hours until closing time, then stumbling home for a hot shower and an early bedtime to start over the next day. He doesn't even know where to *park* around here.

Newspaper fragments bleached by sun, wind, and rain coat the lower half of a chain link fence one street closer to the river. Dead yellow weeds poke through both sides. The rust-red iron of the train tracks bleeds in the December light.

Yet the workers here have their own dreams. Ben stops. Every goal he thought he had has fallen. He's not spectacular. He doesn't stand out. He's not an example for neighborhood children to emulate. No one pores through copies of his high school yearbook to sell his senior photo to celebrity news shows. Why not disappear? Why not give in? Why not admit that the best he can do is find some satisfaction in earning his keep, if not in how he makes his living?

The fulcrum appears again. He starts west, more slowly. There are two blocks of warehouses, then two blocks of little shops before a main street. He's not in the mood for surplused furniture or office supplies, but it's a warmth to know that he could explore dozens of types of discontinued carpet.

What if mind-readers exist? If he were with other pedestrians, could they tell his questions from the look in his eye? Might they identify his inner gap, an electric burning almost inflated so that if he fell on a sharp stone his inner being would spill out and evaporate?

He's been an adult by number for eleven years, in the eyes of the government for eight, and according to his insurance company for four, almost five. Where is his confidence of age 18 or the bravado of 21? He's less himself now than ever.

He's between two bridges now, great concrete and asphalt monsters that could swallow his house many times in their shadows. It's no less impressive across the river where he can crane back his head to look up over thirty stories. When he first learned of the ton as a unit of measurement, his world was so small that he could barely imagine anything weighing two thousand pounds. His imagination still fails when he considers the magnitude by which any tiny spot on the surface of the earth can hold up so many tons of tons. The size of the earth makes him so insignificant. Not even solar system sizes and distances humble him, but only the fact that eleven of him jumping up and down atop a skyscraper would weigh, in comparison, less than a few of the hairs on his head.

Is there any project to which he can attach himself to build anything so substantial? Even something as mundane and well-distributed as an office building has a permanence that he could never achieve on his own. Less so is the significance of a freeway, a ribbon of asphalt of which he turned a shovel of gravel or flattened with a steamroller or painted achingly painstakingly. Yet drawing a part of the network of maplines colored in blue and red across the United States is significant; every day a thousand people reach their destinations more smoothly because of thousands of anonymous somebodies.

Who invented the cupholder? Who devised the rear-view mirror? Even the humdrum routine click-and-go over-the-shoulder seat-belt deserves some attention; countless families ignore blissfully the lives otherwise lost.

Ben waits at a crosswalk. Five-story brick buildings hail each other across the street, one painted in the style of old traveling-show advertisements and the other a smart, modern bar with neon beer signs. He sneaks up on his car from a casual southerly route.

In one sense he can't help but affect the world, but it holds no satisfaction. Has he taken a breath in his life that didn't contain at least one molecule of air from a dying Julius Caesar, Alexander, or Xerxes? Has his presence on the road prevented an accident or a traffic jam or delayed someone from a painful and unpleasant meeting? He's downed enough tea in the past few days to have had an immense effect on at least the local water cycle; he idly scans the high overhang of clouds for anything familiar.

His assets are scarce—neither a huge array of classic literature, either owned or remembered, nor more than a few tens of thousands of dollars of wealth, minus the two-story chunk of equity squatting on a slab of admittedly prime real estate. He sees few opportunities for charity and philanthropy in the large, and finds the volume of needs even locally too great to consider, even as he writes it off as a convenient and shameful excuse.

Another left turn points him north and leads to a quieter section of town, even only one block over from the major northbound street in the area. The noise strikes mostly at major intersections. Everything farther back relaxes, confident in comparative obscurity. He dislikes the pace of action otherwise, with something always in motion and no moments of perfect rest even long enough to draw a deep breath. He envies the anthropomorphic confidence about the other shops and businesses that acknowledge their places and *be* exactly what they are.

He can't imagine himself as a child setting a life goal to own a knitting supply store, for example, but that kind of dedication of purpose elicits a jealous glow of admiration.

His parking garage is mostly empty, though it'll likely fill up with shoppers and clubgoers as the evening waxes. Walking through a building devoted to drivers always turns him nervous, as if the bored booth attendant is moments away from chasing him down and berating him for brash pedestrianism. Even the boring, squat sandwiches of slanted concrete and air pay homage to the vision of someone who's attracted enough people here to raise their cars to the air in supplication and $8.50 a day with a monthly permit.

Ben approaches his truck from the passenger's side. The early afternoon light and relative position within the garage replay an unbidden memory. He tries a new trick, ignoring his keyless entry and first unlocking Emily's door to see her safely in before embarking himself. Would she unlock his door?

He can't remember. He has only the flash of closing her door, watching her smile at him through the window. Is it a dream? Is it a memory? That day stands alone, apart from other recollections as if the single image had come unattached to skip and bounce away adrift on a breeze.

He feels detached, almost dizzy. The world threatens to spin with him as Charybdis swirling reality into a tiny point. It deposits him in the center of a vast white horizonless nothingness, alone with his thoughts, alone to paint his own false memories on the canvas of the universe.

"You wanted significance," it mocks him—or he himself—"now write your life."

He steps back. Grief rushes in. Everything he's given up: football, the flute, a perfect college GPA, and everything he's lost: a broken arm at age 12, both maternal grandparents in a house fire, and the feel of Emily's heart beating in her wrist as they hold hands while walking barefoot in a waterfront park one summer day. Everything but the emptiness bursts out of his heart through jagged tears.

Vainly, he wrings his mortgage and the project into bandages, tying them around the hole, but they sag and fall and he's empty again. A cold, black sea rises.

He blinks and really looks. The world rushes out of his head and stretches to fill his normal vision, colors washed charcoal gray. He shivers though his heart pounds and his face has flushed. He pushes against the fender where he'd somehow laid his hand for support, straightening himself, setting his jaw, and manages to make it into the driver's seat before the sobs begin.

o o o

Pruning

A hundred-twelve-pound blonde woman wearing two-hundred dollar sunglasses sips a six-dollar coffee and drives her two-point-four children past in an SUV the size of Ben's kitchen. He waves his gardening clippers idly after her. "Sorry Mom, could you repeat that last part?"

The rosebush by his front steps went wild since he moved in, mostly because he's neglected to prune it in any of the springs or autumns he's lived there and partly, Ben suspects, because Randy's friends secretly fertilize it after parties. When the thicket threatens to take over the stairs as well, he calls his mother for advice before it consumes an actual human for sustenance. The first frost has struck, and he feels less guilty now that pink and yellow petals have fallen and wilted all over the steps and sidewalk.

"So my son's now a gardener? Finally all of that weeding I could never get you to do has some benefit for someone! I'm so proud."

"Ha ha. Just help me not cut my fingers off or kill another plant, okay?"

He thinks he understands by the second run-through, but he still can't believe it.

"I cut it down *how* far? Mom, this thing is huge!"

"That's what roses like, Ben. They grow in a hundred different directions and send out dozens of blooms, but they can't support all of those branches at once. You have to prune them way back to their cores. They'll be much happier and grow better and bloom more next year. I promise."

"That's cutting everything out! It's as tall as I am."

"It's the only way you'll be able to see which branches you want to keep. You're trying to keep it off of your steps, right?"

"Right, but can't I just lop off those branches?"

"Sweetie, first of all, it's a mess and they'll just grow right back that direction. Second, you'll never get in there to get all of them. Don't worry, it's healthy for the plant. They love it."

"Who trims wild roses? They survive just fine without pruning!"

"What's a wild rose anymore? *Someone* planted it, and I'm sure it's the result of several generations of highly selective breeding. This is what gardening is all about. You take a whole mess of life and possibilities and choose what you want to encourage and remove what doesn't fit with your vision."

"Sounds all planned."

"You can only encourage things to grow or discourage them."

"This to you is relaxing?" Ben releases his grip on the cutters. A bead of sweat slides down his arm to drip off the end of the handle.

"It's a different kind of work. There aren't any deadlines or meetings. You just decide what might look nice and do some research if you want to plant something or discourage an insect or whatever.

160

Then you do it and see what happens and try again next time if you didn't like the results."

"Okay, I'm looking for the branches that grow in the wrong direction and the dead ones?"

"That's right! They're brown and woody, not green and tender."

He's already chosen the first branch. "And I cut downward, toward the center?"

"Yes, and if you see a little bulge, cut just above that."

"I can do this, Mom." Ben blushes at the thinness of his confidence.

"Yes you can, sweetie. You'll do fine. It's surprisingly difficult to kill off roses."

Ben raises the clippers and lets out a deep breath. "Here I go." The first cut is surprisingly easy. Several feet of a branch fall to the ground and already the way into his house is less dangerous. He kicks the thorny bundle off of the sidewalk and kneels to cut it in trash-sized pieces. The last thing he needs is a pile of pokey branches on his lawn for months.

"Good! December pruning is a little late, but your plant should handle it. So what else is new in your life?"

o o o

Beautiful

Moment

She's fallen asleep and he hates to wake her.

On the TV in the rain, Humphrey Bogart reads a letter from Ingrid Bergman at the train station. The ink smudges, then washes off of the paper. The sentence "You must not ask why" sticks in Ben's mind as the final train whistle blows and Bogie reluctantly boards, crumpling and throwing the letter.

She, half-turned, rests her head on his chest and right shoulder. His arm tingles, tucked in the curve between her ribcage and her hip. She breathes so slowly that he can only feel the rise and fall when he concentrates.

It's mid-afternoon, Sunday, a gorgeous May day of clear skies, warm sunshine, and the thought of a hammock for napping before breaking out the barbecue for hamburgers or sausages. Spring stretches lazily into an endless summer, lawns emerald-green, tomato plants inflating delicious fruits, and ponderous late thunderstorms spending fierce furies all dark-browed and wet-warm before rolling on and on away, having made their point. The sun then punctuates the conversation and smoothes out the colors into lingering twilight.

Ben savors.

Emily had laughed all of the way through *The Princess Bride*, though the oh-so-'80s framing story nearly failed to capture her. He expects that if she can make it through the first ten minutes of *Strictly Ballroom*, she'll enjoy the rest of the movie. Even *Casablanca* had been too subtle or the day too lovely or the moment too peaceful. She'd relaxed and let go and curled up so gradually that he only noticed when he looked over to watch her watch his favorite scene for the first time.

He also likes the spotlight near the end.

She chose *The Little Mermaid* and *My Best Friend's Wedding*. Despite distractive redheads in each, he'd managed silence during the songs in the first movie and for the entirety of the second, mostly by thinking that she would love him more for not saying anything. At least, she'd like him less if he did say what he was thinking. On the whole, The Little Mermaid was entertaining.

He'll never appreciate movies about weddings, though.

A sudden dilemma flashes. Ben wants popcorn, needs to move his arm before it starts to twitch, and feels an obligation that Emily not miss too much of the movie. She's small in comparison, him solid and tall and her elegant in frame but neither delicate nor fragile. He leans toward her just enough so that she adjusts in her sleep to tip her head the other way. He catches it and eases her down to the couch, placing a pillow in the crook of her left arm. She clutches it, smiling in her sleep as he covers her with a huge afghan his grandmother had knitted for him as a baby.

He stands and flips a corner over her tiny bare feet. Ingrid Bergman has frozen on-screen just as she refuses to count the days in Paris. He turns back from the kitchen doorway. She's a vision, honey-gold hair tucked neatly behind one ear, as composed and graceful as ever. When he sleeps, it's a wrestling match with both bedding and wakefulness, but she remains undisturbed, perched in a safe corner with feline peace.

She's attracted a stray sunbeam. They must navigate through light, single-brushstroke-thin clouds and miles of thickening atmosphere before dodging rooftops and powerlines and budding tree branches, aiming directly for the peace and comfort of her contentment.

He prefers to think of it as celestial approval. His only truly memorable religious experience occurred after entering a nearly-abandoned downtown cathedral while carrying camera equipment for his younger brother on a high school photography assignment. The motif was dust; everything held the color of old marble statues of saints. Empty hard-backed pews and stone walls echoed their footsteps. The vaulted ceiling reflected every noise into every corner of the room. It felt old and unmoving, with candles and incense and saints and stained-glass scenes he couldn't identify coating the interior with layer after layer of intimidation and history. The overcast sky dulled the great windows, pulling at the walls so the huge room felt cramped. If he closes his eyes while listening to a Bach organ mass, the scene repaints itself.

As they turned to leave, sunlight blazed across the sky as if God had wiped a hand across the eastern windows to remove accreted years. Jeweled light jumped from the wall to the floor in bright columns of dancing blues and yellows and reds and greens, and the scene turned inside out. Where the cathedral struggled before to hold in a claustrophobic reality, now it housed heaven's very pillars. He tried and failed to unsee the change; space had unfolded to reveal itself far larger.

A breeze shakes the tree branches outside. Dappled patterns of shadow play across Emily's cheekbones—just a taste of the jewels of light and colored glass of his memory. It's enough.

o o o

Dreaming

One spring day he sees himself dressing in a mirror: a solidly-starched white shirt with buttonless cuffs and a high collar. He leaves the top button undone for now, but threads silver cuff links through button holes on the sleeves. He shrugs into a vest he names blackish, buttoning all three buttons, its color more charcoal than the black of a deep, dark cave at midnight. A black jacket hangs carefully over the back of a straight wooden chair; it feels thin and flimsy compared to his usual leather jacket, but fits nicely when he buttons the lower two buttons.

Ben only remembers the pants when he finds them hanging in plastic from a hanger on a hook on the back of a door he hadn't realized he'd left open. Apart from the wooden chair and assorted flowers, the whole room is white, from the classic dresser with its oval mirror to a huge wicker chair in the corner that looks far more decorative than comfortable. A brass bed finishes the room, lengthwise, with one window near the head painfully bright with the sunlight outside and the other window at the other end of the room less so. It's a single bed, still made, with comforter ruffled and wrinkled gently from a nap, not a night.

The pants are serviceable, slightly stretchy with a good give, if snug around his waist and hips. In contrast, his bare feet, relishing the deep pile carpet, look out of place. A pair of dress socks press against him from the right pocket, either a navy blue or again a black too subtle for him to distinguish. They hug his feet.

His final task is the pair of shoes in a box beneath the wooden chair. He hasn't owned a nice pair of shoes since he wore out the results of his father taking him shopping at the bequest of his mother for "just one decent outfit that doesn't make him look like a hooligan, please!" at around age 12. Even then, the wisdom of sending two males out for footwear when they'd rather have raced go-carts leads them to bring back the first utilitarian pair that fit well enough and cost a reasonable amount.

These shoes are different. They're formal, commanding. They lend him seriousness and dignity. The color is deep, a nutty brown. The grayish-black soles somehow match the vest. The laces are soft and new, with clear and unfrayed needle-like aglets. He ties two bow-knots so perfect that regret stabs him momentarily that no men's fashion magazine photographers are present to record how handsome his feet finally are.

He stands again to brush imaginary lint off of the pants and pull the shirt cuffs down just below the jacket sleeves. He closes his eyes and faces the mirror, breathing deeply before squaring his shoulders and standing up as straight as possible.

The little rooster tail at the crown of his head is behaving and his normally frantic fake smile has relaxed. He looks as peaceful as he feels. Even his shave is perfect.

By his watch it's 10:30 am. He removes the bow-tie from the dresser and pulls open the door. To his surprise, there are two small ring boxes in his left pocket. Light from the windows behind him spills into the hall and everything saturates and washes sharply to white.

o o o

Pain

Emily squints in the sunlight. His left arm lies across his eyes; she clasps her hands on her belly. They lie in a hammock in his backyard, him in a faded navy blue T-shirt and denim shorts and her in a white tank top and tan cargo pants. She's barefoot, so he pays close attention to the locations of his huge, ubiquitous boots.

He laughs inside and chuckles outside as their shuffling motions rock them back and forth. When he shifts his weight, she starts to roll toward him and he steadies himself with a hand on the ground. He so far has resisted the urge to rock the hammock on purpose, but temptation wells up like the joy of being outside on a clear spring day with a pretty girl and nothing else to do until dusk.

Emily turns her head to the left and rolls her eyes at Ben. Even when he really sleeps through the night, his eyes are pinkish around the edges. When his dreams chase him away from slumber and rest, they are a horror show of veins. Hers, now as ever, are clear and white, polished orbs; it's yet one more beautiful thing he loves about her but will never say. "I love your eyeballs." "What?" "I love your eyeballs." "You're weird."

"Ben?"

She's caught him watching her. He says, "Yes?" and his upper lip stays smiling though he bites down on his lower lip, just a little, in his sincerest, most mischievous smile. He's practiced in the mirror to figure out which way to tilt his head. He imagines little pinging noises as the light reflects off of his teeth and his eyes. These are his own clichés of charm.

Emily's voice is low. Something dark moves in the depth beneath. "I have to tell you something." He hears her catch water barely overflowing from a fountain in her hands, putting it back and chasing down new rivulets of moisture.

He angles himself up on to his right elbow, nearly tipping them both off. She holds on to her side of the hammock while he throws his left arm over her. When it settles, she starts again.

"Ben, I really like you, but I have to tell you something. My last relationship was..." and her mouth bunches up and her chin quivers. "It was really painful. I didn't realize how painful exactly until I met you."

He sees somehow her double-fisted grip of something terrible. His stomach falls from the fear that she'll cry. He forces himself to look her in the eye but she has unfocused somewhere in the vicinity of the drainpipe on the roof. She pulls in a giant breath and they sway gently again.

"My parents used to fight. I mean a lot. It was bad. I used to fall asleep hugging my little brother and him hugging me just so we wouldn't be alone while they yelled at each other. I couldn't understand why they hated each other so much."

Emily leans back now, eyes closed and face toward the sky. She balls up her left hand and uses her right hand to massage it, thumb over thumb. "This one time, I was twelve, I guess, and Momma was visiting Aunt Agna and I forgot to pick up the dishes after supper and he came to my room and looked at me in the same way and said in that voice, 'I guess I can't count on you, either' and walked off. He moved to a hotel room when Momma came back and that's when they divorced for real."

Her right hand works its way down the back of her other hand, past the wrist to the elbow, squeezing gently. Somehow then she clasps opposite elbows with both hands and hugs them to herself.

"They had problems, real ones. Now I think Momma left when she did to figure out what to do next. Then I let him down, too. He looked so hurt and angry."

"You were twelve."

"It was my job to clear the table that night."

"Everybody forgets." He's had to scavenge through the pile of dishes in his sink for spoons the past two mornings, as neither he nor Randy has had the courage or inclination to invest ten minutes in loading and, after an hour, unloading the dishwasher.

"How do you look at someone you've disappointed? How do you look in his eyes after that ever again? You can't take it back. You can't undo it. It's always there. Every time he sees you he sees your failure." She has clamped her eyes shut, but a tiny trickle of moisture escapes the very corner of the left one and dangles on her eyelashes. A pure, sweet transparent jewel scatters the sunlight.

He could write a perfect mathematical proof in chalk on a blackboard for her to stare at and puzzle out and come to admire its flawlessness and towering syllogistic combinations of first principles and derivations, to know that it's not her fault, leaping lemmata adorning his argument with garlands of grace. He files that in the teeth-clenching file. He doesn't even *like* proofs.

"Your last relationship?" he prompts instead.

She breathes two deep breaths. "At first it seemed so wonderful. He gave me so much attention, always calling or coming over. I'd never felt pretty before then, or never really believed I could be beautiful or talented or worthwhile. I started to believe it then."

"But you are. You really are."

"I felt wanted, chased maybe—not in a bad way, but maybe part of a big adventure. The beautiful princess who helps the handsome knight on his quest after he rescues her from the tower."

"Every girl wants that."

She's silent for a long time. Her eyes keep trying to read his face, but she won't catch his eye. She speaks again; his heart starts again. "I don't remember when I first saw that look in his eyes. Maybe it was too gradual to notice or maybe it was there from the start and I didn't want to see it. I let him down, too."

He watches her breathe. Her chest shudders as something catches inside, not completely willing to exchange for new clean air.

"He didn't yell. He didn't have to. He could just give me that look and I would feel dirty and ashamed and..." She covers her face and shakes, twice, then puts her palms together flat to cup her nose before folding her hands and fingers together beneath her chin.

"My brother was 16, almost 17. When he found out, he cut class, drove up to school, and parked his car sideways in front of the driveway to my dorm, to sit on the hood. Erick came by that afternoon. Andy told him to go away, that I'd never have anything to do with him again. I didn't find out until the Dean called both of us into his office. He called Momma to tell her what had happened and banned Erick from campus.

"I transferred out here the next semester. That's when I moved in with Shelly. She's Andy's girlfriend's older sister. She's someone I trusted."

Emily is silent for a long time. She keeps her eyes closed and rests the first knuckles of her thumbs on her lips. When she opens her eyes, they're moist and still perfectly clear. She stares straight ahead.

"Emily?" he says. She blinks a long blink and turns to look at him with fear and guilt. "Emily, you've never let me down."

He reaches for her hands. She doesn't pull away. "I will always, always forgive you." He folds his hand over hers and she crumples on his shoulder, hands clasped to her face and halfway lying on him. After a long silence there are sobs, genuine sobs, sharp sounds but soft in the middle. They fill the backyard from fence to fence.

He lies back with awkward arms around her, as she lets the fountain bubble and overflow. Tears run out of her hands to soak into the ocean of his shirt. He counts them. He wants to say something.

An age later, it's quiet. Her breathing softens as she falls asleep. The sky is blue. Powdery clouds wisp and evaporate as they cross the face of the sun.

o o o

Memory

Ben drives west. Sunlight streams through his back and left side windows. This is the kind of day that memory detaches from time. On the stereo, Michael Roe sings about how long a day it is from Heathrow to Humboldt Bay.

West is toward the ocean, though he might not drive that far. It's too beautiful a day to stay in the city. The late May weather is the kind of perfect that lasts through August, except for the seven or eight days every year when the temperature suddenly jumps into triple digits and everyone prays for rain. He still feels the urge to drive, to go, to shrink his own world to the cab of his truck, alone with his thoughts, as the world unwinds in a thin black ribbon of asphalt, one curve at a time.

Clouds always come from the west, to cycle through palettes of grays and oranges and pinks as the sun sinks from sight. Today, there's only pale blue sky. Trees run on and on at the edge of the valley. Older ranch-style houses and newer estates poke out over the ridges.

He's as light as he's ever felt. Even as he fought to leave town, up and over the mountains to the west (he avoids the tunnel, when possible, preferring the detour through and around the park), he found everything beautiful as it is. He crossed a bridge over a creek and looked far to the left in the leaf-covered banks to see a sleeping bag and a folding chair tucked away under a tree. The image remains; he sees it when he blinks. It is as peaceful and serene as the notion of sleeping on a discarded refrigerator box under an evergreen tree during April rains. It's a beautiful ache.

During a camping trip at the start of his junior year in college, he stared one night at the campfire, really stared, to wonder at the chemical processes converting logs into heat and light. The smoke and little ghosts of heat distortion escaped from the cells of wood as the pops and snaps of sparks. He followed a twinkling ember on its thermal into the sky where it vanished into deep folds of space and night.

Ben wants to lead Emily there, blindfolded, and point wordlessly to the fire, to show her what he'd seen and then direct her gaze up, with stars as crisp and clear and cold as ever and one tiny satellite, maybe no larger than he, accelerating forever as fast as it falls, winking red on and off and tracing its path across the heavens. Deep space is seventy miles away; he could take her there and further in moments.

If she could see what he saw, that memory of beauty and insight, would she love him more? If he can show her, tell her, and demonstrate to her the things he finds beautiful, can she understand how deeply run his emotions?

The world is a bowl; he chords the northern edge. The highway sends one lane each way from the sea to the city. Every car holds its own stories, years of hopes and fears and pains and joys. He finds this beautiful too. One more ridge of mountains guards the plains that stretch to the ocean. He'd gone up there a few years earlier with his parents after Christmas when they all missed the thick, comfortable blanket of snow the Midwest always pulls over itself.

Michael Roe sings of the impossibility of a beautiful heartbreak.

Above all, he feels alive. He understands the desire of migratory birds to flap their wings northward. He imagines himself as a mighty tree, digging his toes further into the rich soil as sap looses and then runs freely throughout his veins. He catches himself and backs off on the accelerator until the needle dips back under 75.

Ben welcomes the solitude not just for the chance to feel echoing guitar and bass and drums shake his bones. He likes feeling her with him in his mind almost as much as he wishes he could turn his head and trace the curve of her jaw with his eyes or run the back of his fingers up and down her arm. He misses the way she makes absentminded slow circles with her thumb when they hold hands. His own thumb seems to feel it now, his nerves singing the memory again.

The first time she ever rode with him, the truck smelled lightly of her perfume for two days and he couldn't stop smiling even as he commuted. Her presence also lingers around him when he sleeps and when he wakes. When he finds himself noticing something new or amusing or different, his first thought is to turn, to look beside, to point it out to her.

In the middle of nowhere sometimes he wonders about the people who move so far away from city amenities—Thai food within walking distance, supermarket trips without elaborate plans to maximize a ninety-minute round-trip driving time, and a sense of connection to a sea of humanity far greater than the sum of its individual stories. Then the view and the quiet glory of the solitude whisper that some-day he'll pad, slipper-clad, into a hardwood living room with huge bay windows and a tiny gas fireplace in the corner to see Emily curled up, legs beneath her on the couch, reading a magazine and smiling good morning as he hands her a mug of hot apple cider. Perhaps the presence of humanity will linger around them too, then, or perhaps they will find it sufficient in each other.

Lines connect people, now. Strips of dirt road, highway stripes, and swathes of pavement criss-cross the country, bounded always by power and telephone lines. There's always a connection, everywhere. He could stop at the side of the road, look up, and with precise enough control over matter and electrons, send a message with his mind alone to where Emily right now studies for a test or performs her morning stretches or sleeps late on this glorious Saturday morning. Yet he has no need for physical wires; a strong elastic cord stretches from his heart to hers, no matter where he goes, no matter where she is, and it vibrates and jangles counterpoint harmonics that only they can hear when they're quiet and alone.

Ben sees himself yet again on the beach, where wind whips up the surf and chases the salty fish-scent of foam and sea creatures past his nose. A well-worn trail tracks through weedy growth up a hill where, at the crest, the horizon drops away into a gray-green that stretches across the entire horizon. He hears it before he sees it, a roar so subtle that no one ever recognizes its immensity or its ubiquity before the two senses combine.

The base of the hill is rocks, head-sized and larger, thrown by violent storms and never carried away by gentle tides. They quickly give way to deep, dry sand that sinks his feet and fills his shoes. Then comes the tide line, marked both by a layer of drying brine and sturdy, wet sand where his footprints squeeze out water that rushes back in as he steps away. It's his game, when the tide returns, to walk a straight path across the curve of the beach, avoiding encroaching water.

On a day like today, he expects low-wind kites and beach football and families with plastic buckets and shovels to mold low lumps of castles and rivers and moats and ponds and to collect piles of shiny rocks.

He just wants time to think. He'll return with her in August, when the city's stifling heat refuses to escape even at midnight, when they can walk barefoot in the sand at the water's edge, unafraid of the weather, unmoved by the waves. Then he blinks away the image and resolves to keep his eyes on the road. Her memory still lingers, and he plays the song again.

o   o   o

Leavings

The dusk settles around them at her doorstep. It's almost 8:30 pm. It's warm and comfortably humid; fresh blades of grass exhale excitedly as trees sigh and settle and flowers fold themselves up for the night. There's little to say. There's nothing they have to say.

Soon it'll be night, when the radiant heat fades and a gentle chill dances delicately on his bare arms and across her pale, perfect cheeks. Soon the blue watercolor wash across the sky will stick to the dome, every minute a deeper, richer shade, until a million jewels reappear. If he could, he'd count them all again and again from their reflections in her eyes.

Their hands clasp, his right and her left. Their intertwined fingers curve over and under and between and through each other to form knots of touch and humanity and connections. Their beginnings and endings all sweetly pile together until he forgets where he ends and she begins. The transcendental union leaves him not numb, but still himself, floating in an electric sea.

She stops, just under the light, and tilts her head to look back and up. "What are you thinking?"

Don't let this moment end, he answers silently. "You look beautiful right now, so soft in this light."

Emily blinks slowly. Her lips purse as a tiny grin stretches the sides of her mouth. The smile continues to reveal her upper teeth. "You are so sweet. You always know what to say. You're always thinking about it, aren't you?"

175

He shrugs, carefully, not to pull on her hand. "I say what I see."

She whispers now. "I love how you see me. I love...seeing myself the way you see me. I feel so beautiful."

He brushes a stray hair away from her left eye. "You are...and I like feeling handsome and strong and gentle when I'm with you."

She tries, but the flicker is too fast for her to hide. He catches it and grabs her other hand, pulling them both to his chest. "...and love. I love how I feel right now."

Emily looks down at their hands, folded together, for a long moment. She looks back up and he finds happy and sad all together there and draws her left hand up to kiss it, never looking away from her expressive eyes. It's cool and smooth and warms immediately as his lips brush it. He's more aware of her heat now on the tiny porch, under the warm yellow bulb.

She smiles. "Always thinking."

Visions and possibilities dance: to sit here on the step until their shivers drive them inside, to walk around the block hand in hand, to go inside and make pleasant conversation with Shelly until she takes the hint to go to bed early and leave them side-by-side on the overstuffed couch. Ben won't sleep; he'll replay every moment in his head until he can recall the bittersweet of their leaving at will. It's the best kind of pain: a temporary respite from greater joy than he has ever imagined. It's not an ending; it's the soft sigh of a period—or a comma—before the next, more beautiful phrase begins.

He untangles his fingers and lets their hands drop. She watches. He rests his hands on her hips, bases gently just above her pelvis. His thumbs ride gentle curves inward and up to her rib cage, and his fingers fold around behind to her spine. She's tiny and smooth and soft and beautiful and smells so wonderful as he leans down to rest his chin on her right shoulder. His left hand moves up to the spot between her shoulder blades where she purrs when he massages and his right arm circles her waist. She presses in closer, throwing one arm around his neck and another across the middle of his back. She always squeezes them closer together than he does.

A moment, or two, or ten later, she relaxes, then squeezes once more. They ease apart, him straightening and her rolling back from the balls of her feet. He smiles and brushes away a few strands of golden hair from his goatee; she smiles and says nothing, watching and waiting.

An idea shaped in pure language passes between them wordlessly, hearts and minds together in the fading light. They lean together, eyes closed and heads tilting. Their lips touch gently at first, both parted, hers gentle around his upper lip and his around her lower lip. It's soft and sweet. He turns to kiss the corner of her mouth. He feels her smile and pulls back, as they both chuckle. Their eyes close again and they lean together once, twice more, first with the hunger and thirst of desert wanderers, then with the satisfied satiation of banqueteers after the first tiny spoonful of a perfect creme brulee.

There's another pause, this one awkward. He finds one hand at the small of her back and the other curled in her hair. Her eyes ask for guidance when he opens his. He'd like to stay until sunrise, to watch the sky darken then lighten again, feeling their warmth grow stronger through the night, but he smiles a sad smile and pulls her in for one last hug. He whispers, "Goodnight" in her ear. She smiles a quick smile, then looks down and smiles a strange, beautiful smile at nothing in particular.

Then he's down the single stair, halfway to his truck, with the image imprinted of her leaning wistfully against the door, watching him as if she'd also come untethered from time. The tingle of the evening lasts through into his dreams until he awakens, still smiling into his pillow.

o o o

Fear

Ben wonders.

He sees the trap of a perfect dilemma. Every moment he thinks of Emily is a beautiful, delicious ache. He has a list of ideas, song lyrics, poetry, and passages of books that he wants to leave lying around casually so she can stumble upon them and feel the same soul stirrings. He holds the desire in his hands, thick as ropes, that she'll admire the beauty of his true self the way the moon admires the earth.

Yet when it grows dark and the bedside lamp throws soft yellow circles around its shade to the walls and ceilings, his bedroom seems at once both cave-like claustrophobic and comfortably snug. Then he feels alone and wants to reach out, to cry out for her.

He remembers his grandmother's lectures about good posture. His mother once remarked that at least his heavy sixth-grade back-pack would pull his shoulders back and his head up. Some days he transforms in the mirror as he imagines a string stretching his spine straighter, gathering his muscles and confidence and pulling him to his full height. He glides from room to room, power fully controlled and ready for anything: a perfect being of pure will. He feels the same way when she looks at him, or walks with him, or says his name.

His only memory of being thirteen is of the junior high boys' locker room, undersized and voice-cracking, awaiting the inevitable and unstoppable teasing that separated the individual weak from the group strong with little pattern and no reason except its heritage and the desire to identify and mediocritize the unique. His only solace was to bear it stoically until the period-ending buzzer sounded and to hope for the next twenty-three hours and ten minutes that the hammer would fall on someone else the next time, when his only social requirement would be nervous laugher.

Beautiful

Somehow, it's worse now, as he recognizes the chromatic abstraction of his splayed emotions. Cola-colored fear provides the base, a fear of loss of pride, stability, and peace. Cinnamon anger dashes in and out, railing against the injustice of the world and the frustration of being so powerless toward his own destiny. Cream hope bubbles in small clumps. No amount of mixing can beat it out of the mixture. They espouse patience, knowing that somehow, sooner or later, everything will come around for good. Pollockian yellows and blues of betrayal and loss and pride drip in. Where once he'd have surveyed a vast sucking muddy muck, now his vision has cleared and his sophistication increased to the point where he can identify the beautiful individual pieces and even trace them back to source events for almost each individual hue.

His pain and fragility terrify him. They're beautiful, fragile glass structures built slowly through time and trust; he fears wind and water—even gentle spring rains—will throw them down into jagged, terrible shards. A careless word could raze the plains.

He wants to gather her. He wants to sit silently as she surveys his crystalline terraces and sweeping archways. He longs for her to smile, to touch his hand, to smooth his hair, and to say that it is good and beautiful and worth preserving.

Yet as the desire clenches his hands, he sees himself at thirteen again, struggling for identity and attaching himself anew every day to a different group and ideal. He wondered then wordlessly if he would ever be strong and silent and the kind of masculine from which fears turned away. Can he crawl to her, cradling failures and flaws, to offer the pock-marked glories and imperfections of his humanity? He'd clutch her to his chest, softly and silently, as her flood of tears bathed them in a living ocean of pain and sorrow. Can he be broken, beautifully afraid and vulnerable, and ask for the gift he doesn't deserve? Could he walk on if she said no? Would he let go if she said yes?

When they talk on the phone late at night, both lying in bed, his arm shields his eyes from even the gentle glow of the light and he lies back to listen to her breath. Full and rich silences swirl between the sounds and he smiles; neither has to talk. There's nothing left to say. Even when they both yawn from exhaustion and their voices fade and soften into dreamlike contentment, he wants to hold on for one more moment, just one, so he never feels the immediate fade as that connection moves from its prominencee into the warm background glow of love as he understands it.

He recognizes the pause as she begins the delicate process of saying goodnight and waits for him to say something. It's a silence tinged with expectation and a little sadness. He can never see its words. He wrestles with them, his hands slick with sweat and unable to grasp the argument as it shifts and phases in and out of form. It's too ideal, too abstract. His best attempts sound high and lofty, words used to build a cathedral around the world's most perfect rose, or to write a symphony about writing symphonies.

How can he tell her such a flawed understanding of his love? He barely finds himself lovable. Who is he to intrude into her goodness and patience with failure and fear? She is delicate, neither fragile nor breakable, but filigreed and fine and feminine. He is masculine, all clomping boots and incautious laughter and mayhem. He'd leave greasy fingerprints all over a Faberge egg.

Emily fills him up. Something melted the first time she looked at him, head tilted to the side and eyes widened just a little and mouth open in a tiny, breathy smile. Something hard gave way to something soft and warm and he knows how the maple trees in New England feel when spring sunlight awakens them and whispers to bud, to bloom, to lift their limbs in canopies of applauding leaves. His heart pounds once again and every artery leaps to attention as blood flows faster and freer. Warmth radiates from his core and life tingles throughout his body.

Her touch, too—he now knows why soldiers in foxholes grab stubs of pencils to scribble notes to their sweethearts while waiting in thin, wet muck for battles to fall. She connects him to humanity with an unbroken line through countless generations, each rediscovering the simple and complex joys and pains and sorrows and heartbreaks and bittersweets of the union of two lives and two souls. She sets him on fire; even an accidental brush of shoulders can burn so beautifully on his skin for days.

Somewhere across the city, she waits for him. He straightens again at the thought. Somewhere she feels the same beautiful ache when they're apart, dies the same little deaths when they leave each other. He never knew he felt incomplete and unsatisfied in his small orbit of work and home and hobbies, until her gravity drew him higher out of unstable, untenable orbits, somewhere he doesn't yet understand to some place with a greater view of celestial wonders. He sees himself from above, in a true context within his neighborhood, the city, and the world. For the first time, he feels a connection to the age-old thread which spent countless generations to produce them now, at the right time, in the right places.

It's a huge weight to bear. The future of the race depends on his decisions; mankind is always one generation away from extinction. Then he smiles again. He can carry the weight of the world if she stands with him.

Ben leans out, far to his right, and turns off the lamp. Darkness fills the deeper spaces until his pupils readjust, but there's no emptiness now. He turns onto his left shoulder and puts his hand under his head and tries to clear his mind of everything but the radiating warmth pulsing out and from his heart. Then he sleeps, eyes closed lightly, worry-lines erased, and wistful.

o o o

Beautiful

Their youth is indelible; they dance on the tracks of a train named June.

The sun hangs high overhead; noon's protector chases away shadows. It's quiet by the river; reverent crowds hush as they walk a green strip separated from downtown by a buzzing ribbon of asphalt. Huge bridges span the river to the north, north further, south, and much further south. Colorless clouds rearrange themselves as they sail lazily west to east.

Ben's given up on black today in favor of a forest green shirt and denim shorts. Emily has her hair pulled back in a loose ponytail, with a pale blue tank top over white pants. He loves the freckles where the sun kisses her nose and shoulders. They pause at a railing to look down at water lapping against smooth river rocks.

They say nothing. There's nothing to say; it's only them, there, with the river in front, the waterfront park behind, and miles of perfect blue dome stretching horizon to horizon above. It's a silence with very little fear. It's Flag Day.

His birthday's on Father's Day this year: tomorrow. Everything's all ready for the barbecue, hamburger meat and sausages tucked safely away in the fridge, Randy en route to find various beverages right now, and two dozen friends and well-wishers bringing their own necessities. Yet Ben wanted to celebrate early, with her, in silence and peace and a shared moment of beauty. The river stands in for sea and sky.

As he watches the sunlight sparkle a thousand times per second on gentle river ripples, he cannot resist the lure of her waist for his right arm. Silently, they tilt their heads together. When he closes his eyes, it's exactly as he pictured it. He has more than he ever wanted; he has everything he never imagined he needed.

To Everyone a New Ending

A Solid Bliss

Jerry performs an impressive feat of magic.

A management pattern had appeared in recent years. To save money and to give the financial department time to finish off the year's accounts, both of which excite financial departments in peculiar and frightening ways, many companies hint strongly that their employees take vacations in the dull groove between Christmas and New Year's Eve. They accomplish very little, goes the argument, due to vacation overlaps and tryptophan- and chocolate-enabled drowsinesses. Practicality so rarely overlaps business sense.

The client offers this justification to delay its work on the project for a single, glorious week. Jerry clads himself with persistent avenging righteousness and climbs the stairs, logic and reason in hand. If the client has no one available to answer developer questions, why force the current pace of progress? Why not back off to let people

183

take vacations if they wish or mop the edges of the current project if they really want to come into work?

The stars align. Jerry's cherubic face shines with heavenly approval. Even with a full beard and bright red suspenders cutting bloody stripes down atop a tie-died T-shirt still effervescent after hundreds of washings, he descends from the seventh floor with the word of truth. His face shines from the miraculous coup of his divinely inspired pitch.

Ben contrarily works figures to devise how a giant Santa boot can burst through two stories of windows on the north side of the building and punt him over the mountains to the south in a cartoon-perfect parabola with an appropriately accommodating thump that bounces buildings off of their foundations and kicks up small dust-clouds. Where he'd normally imagine the scene from different angles until he could identify the buckle in a shoe-only outlet mall fire sale and replay his trajectory so accurately that he counts vents on top of the buildings as he sails over the warehouse district, past the concentric circles of neighborhoods of lesser influence surrounding the rich section of the suburbs proper, and, finally, rivers, trees, and minor wrinkles in the landscape, this time he takes it as it is and refuses to chase down the image for more than mere stomach-clenchingly bad news.

He stares down at traffic through the blinds, blinking in abnormal winter sunlight, for a few minutes before he considers what to do with his vacation. Visiting his parents means dealing with thick blankets, both of snow and actuality, while remaining in town runs the risk of a once-a-decade snowfall of an inch or more turning all of the television and radio news in the city into a free-for-all of reporters wog-boggled at the idea that, yep, the white stuff is still coming down. A couple of years earlier, the apparent newsworthiness of frozen precipitate still hadn't worn off after two days. Then again, he'd sworn off of television news when the 11 o'clock preview during the *X-Files* series finale used the bump, no kidding, "Now that the *X-Files* is ending, what has the show taught us about *real* aliens?"

He decides to mitigate his risk by inviting his parents to visit, if they want, if they have time, if notice of a week and a half is sufficient.

It is.

His older brother and his wife have plans to visit her parents, and his younger brother is in the UK to study for a year and has neither money nor time to fly home. It isn't the first Christmas they won't all be together, but in Ben's mind, it is the loneliest.

Ben resists the urge to re-re-arrange his kitchen. He lies on the couch in Bermuda shorts and a Hawaiian shirt and sucks cranberry-raspberry juice through a twisty straw, with the heat turned up to 80. Leigh Nash's "You're a Mean One, Mr. Grinch" echoes through all of downstairs. It's on repeat. Randy had stopped halfway down the stairs about forty-five minutes earlier, judging the expression on Ben's face as much as his posture—one bare foot pressed against the arm of the couch and the other dangling almost to the floor—and locked himself in his bedroom to play computer games.

So far, he's dusted underneath the fridge, atop the range hood, and both sides of the plastic blinds in the kitchen. He's resolved to put all of the recyclable materials in the laundry closet by the side door as soon as he's emptied them, rather then letting them pile up on the clean dishes side of the sink. He even cleaned under the burners on the stove. He knows nothing else to make his house sparkle; the kitchen is its heart, radiating out life and purpose. Today he is a whirlwind of excitable cleaning power.

The song starts over. By the clock he still has two hours before he must leave for the airport. He halfway ponders rearranging the furniture in his living room, but then switches discs by remote control, this time to a little-known band he saw perform in Cincinnati one December at the Taft Theater. The final song rumbles like a

185

coal train through a sleepy town as the winter solstice descends. He figures that it's at least as aurally disturbing as the twenty-ninth repetition of the phrase "thirty-nine-and-a-half-foot pole", but he can't hear Randy walking around upstairs.

Ben sighs and almost allows himself to relax. He's spent too long away from the couch lately. A nervous tension twitches in his muscles; a buzz in his mind refuses to admit that for two hours he has absolutely nothing that he absolutely must do. He can't conceive of any longer stretch of time empty of meetings and questions and deadlines. Couches and easy chairs and the heavy entertainment center he'd have to unpack completely before rewiring the television, stereo, speakers, DVD player, and game consoles in reality, shuffle and rearrange themselves in geometrically pleasant ways in the dull rectangle that is his empty living room, but he waves them away combinatorially and visualizes billowing clouds of coal smoke and steam. Whistles and pistons and clacking rails and wheels keep time.

o o o

Christmas Dinner

It's quiet around the table. Ben puts out his only tablecloth, then hovers over the ham in the oven. His mother convinces his father to disappear with the car and he returns with a pair of candlesticks in lieu of a centerpiece. "They do look festive!" Ben admits as he wonders when he can ever use them again.

His house expands and contracts in ways contrary to his expectations. Now he's the one worrying about doing laundry to have enough clean towels and stocking the right food in the fridge and finding them comfortable places to sleep. It's uneasy, almost unnatural, being the person on whom the people he's relied most must now rely. Perhaps it would be different if Andy and Crispin and, now,

Ellie were here, so that the children would outnumber the adults again.

He throws himself instead into the meal. Besides the ham, he cooks pounds of green beans, garlic mashed potatoes, dinner rolls—cheating; from a cardboard tube—and an Italian salad. He laments the lack of sweet potatoes, starting from when he remembers them, ten minutes before the final ham timer beeps. There are two kinds of pie: sweet Northwest berries and classic pumpkin.

Randy ducks out to drive to Vancouver for the weekend after decorating a small pine tree in the corner with a handful of ornaments and more tinsel than a tree twice its size could wear proudly. Its aroma mixes with the ham all day to put Ben in a Christmasy mood.

Ellen suggests saying Grace and offers the honor first to Ben, who finds the suggestion shocking and surprising and passes to his father. They hold hands, again Ellen's idea, and he feels how thin her hands are becoming and how strong Daniel's remain.

His eyes snap open. He's forgotten to cut the ham. It sits on table untouched under its cooking foil. His father finishes. Everyone watches Ben.

"Uh, Dad, would you like to do the other honors?" he starts. He pushes his chair back, remembering to say, "Excuse me, please" to his mother, before pulling the serving platter he had searched every cupboard for last Thursday and finding a clean knife.

"I could do it if you're uncomfortable, but you're the man of the house."

"Dad, I appreciate your confidence, but I don't know how to carve a ham." He used the same phrase when he learned how to ride a bicycle, swing a hammer, hit a baseball, change a tire, and replace his oil. It's their symbol. Only when he admitted his limitations could Daniel start to teach him.

He never needed that direct and helpless honesty with his mother, not in those terms. She never looked at him differently if he failed. He could call to thank her for the lovely new cookie recipe and then explain that they turned out nicely except for sticking to the pan and now he had a plate full of delicious but rumpled cookies and a cookie sheet that he thought might need a good dose of attention from steel wool, but he wasn't sure and how would she handle it, if she were there?

Ben grabs spare pot-holders and rushes the ham pan to the kitchen cupboard. He stands with the foil cover in one hand and the knife in the other. His mouth waters at the first ham he's baked; it looks and smells fantastic, with a gentle brown crust and clear juices puddled around the bottom.

"Grab a fork too, son," his father advises from the table. "Hold it in place and slice horizontally just over the bone."

More juice flows out.

"That looks good. Stop there. Now cut vertically, down to the horizontal cut. Cut it as thick or as thin as you like. It's just a matter of taste. I like an electric carver, but this is fine. Don't go as far as the bone, though."

He bites his tongue while trying to keep the knife even between slices. The first few slices tear off raggedly at the bottom, but he persists and soon has a steaming plate of meat. He sighs and replaces the foil covering before transferring the platter to the table.

"Good work, Ben."

He glances at a mountain of soon-dirty dishes. He and Randy would take a week to make a mess that size. "Thanks, Dad." He turns to his mother. "Does Dad need to bless the meal again?"

Ellen's sad little smile becomes a grin as she holds out her plate. "No, of course not. May I have a piece of ham?"

"Absolutely, but you two are going to have to slice the pies."

o o o

Festival

In deference to sensibilities that take offense at the notion of possibly giving offense, the annual holiday party moves from early-to-mid December to mid-January, when the only thing to celebrate is the arrival of credit card statements and nine more weeks of winter. Ben tries and fails to accept this. The proper place to celebrate is the end of a year, when everyone can reflect solemnly at the end of twelve short months instead of pondering somberly the stretching possibilities of twelve, eleven, or eleven and a half long months. Worse, spending time with his coworkers outside of normal working hours invokes miserly accountant feelings, as if he should deduct every minute spent exchanging awkward pleasantries from normal working hours next week. He adds to running notes for the work-party-flex-time protocol, intending to explore how to maximize his appearance to meet the expectations of people who intend to see their coworkers in odd situations, strange outfits, and abnormal places, while minimizing his discomfort at spending his own time without compensation.

Several floors up in a rented penthouse apartment in one of the better hotels on the west side of the city, an open bar helps the sales department cope with the situation far more than their numbers deserve, statistically.

It's a small mercy that he came alone. Last year he brought Randy. Ben faced awkward jokes about what an ugly date he had, while Randy happily chatted with a pretty administrative assistant who failed to answer his calls within a week. They spent several more hours at the party than Ben had intended, the main insult being a dull, if drunken speech from the CEO and founder. Interruptions of cheers from the seventh-floor crew only encouraged him. They survived and exorcised the memory during the drive home by planning a series of bizarre pranks culminating in stealing and burning all of the MBA diplomas in the building, one week at a time, corner by corner.

It's a very small mercy. One of his developer colleagues asks, "So, where's Emily?" before introducing his fiancée. He tumbles down several strange mental paths about the hows and wheres and whys and whats of merging these two parts of his life and how she would have had to do the same and mumbles something about her not being able to make it, which appeases the querents somewhat until the girl winks and says, "Pity, she sounds cute!" Only his Midwest upbringing saves him; the reflexive "Thank you" serves as a response while he figures out how to extricate himself to perform obligatory balcony-view admiration.

Ben leans his head way out until everyone else fades into ignorable peripheral vision. He prefers the view from the other side of the river looking west. This view dulls in comparison: a few low hills covered with trees and houses in the distance and bridges and warehouses and traffic in the foreground. It's too dark right now to appreciate the river and too dark to count the bridges, each one a different style of architecture that he can see and name and replay as a drive. For example, the main highway loop around the city swoops across the river two bridges south on the much-maligned double-decker cantilever, before turning north again to join the north-south Interstate, eventually, or, more to his interest, the east-west Interstate immediately. Every time he comes around that corner, the green sign of the exit looms closer before passing over his head. He feels his truck turning and that every-time irrational fear of driving up and over and finding that the road has stopped just past his view now that he's in the sky and it's too late to stop. Then the exit curves gently and gradually down to the ground before turning east yet again and merging toward his home.

To Everyone a New Ending

The sun perpetually shines just after a storm. Gray clouds pass overhead, chased away by thick patches of clear blue. People live in the apartments at eye level of the bridge and raised roadways and he wonders if they see him glance into their lives as he passes. Yet he once saw the very same apartments from the ground after a late afternoon thunderstorm when the heavy clouds wandered away spent, and the dusk threw rose-colored hues on the staggered buildings and that the angle was just so that each car gleamed as it sped up and out of sight.

He'd never live there. Even the rush of traffic from the highway two miles away at midnight in his childhood kept him from falling asleep some nights. He prefers the comfortable comparative darkness of his own quiet, dull neighborhood. He's never on this side of the river. He never bathes in the glow of the skyscrapers and confusing snarls of one-way streets and the steady march of clubs each too hip to stay open longer than three months. He prefers to admire from a distance.

Ben turns away from the window, unable to pretend further that the view has transfixed him and making him a prime target for roving soi-disant raconteurs. He swirls the pineapple juice in his glass, willing the ice cubes to melt faster so that he can nurse the drink longer to avoid facing the sea of roiling and reforming conversations empty-handed. It's easy to find developers at a mixed office party; find the corners, televisions, stereos, and laptops. Listen for comparisons of cell phones, PDAs, and raucous discussions of operating system advocacy of interest to non-developers in the same way that, for example, the average candy striper never considers the relative merit of one stethoscope manufacturer over another. Other sentences drift over and above the sea of sound, comparing golf courses and scores and the virtues and pitfalls of owning a house that backs on to the river in the affluent southern suburbs, where it's possible to boat to work when highway traffic crawls, if you can find a dock on the east side of the river. Ben interpolates the punchline.

He scans the room for the least offensive crowd. He attempts to predict the discussion most likely both to last until and break up closest to the time at which he promises himself to leave, but his sea-legs stay land-bound. There's a point in every party where the first person to leave breaks the ice and, ten minutes later, a puzzled host looks at the clock and wonders why he has an empty house at a quarter 'til 10 and decides that he really might as well tidy up now, if that's all that will happen tonight. Ben's plan B is to volunteer to accompany someone sent to fetch libations and disappear after pretending to bring in one more bag of snack food.

Hotel bars make that difficult.

He's not sure why he's here. He's an outsider. He resists the temptation to turn back and rest his forehead against the glass, hands and nose pressed to the window. His shoulders slump as he wonders where and how the world goes by outside, hoping someday to escape into the night air, maybe to follow the river for a time, perhaps to wheel untouched above city lights.

Somewhere in that ocean of lights and trees and buildings and cars and motion, his light burns. The darkness laps against and surrounds but never quenches it. He can't see it from the window. He can only guess.

Why is he here? He can't answer the question in any way that points to any one person or any one relationship or any single obligation. It's all a ball of unease, of conflicting desires—not his own— that raged less dramatically when he gave in and agreed, in his head, to go. He sees himself on New Year's Eve, surrounded by friends and connections tenuous. Couples clutch each other around the waists to await the New Year's first perfect kiss.

What could midnight bring tonight? He lists the people he would talk to if they were here: Eric, Jerry, Andrew. Their lives all overlap professionally between the weekday hours of approximately nine to five, but they're mere slivers and arcs of full, healthy great circles of actual human lives. Ben hopes for a connection to someone he occasionally passes in the hallway or the lobby, even someone with whom he's shared a moment of recognition.

The inevitable sad end there, too, is unwrapping the last of the leftovers for a lonely Friday night meal to find that it's barely enough for a snack after picking out the mold. His disappointment has already settled for second or third or fourth best. What possible conversation could he make? What small talk does he have now?

The conversation in another corner reasserts itself with raucous laughter over whichever punchline has slithered into the sunlight of its attention. He doesn't understand it. He doesn't even want it. Ben sets down the glass he didn't realize he's emptied and walks out the door. After a step he stops again to slump. Noise pours out in liquid streams; they combine into a rush of white noise.

The elevator is so close that he can give up and go home and pull the covers over his head, taking back his weekend in defiant unconsciousness. Yet some obligation still draws him. The president always speaks at midnight. Perhaps the sacrifices of the past few months will not go unnoticed. His hard work will have made a difference. Maybe it won't be a small sun that drives away the darkness. Maybe it won't be even a neon sign that draws the eye. Maybe he'll stand apart from the recognition, to stand when he hears his name, and to point at his accomplishments, saying, "Look! I did this! I made a difference!"

Ben turns away and closes the door. The elevator fails to reach the top floor after thirty seconds, so he takes the stairs down to the lobby, then drives home.

o o o

Resignation

For the first time in recent memory, Randy is quite single. He suggests celebrating on Tuesday—Valentine's Day—with a game of pool and a beer or two. Ben agrees.

Jerry and Ben review the week's plan in that afternoon, laying several graphs across Jerry's desk. The current progress is adequate, even surprising. There's still too much work to accomplish by the first of March, but they have a solid product that meets their basic obligations. The customer could use it right way. It's not perfect and it doesn't do everything it eventually must do, but it's a definite improvement over the current system. Ben's happy. Jerry's happy. The customer is happy. Everyone's happy on this floor.

Half of the seventh floor is happy, or at least content. Despite Ned's protestations, there's been little overtime and the customer has been very flexible about the schedule. Some of it is Jerry's magic: convincing them to start migrating to the software now for what it does and delivering reliably new versions every other Wednesday afternoon. Both Eric and Ben punctuate their warnings not to deliver new versions on Friday afternoons for weekend installations by drawing their fingers across their throats and making choking noises—in separate conversations. They've slowly added new features. The first upgrade is a near-disaster, but the team fixes the single serious bug that had escaped everyone's notice at just after 5:23 pm that Wednesday night, averting almost certain disaster.

Ned continues to make his displeasure palpable, stomping downstairs and storming into Jerry's office twice daily. Jerry closes the door a couple of times every week but their opposing points of view leak out around the edges. Part of Ned's reluctance to let developers talk to the customer directly is that the contract specified a generous fixed fee for the work; at the original, impractical three-month estimate, the company would have made a very healthy profit besides gaining a foothold in a difficult market and a good working relationship with the client. This was at least half the price of all of the other bids, for good reason. As things look now, the company will be lucky to break even, and Ned will be very lucky to keep his career. It's a valuable lesson to learn, but every week that passes makes Ned less of a hero and the experience more expensive.

The second year in a row of mild winter helps too, as the normal February gray skies give way to beautiful May-type clear blues with temperatures in the 50s. There'll be another painful summer, no doubt, but the short fury of November and December grew mild in January. Winter has all but fled.

Jerry brushes an invisible speck of dust off of the picture of his wife on the corner of his desk for the second time in fifteen minutes. Ben ticks two more mental checkboxes as Jerry smoothes his shirt and flicks his eyes toward the analog wall clock every few minutes. "Okay, what's your plan for tonight?"

"Hmm?"

"You're distracted. What are you and Karen doing tonight?"

A blush spirals out from Jerry's cheekbones. "We haven't had much time together in several weeks, but my sister's taking the kids and we're going out to dinner... and spending the night at that hotel out of town, where Eric had his birthday dinner this summer."

Ben nods, then rolls his eyes at a scraping, stamping sound from upstairs. "Sounds pretty special."

"After, what is it? It's twelve years now. After twelve years, even just one night is a vacation." Jerry's expression softens further.

"That's great. Dad did the same thing one year. Mom didn't know whether to strangle him for keeping the secret or call the sitter to come over early and convince him to leave work at noon. I've always remembered that."

They're both silent, Jerry in anticipation and Ben flipping back through every Valentine's Day he can remember for his happiest memory. Nothing tops eating a cupcake with pink frosting and a huge heart-shaped gumdrop at age seven. This year, his mother's annual Valentine arrived the day before and he clings to that as the high point.

A telephone rings in the distance.

"Are your parents still together?"

"Yeah, thirty-uh, five years, I guess. Long time."

Jerry leans back in his chair and puts his hands behind his head. "I hope to get there someday. It does seem like a long time, though."

Ben spins his pen with his right hand and re-reads the weekly plan. If he found the right girl and eloped today, he'd be well over forty by the time they celebrated their twelfth anniversary. The likelihood he'll have a fiftieth anniversary slips further away. He can't think of the last time he even glanced at the engagement, wedding, and anniversary section of the newspaper. A different phone starts to ring and he replays the last several seconds, recognizing first the sound of his cell phone in his office and, second, the sound of his office phone. They both came from the same location.

Jerry's phone rings. They both stare at it for a moment, then Jerry answers. He studies Ben's face. "There's a call for you, something about Randy. Go ahead and take it." Ben reaches for the phone. "You might want some privacy; I'll be here when you finish."

Ben walks to his office and shuts the door. In the distance, someone disembarks from the elevator and whistles happily off-key. He dials the reception desk.

"This is Ben."

"Ben, it's Annie. Someone's on the line for you about your roommate. I'll connect you now."

There's a click and a hum and a moment later another click unmutes the silence.

"This is Ben."

"Hi Ben. This is Dr. Miller. You're Randy's medical contact, right?"

"That's right. Is something wrong?"

"Randy was in a small accident earlier today. He's fine, except for a concussion and a hairline fracture in his right tibia. We've set his leg and want to release him in a couple of hours. Can you find him a ride from the hospital?"

"Wait, he's fine?"

"He'll have a cast for a few weeks and some discomfort for a while, but otherwise he's fine. I understand he saved a small child."

"Randy saved someone's life?"

"He can tell you the whole story, but yes, he did."

Ben pauses. Right; Randy needs a ride. "I can be there in half an hour."

"Thanks, Ben. There's no rush. He's already popular in the emergency room. A couple of nurses and at least one intern will be very sorry to see him go; he's charmed my staff."

"Yeah. That's Randy. Uh...I'll be there soon."

"Great! Thank you, Ben."

He leans far forward in his chair, elbows on the desk and both feet bouncing up and down. If anyone were immortal, it would have been Randy. Maybe there was blood. The worst he's ever been sick is sneezing a few times during allergy season. Of course he'd found a way to do it dramatically, probably throwing a toddler heroically to her mother out of the way of a bus that's lost its brakes before diving out of the way and clipping the right front bumper and taking out a hulking blue mailbox, impressing all of the women in the emergency room with his toughness, good humor, and charmingly unkempt hair.

Ben sees himself losing both front teeth and tearing his pants in that situation.

If the mayor gives him the key to the city, Randy can find another ride to the ceremony, Ben decides, just before resolving never to bring up the idea again, at least, not while trying to extract Randy from a parade of female well-wishers clustered around the complimentary wheelchair to the parking lot. The cast can't be dry and it's probably full of phone numbers already.

Ben shuts down his computer and gathers his phone and jacket. He turns the door to the stairway before the thought he suspended in Jerry's office continues. Jogging back, he bursts out, "Sorry, I have to go to pick up Randy from the hospital—" before catching Jerry's red-faced expression, and not the peaceful anticipatory comfort he'd had a few minutes earlier. Then Ben sees Ned perched on the chair, frowning and glaring at his watch, and begins to understand.

"Pull up a chair, Ben. You can give us a few more minutes of work today." Ned's grin has far too little mirth.

Jerry won't meet Ben's eyes as he takes the other chair in the room, a nasty plastic thing with no arms, wobbly casters, and a back that can't decide whether it's better to pitch forward uncomfortably or lean way, way back. He crosses his legs at the ankles under the chair, between the perilous plastic legs, and arches his back; it's this chair's posture of least pain. He traded the sibling in his office for a nicer wood and plush cushion model discarded from a previous seventh-floor remodel last year before actually sitting in it. Perhaps it's in a fatal furniture exhibit somewhere where no one will confuse it for something functional and will instead appreciate its modern reimagining of good-for-your-soul Puritanical suffering.

Ned waves their way a thick sheaf of papers as if he were the final torch carrier of the Olympic opening ceremonies. "I was just going over your velocity reports with Michael and Gabe."

Those names sound familiar in the sense that they're actually invokable titles, as in, "oh, I just had lunch with Michael—you know, the CEO" or "Uncle Gabe thinks the finances for this quarter look good, so there's a possibility of raises, but don't tell anyone". They're the business process equivalent of punctuation. "I don't think Gabe would agree" not only ends a sentence, but underlines the speaker's point and doodles exclamation points in the margin.

Ben sees Jerry's face reflect the same understanding even before he tries to resume the argument from before the interruption. "I was just telling Ned that the customer needs no major features until the start of April, for fiscal year-end preparations in June and in November for calendar year-end calculations."

Ned returns fire around a wickeder grin. "And I was saying that both Michael and Gabe agree that we're spending too much on this project."

"We can scale back. We've talked about this. We can switch some developers to the other projects we've delayed. It's not too late to go back to our regular customers."

"Michael feels that that's not a strategic goal anymore."

Ben regrets scoffing but can't stop the words. "Having customers? Satisfying customers?"

Ned shakes his head nastily. "The future's not in custom jobs for small fish. The future is big projects for big customers—glorious migrations and conversions."

Having lived through the original Internet gold rush vicariously through the stories of coworkers and fellow students who'd dropped out to make and lose fortunes, Ben recognizes the theory of building mindshare through carefully crafted press releases announcing strategic partnerships with large companies (partnerships only to appear together on the same press release) as unworkable. Jerry rolls his eyes and Ben realizes that this is still a review for his benefit. He stifles a yawn, then remembers Randy at the hospital and stands. Ned is faster, throwing out the hand holding the papers to catch Ben in the chest and counting on Ben to grab the stack reflexively.

"Don't go yet. You might as well help Jeremiah. Here's a list of headcount costs correlated with time to task ratios for the migration. Gabe wants a plan for a 25% reduction in employee expenses on his desk by noon tomorrow. You have until 9 am to have it on my desk."

Something grows inside Ben during the explanation. Something new or very old but never used shakes itself free of cobwebs in a long-forgotten mental corner.

He looks at Jerry, who's not saying anything.

He looks at Ned, whose look of triumph is too heartfelt to be real.

"It's right now," Ben pauses to hand back the report, "4:30. Jerry has plans for tonight. I don't share your sense of urgency. If you'll excuse me, I have a real emergency that actually requires my attention right now."

He pushes past Ned, who squeaks but stays seated, and halfway jogs to the stairs, hoping but not waiting to hear Jerry make a similar pronouncement.

○ ○ ○

Every Today is an Ending

"I don't know. Do you think Sharee is a fake name?"

Ben grunts. Randy's more chipper than he ought to be for as pale and awkward as he looks as he angles his right leg into Ben's truck. The seat is as far back as it can go. He's pulled his ragged jeans down over the cast. Speckles of blood from asphalt abrasions make them less appealing. The significant group of female ER staffers has gone back inside; Ben could find little pattern in the group as he waited for Randy to finish signing the release forms. Several appeared to be appropriate surrogate mothers, though their attentions seemed somewhat. . . different from the last time he needed medical attention.

"I guess it could be a real name. I haven't had a lot of experience meeting women in hospitals, but I wouldn't expect it to change their standards of truthfulness, well, except for terminal illness wards or something like that, but these weren't patients. Well, most of them weren't patients." He's on a roll now.

"Did you really save a little kid?"

He stares out the side window. "I don't remember very well. There are flashes, you know? I only see snapshots. I'm out for lunch, waiting at a crosswalk, and there are people all around and traffic, sure. Then I'm looking up from the middle of the road and there's a bus and everything's really supernaturally quiet and then there's blue sky and people leaning in over me. I don't really feel anything right now."

This is more honesty than Ben expects all at once; he scrambles over the transition between the manic bubbles of being everybody's friend that wins Randy admirers and the vulnerability of what he interprets now as slow-burning shock. "You're not in pain?"

"No, not really. They gave me something good but I wasn't paying attention. They called you because I'm not safe to drive. It'll probably kick in sometime tomorrow morning."

Ben signals and pulls out into the street. "When I was twelve or thirteen I went to race bicycles with my friends around the creek down the road. We built up the bank on one side as a ramp and spent a couple of hours piling rocks and dirt into a slope. It was only a few feet across, so we thought we could pedal as hard as we could and jump completely over it.

"The first guy chickened out and we teased him and I didn't want that. I backed up and went as hard and as fast as I could and just at the last minute, I don't know, my back tire slipped on a rock or something and I went off sideways and landed on my right side and broke my wrist in two places.

"I don't remember it hurting much. My ribs hurt more. I scraped them pretty badly. Anyway, the worst part was lying in bed with the weight of the cast on my chest thinking that I'd never broken anything before, that I'd crossed some kind of irreversible threshold. It woke me up at night, not just replaying the crash in my head, not that that was fun, but the thought that I'd lost something. I could never think of myself as someone who'd never broken a bone.

"It was never a *goal* that I could reach age 80 or whatever and tell my grandchildren that I'd never had a broken bone, but I still had a sense of grief. That was the worst thing. Well, that and trying to roll over in bed or take a shower or play basketball or something and think that that cast would never come off. Six weeks is a long time for a kid."

Randy hasn't stopped staring out the window. His voice has a careful, even tone, mathematically precisely between his earlier euphoria and the dissembling. "Do you still have those kinds of dreams?"

"I haven't thought of that in years. It was a big deal at the time and I didn't know why—still don't—but now it's just a thing that happened. Bones heal. You move on."

202

Silence pulls more words from Ben. He resists; something in Randy's tone suggests that it's not a random question, that it leads somewhere painful or hard to phrase.

Randy chews every word thirty-two times before releasing it. "I really did save a kid. He couldn't have been more than eight. I didn't even see him, didn't know he was there. I was fiddling with my backpack and looking up at the clouds and must have hit him with my backpack and knocked him into the street. I didn't get out of the way from picking him up in time to miss the bus. I don't think anyone else saw me knock him down; I don't think he knows or remembers. All I can hear right now is some lady yelling, 'He saved that kid! He saved that kid!'"

Ben blocks the scene per the script to work out an apologia for how it's not Randy's fault, how accidents happen, how saving the boy more than made up for the mishap, how the bus driver would have found it much easier to see Randy than an eight year-old, how sometimes dumb things just happen and you have to deal with them, but the abstract concepts of doubt and blame and free will phase in and out of the material world and every sentence he starts to assemble ends up hollow. Even "So, change of subject, you should have seen Ned's face when I walked out of the office halfway through a lecture" crumbles halfway through.

He starts to say something else, then feels his heart pound its way through his T-shirt. Surely Randy can hear the noise. Ben forces his attention through the sudden anger and his confusion over the same to concentrate on the red stoplight from a left-turn lane. No matter how unfair the situation seems, he *knows* that stupid things happen for indeterminate reasons. The other half of his mind screams back that this is unacceptable, that there must be meaning and that he deserves justice and plain, simple rationality.

Randy exhales sharply as he leans back to straighten his leg, forcing Ben's attention back to the moment. The debate remains unresolved in the face of the events that actually occurred, and he can't say that he minds.

In the end, they can only agree that neither of them ever really had the hang of Tuesdays after all. It's a cliché, but they trade wistful smiles and Ben decides that he really means his.

o o o

Unity

Ben sits in his office on the morning of Friday the 17th, proofreading his letter one more time. The words turned into meaningless symbols an hour ago. St. Patrick's Day will be his last day. Thirty days seem like more than enough notice, especially because Ned's plan had proven superior—not ultimately, but enough that he has tired of fighting and now sees the implied layoffs as his opportunity, not Ned's final blustering bludgeon. It's not a threat. It's liberation.

He's phrased and rephrased the letter dozens of times, starting in the shower on Thursday morning and continuing as the last thing before he fell asleep and the first thing when he awakened. When he finally sends it to the printer down the hall, his office feels small. Every familiar corner and landmark his eyes have wandered over thousands of times while distracting himself from work shrink into a scale model.

He pauses at the doorway to absorb the lifelike details and wonder at the change in his mind. Early rays of sunlight push through the blinds, golden hues seeping in around the corners. A touch on his shoulder startles him.

"I wrote one, too," says Jerry. "I shouldn't have read yours, but I printed mine at the same time."

204

Eric says, "Jerry told me in the elevator. I hadn't decided yet what I was going to do, but I'm not staying if you two are leaving."

By twos and threes and ones the mini-meeting in the hall grows to an informal quorum. Then Ben rewrites his letter to pluralize some of the language and add places for other people to sign and, before it really sinks in, presses the button for the seventh floor. He didn't want to make a statement and hadn't planned to make a scene, but all anyone really needed to speak up was one last push. Not everyone is ready to leave, but the final consensus is that Ned will have his 20% cut—and more.

Ben secretly smiles all the way up.

o   o   o

What Happens in the Past...

Unexpectable

HE doesn't understand *again*.

He's missing something. He's gone over the situation a dozen times, each time from a different angle. He's decided to do or not do a dozen different things. Every time he probes his feelings, something else leaps out and knocks his thoughts askew down a different corridor.

He's in space. Gravity fails. He bounces off of walls and ceilings and floors of uniform whiteness, where Down is Left or South or Up and his frame of reference nauseatingly shifts as he attempts to put himself perpendicular to *something*. Every few seconds he feels certain that he has put Down beneath his feet, on which he can stand. Then the world readjusts and everything changes and he peruses, yet again, the idempotent bulkheads.

Perhaps it's not the world that's changing.

Emily is beautiful and so foreign. Ben has started to take notes on their conversations, following a suspicion, and it disturbs him to graph the frequency at which beautiful moments end with her growing silent and sullen and he feeling stupid for no reason he can identify. There is no pattern, no math. He can't extrapolate a series. He can only sense an invisible lattice overgrown with invisible vines.

In one knock-down killer fight, she accused him of being cold and unemotive and he suggested that she tended to withdraw from potential conflicts until her frustrations built up into an explosion of ultimata. Emily gradually unpeeled herself from the corner of the couch as the argument heated to lean in, eyes flashing, and finger finally stabbing once, twice, thrice at the air in front of his heart. She was most alive then, when she cried, "Don't you feel anything?"

He can't see where he went wrong. He has forbidden himself to write a list of his goals for the relationship. Every time his awe and wonder become ponderings of practical matters and contingencies, he closes his eyes, breathes in deeply, and repeats his mantras. "Let it be. Let it go. Live and love as it is." The single luxury of his obsession is the knowledge of his only plan: the resolution to breathe in peace and to breathe out the need for control.

He enjoys himself, mostly. When it works and they're really together, he loses himself in an unselfconscious comfort where he feels strangely more himself. Yet her thrown verbal puzzles and his lack of words combine sometimes to balance him on knife-edge tiptoes, if he wishes to retain her good favor. His gratitude has acclimated to a constant ache.

It covers the side of his vision like ink or blood from a forehead wound, but then it washes away as he swims in the cool, deep waters of their commitment. They've never discussed it seriously since it became an implicit possibility. Still, she puts her little hand atop his big hand and her little thumb curves in between his thumb and index finger and her palms barely close over his knuckles. They both know what neither of them say: something good and beautiful shines where they both can see it. It's in their hands.

Ben still wonders. He lies on his bed late at night when late November winds howl through whispering trees. The days grow shorter and nights encroach on everyone's plans. He weighs two plates in his heart, one jewels of life and joy and living and love, and the other ashes of pain and fear and loss. The pans tip and tilt, but always balance. Then her touch and smile and looks of joy add another gem. Another speck of dross melts.

Emily has the power to destroy him. In a sentence she could spill the jewels to the floor to shatter and blow away as worthless dust. She could end it by smearing her victorious ashes across his face and clothes. Ben knows that that's never the end. He's lived through it before. The corners of his heart remember each little death he's died before. Even Emily's wounds will not be fatal.

If he could, he'd tear away all of the words he uses to hide his real intentions and live freely, a creature of transparent honesty and will. If there were no confusion or regret or reconsideration, he would stand on every word he ever shouted as foundational truths. How tall the tower he builds! He brings down fire from heaven! Yet the faces of the people he loves burn as they turn away.

Honesty pulls at him. He wants to strip off little deceptions and tiny secrets, protocols and politenesses that sometimes hold her away. Is it the shock of diving in to ice cold or boiling water? He wants that shock—the opportunity to acclimate to an environment far better, far more alive, than his perpetually tepid. Maybe he's right. Maybe it's right. Maybe it's right now. Maybe they're the right people in the right ways at the right time.

He still doesn't know how to tell. The pieces spin and flip as he shakes the image, hoping they'll fall into place on their own. Now he replays again something she said to listen for the point where the tone of her voice went from happy to sullen, to wonder again if they ever really do communicate. He considers again sending her a rose, but can't decide on the color.

○ ○ ○

Endings

This is the end.

Ben sits in his truck outside of the main post office downtown. The three-story monster squats on a full city block. A narrow strip of parking spaces on the south side angles toward the west, past a parking garage.

It rains now mostly from spite. Ten minutes of watching the light at the end of the street cycle through reds and greens and yellows, have turned the individual drops on his windshield into rivulets and streams. Now a collective sheet of water holds fast to tiny imperfections in the glass.

The driver's side window still holds mottled drops. Individual amber jewels glow the yellowish-orange of parking lot lights. Ben feels a sense of unease every time the nearest pole tickles his eyes. He stares until it becomes a giant praying mantis ready to strike his head from his shoulders. Maybe that'd be a mercy.

Emily remains inside, still mailing a package to her mother. She'd insisted that he drive her across the bridge to a square formed by the train station, the bus station, a bridge, and the post office. He hates this part of town; it confuses him. Apart from some river shipping, it's the city's spine. A tangle of one-way streets move people and cargo here and there, never stopping, rarely slowing.

Ben can see two or three people moving through the big glass windows. None is Emily. A scowling blonde woman, who might be pretty if she smiled, parks to the left of his truck, more gently than most people who roll up against the curb and cause their cars to bounce back on their springs. She shoots a look his direction as she opens the rear door to retrieve a small parcel.

Besides the three insectival light posts, he also worries that the postmaster will chase him off with vague murmurs of terrorism and federal buildings. It's more pervasive than accurate.

The drive was silent, partly because Ben chased everything out of his mind but a chant of street names on which to turn once he crossed the bridge and partly because there is so very little left to say. She's stuck here for the holidays, apart from her family for the first time. He feels her stress knot the muscles of his neck, even with only her cold stone silence for guidance.

Neither wants to explore a deeper silence. He sees a thin film over the surface of a deep, dark hole, where they may not touch bottom before their breath runs out. If they dive down, not knowing where it leads, will they die? Will they find something or anything they seek? He paces slowly, kneeling for a closer look but always pulling his hand back before he can make contact.

He cups his chin with his left hand, not really feeling the four-day stubble of a goatee in progress, and rests his left arm on the armrest on the door. A postal service employee, unfortunate to have to work on a Saturday night, wheels a cart full of mail from the parking garage under the dull-gray sky into the building and across the front. Ben watches him through each subsequent huge pane of glass. There are rows and rows of PO boxes just in view. The self-service parcel mailer is around the corner.

A tan minivan replaces the blonde's car. Three small stuffed monkeys slump in the dashboard cupholders. Ben flashes back to the late '80s, when family cars were boxy with no sleek, smooth curves to ease a young father out of his sports car and into responsibility.

Near fifteen minutes now, Ben catches the traffic's rhythm. Just behind him, a faded yellow arrow on the pavement directs cars one way. He can follow the road all the way to the end and make a left turn onto the road, turn back onto the bridge at the next light, and drive back home. He has to back up carefully; the spaces are narrow and angled enough that every car owner watches through narrow-slit eyes as the people to his or her left leave, as turning too sharply can birth scrapes, dents, and dings. He hates those parking lots.

The idea of driving off feels more and more comfortable as other cars leave. They all seem so confident, the self-service mailing center post office regulars, every Saturday night at 9 pm when there's nothing on TV anyway and all of the good bands have yet to go on stage. Maybe they have meetings in the back, with nametags. Maybe Emily right now is introducing herself as Emily L., with a Styrofoam cup of strong, bitter coffee in one hand and the other waving off offers of cigarettes.

Another thought shakes him, in urgency somewhat less than the mantis-poles and angry pseudo-federal workers chasing him away for abusing free parking in the land of pay-as-you-go lots. He replays the image of Emily walking up to the steel and glass foyer. She yanks the door outward, flinging it open so hard that it hasn't time to close before its inner door cousin, complains about the same treatment. She turns a corner around the other side and he loses her.

In his mind's eye, she just keeps walking. He's never been in that hallway before, but he sees rows of tired posters extolling the virtues of shipping and parcel wrapping services or new and exciting stamps featuring dead celebrities. Scuffed industrial tile reflects dull fluorescent bulbs. Rows and rows of columns of PO boxes are easy to imagine, and rows and rows of tall, floor-to-ceiling windows draw themselves in rough outline, as he's seen that that side of the building is nothing like that. She walks in early afternoon daylight past diagonal columns of sunlight that hold up the sky and pool in her path. He can't see the end of the hall. She shrinks as she walks on.

Ben pulls himself back to what he can actually see and closes the hand reaching for the key in the ignition. If she comes back, she'll need a ride. He can't say now though how he cares; a fuzz in the front of his head dulls his vision looking through a cotton, third-person view. That's all he feels.

Right now, at this point, if she comes back, it will all be mechanical motion. She will open the door, shiver, and brush away petulant raindrops. It will all be deliberate, sturdy motions all the way to her house.

If she keeps walking...if she doesn't come back...if the hallway keeps going...he'll drive back to his house, flipping on the turn signal when appropriate, changing lanes only after glancing ahead and then over his shoulder quickly, parking in his garage and walking right upstairs to fall into bed. He's spent ten years practicing these motions into silent habits.

It's the end of the day. It's the end of the week. He feels their full weights on his back. That's all he feels.

The door opens. Emily shivers and brushes her sleeves with gloved hands. She pauses to stare at his face with a dubious expression, neither content nor sad nor angry. Her eyes are blank. She smiles a tight little smile and sits, closing the door and shivering again.

Ben eases out of his parking space. The driver in the car to his right glares. After a few moments of meticulous concentration, he can turn the wheel and angle his truck toward the exit at the far end of the block past the parking garage. I parked in this inconvenient spot for you, he thinks, because it is night and raining.

Fat wet drops splatter against the windshield. He pulls into the street and the amber and red of the traffic light shimmers in the liquid before the wipers wipe it clean. There's little to see up the street. Thick black ribbons of asphalt punctuated with varicolored lights scream out muted hues. The dark, wet sky overhangs everything. It's closed in, somehow, oppressive. A giant moist hand presses down on his world.

He rounds the block and turns onto the bridge. Normally this would feel like a homecoming, as if the huge arc made tiny by the rush of water beneath marks a boundary where ghosts of conversations and giant insects cannot follow. With night and storm pushing in on him and everything he can't say pushing out, his skin is thin and tired and easy to bruise.

Emily stops staring out the window long enough to flip on the radio. Ambient, experimental music spills out: the province of Saturday night public radio employees untouched by commercial concerns. Quietly furious drums wash into the background. Swirling chords and distorted choruses weave above. Under the partial cover of bridge girders, the wiper blades catch on the windshield to squeak rubberly in time with the main beat. He finds the soundtrack soothing.

He counts in his head again, trying to predict the mathematical pattern of the rhythm. She sighs. "Thanks for driving me, Ben. I hate being alone this time of year. When finals are over it's going to be so quiet with Shelly gone."

Ben holds back. He can't suggest that she come with him. He hasn't told his parents about Emily, half-afraid any hope verbalized will melt away like spilled ice cream in the rain, nor has he told Emily that he's barely told anyone how he feels about her. "I'm sure the quiet will be nice." He has a vision of locking himself in his old bedroom in his parents' house while the rest of the family acts out an old Normal Rockwell painting in front of a roaring fire in the living room or in between fundamental Midwest blizzards outside. He can't unsee either picture, though he dismisses their unrealities at the same time as he considers trading one isolation for another.

"Yeah, I guess so. I can pick up some extra shifts and do a little reading." Idly she rests her left hand next to his right thigh and rubs her knuckles back and forth on his leg. He feels the unconscious connection, the warmth of his leg in comparison to the chill that escapes even through her knit gloves, and longs to find the right answer, some compromise or solution that will make everyone happy. He can't see it.

A mile or two later, he's rejected a hundred different ways to start a dozen separate thoughts and she pulls away her hand to catch two cute little sneezes.

Ben turns onto her street. The thick repavement of giant wet oak leaves skitter behind the truck before rain cements them to the street again. Ben dims the headlights as he pulls up in front of her house. He sets the emergency brake but leaves the truck idling in Park.

Emily unfastens her seatbelt with the quiet grace of well-practiced habit and grasps his upper right arm to lay her head on his shoulder. "I'm so glad you drove me, Ben. Thank you."

His heart is breaking. He smoothes a few tangles out of her hair and kisses the top of her head. "I always want to do what's best for you. I really do." He hates the way it echoes through the cab— hollow, perhaps, and lofty and abstract.

She clutches tighter. "I know you do. I love you for it." She pulls away then to drink in every last corner and wrinkle of his face and to survey all the weight of the world he carries. He thinks he sees beads and jewels of moisture on her eyelashes. She slides her hands down to clutch his hand, raising it and comparing her dainty fingers to his. "Goodnight, Ben."

He offers back a smile as genuine as he can make. "Goodnight, Emily."

She bounces out of the truck then, offering "Call me tomorrow?" and dashing out under the oak tree in the corner of her yard, pausing only to wave and smile over her left shoulder and then she's in the door and gone and he drives home, feeling actually worse for what he thought versus what he said and what he didn't say.

Beginnings

He really did mean to call more often. Despite the ridiculous image of holing up in his old bedroom like a lovesick teenager, it seemed the easiest way to spend time with Emily as well as his family. Then his aunt and uncle and cousins visited one day and stayed late into the night. Another day his father and all three boys went to the forest to choose a tree, leaving the girls (Ellen and Joe's wife Mary) home to bake. Ben would have stayed home to tend the kitchen and decorate gingerbread men, but recognized the rare opportunity for family-wide male bonding. He'd said as much in a quick e-mail to Emily and she responded two days later saying "You made the right choice :)".

Then it is Christmas Eve, and he sleeps late, waking to the smell of waffles for brunch at 11 am. By the time anyone wants to do anything it is already 1 pm: time to decorate the tree and the house and then go to an early church service before coming home to a huge supper. He hasn't a moment to breathe before he yawns at 10:30 pm, all full of hot chocolate and sugar cookies with green and red frosting and relaxing in the luxury of not having to wake up anytime early for the third or fourth day in a row. He feels a twinge of guilt, but considers the time and decides to let her sleep.

He can't bear it by Christmas Day, begging off a round of post-lunch sledding to take an early afternoon nap, but instead curling up on his old bed with a pillow between his head and the dining room wall, whispering hello around a huge grin when she answers. "Thank you for the books," she gushes—a collection of George MacDonald fairy stories he'd handed her in the coffee shop just before he left—"I woke up early to open them this morning!"

He nearly pours out his heart. "I miss you. I wish...I wish you were here sometimes."

"I miss you too, Ben."

He lies back to listen to the comfortable silence of her breathing. The sound of the air in the room fills in the spaces between their words. All of the pain and fear he'd considered drains away and he melts into a relaxed wax puddle. "When are you coming back?" she asks. "I don't work on Sunday."

"Tuesday. I have all next week off, though. Maybe if you have an afternoon free we can get together."

He imagines that he can hear her little nose wrinkle in the pause. "I think Thursday, but I'll have to check."

"Beautiful." He can't imagine anything more perfect, lounging around for a few days to enjoy the snow and his family and freedom from any responsibility more than preparing a meal every other day or doing the dishes, then returning home refreshed and restored only to find amazing, wonderful Emily waiting for him.

"I hate to cut this short, but I promised my mother I'd call her."

"That's okay; I promised to go sledding with my brothers."

"Aren't you all a little old for that?" She's recently taken to teasing him about his age. He wonders sometimes if she's more or less conscious of their differences.

"Dave tells me that life starts at 30."

"I see. Don't break anything. I hear it takes a while to heal at your age." She giggles into the receiver and he scowls, then laughs at himself.

The rest of the holiday rushes by in compressed time—long lazy mornings of wondering who'll be the first to admit to being awake by running the shower and late nights huddled around the fireplace reading, or, once, doing a puzzle. Ben can't remember the last time they were all together to concentrate on making a pristine memory. Every time he had tried to preserve a day or a moment in his mind, all of the effort crowded it back out. Somehow they've all come together

216

with a single goal and the pieces slide into place like bright-colored and smooth-edged child's puzzle. Even an impromptu snowball fight in the front yard includes Mom and Dad and, mirabile dictu, the newcomer Mary. It unfolds like something out of a pop-up storybook, with teams and strategy and loosely packed snowballs that puff into powder on impact.

By the time he starts to pack on Monday night he feels a restoration of spirit. Something stretches and yawns from a long period of somnambulance. His worries and fears have vanished surely as the layers of snowy blankets will by March, leaving life to begin anew again. Maybe he's mellowed, embracing the lean time of winter outside to rekindle fires inside and following the sun's direction to rest more, to prepare always for spring and glorious summer.

He also privately thinks that spending time with his family again as a self-sufficient adult on his own will drive him stir-crazy in a week.

He leans back in the airplane seat with a sigh. Life is good. He has a good job, his own house, a loving family, and a deep peace he's not felt for a long time. Above all, Emily's smile keeps coming to mind.

o o o

Gone

Ben tries the phone again. It rings once, then pauses. The moment drags out. His shirt bounces—ba-dum ba-dum—as his heart pounds its way out of his chest. He's out of breath even merely sitting in the chair in his bedroom. The ground gives way beneath him; overwatered sinkholes pull him down, down, down. He strains to hear a sound, imagining that it's different somehow than last time, longer perhaps or going through a different circuit—the right circuit, relays clicking into place and finally putting through his call.

The disconnected number tones blare out through his head again and he finally believes that somehow Emily no longer answers her phone.

There was no message on the answering machine. His doormat covered no hasty notes. There were no angry e-mails in his inbox nor little padded envelopes in his mailbox containing the Over the Rhine CDs he'd lent her. Randy had picked him up from the airport on his lunch break and rushed back to work. In the three hours since then, Ben has tried to call six times, always with the same results.

Is there a circuit out? Is a powerline down somewhere in the city? It happens, occasionally, in the winter. Did she or Shelly forget to pay the phone bill? He sees them signing a check and licking the envelope.

He pushes down a rising panic, not wanting to acknowledge the worst, hating to name the fear and legitimize it. He fights the urge to drive to their house and wonders if he can explain himself by being in the neighborhood or make a big joke out of being a helpful telephone repairman. The scheme sounds hollow, even now, in a quiet desperation. He catches himself scanning the room without seeing it, casting his eyes about for even a hint.

Ben replays what he remembers of their last conversation. It must have been Thursday night. All he has is her saying that she'd be unavailable over the weekend, working extra hours to make up for coworkers who'd made it home for the holidays. Can he reinterpret something in her tone? Did she sneak a secret into the silence between words? Was it all a test? Is it still? Is the Chinook wind outside a sign that an old evergreen branch had fallen somewhere and severed communications? Shouldn't she be at work anyway at 3 pm?

He stares at the hateful telephone. He curses it as an abominable device full of promise and near-perfect reliability that he trusted before its frustrating and unfixable betrayal. He draws up a full-page newspaper ad recommending that everyone return to renting a rotary wall-mounted phone from the once and future single carrier. In his golden '80s youth, a phone call was miraculous. He stood in the kitchen to wrap and unwrap the cord around his finger. Cold plastic digs into his hand and he notices that his yellowish-white knuckles have nearly burst through the skin.

The only peace he will have, he decides, is in the drive. He watches a weeping sky. Pine trees bow and scrape together. Their whisperings sound like the sea. His skin prickles and chills and he recognizes this weather; snow will come. Inside his truck, he turns the heater to full defrost, hoping to forestall the rapid fog of his breath as well as to turn any tiny ice crystals back into liquid.

Traffic goes his way. The whole city always hushes under a pearly sky. It's touch and go on the rain and snow. Southwestern clouds part just long enough for a sundog to chase the sun down to the horizon. The weak patch of brightness along the low winter ecliptic fades in moments, but he clutches the sign of its rainbow smear.

There's nothing out of order on her street. No white trucks with cherrypickers hoist orange-vested workers to the tops of power poles. No warning cones along the streets mark buried lines. A few loose branches skitter down the street, but they quickly tangle up in storm drains or tuck under the wheels of parked cars.

There are no lights on in the house, which is normal. He parks along the street and breathes a few times, willing his pulse to slow. Everything looks okay, the same as he remembers it, the porch and yard clean in the renters-without-plastic-furniture fashion, but the blinds are open at every window. The whole house gives off a certain empty anti-glow, the equal and opposite of light.

Ben blinks again, then decides that someone may be home. He knocks. It and the doorbell both echo emptily. He can't quite see inside from the porch. As he strains to look in the front room, a minivan pulls into the driveway. He can't see any furniture, but also can't remember if they used that room to store boxes they hadn't unpacked yet.

A young man of perhaps 19 or 20 exits with a clipboard. "You're early. We haven't even listed it yet. Want me to let you in?"

"Let me in?"

"We have to do a final inspection and a cleaning before we can rent it out again, but if you don't mind looking at it early, I can make an exception."

The ground softens beneath him again. "They just moved out?"

"It's only been a couple of days. The owners want us to put it back on the market as soon as possible so they don't lose the rent for too long, but it's December, you know? Who moves in December? I mean, present company excluded." The kid gives Ben a smile intended to look apologetic.

"Do you know where they went?"

"Sorry, I just do the inspections. Do you want to see inside or not?"

"No, that's alright. I'll come back when it's ready to show. I'd hate to cause you trouble." He starts walking to his truck in his mind.

"That's cool. It'll probably be Friday. Oh, and Happy New Year!"

"Yeah. Same to you."

Half an hour later, Ben leans forward in his chair again to stare at the infernal phone with his head on his arms. Surely whatever happened, she'll call.

o o o

Less Alone Apart

On every birthday since Randy's 21st, or so he's told Ben, he likes to visit a different neighborhood bar for two and only two beers. Neither of them drink much otherwise, though one of Randy's ex-girlfriends had brought a bottle of decent champagne to celebrate some occasion and both men had reluctantly agreed that it was the most delicious alcohol ever, even when sipped from paper cups during the *Star Trek* Drinking Game.

This year, Randy vacillated between an upscale bar on the west side of the river which serves designer martinis ("It's my tradition and I can break it any time I want to!") and an old dingy bar a couple of miles from their house. Ben gradually warms to the idea of drinking something that tastes exactly like a candy bar, but when Randy finally makes his decision, two weeks after his birthday, walking distance is the important criterion.

The bar is an inspectacular watering hole that has found itself in the middle of a burgeoning neighborhood becoming hip again for its unpretentious shabbiness. The old sign, "Andrew's Bar and Grill", lies against its alley wall. The new sign hasn't arrived. Inside, it's just as Ben predicted, dark wood interior from the days when wood was inexpensive, not a sign of good taste, with torn barstools and complimentary beer vendor lights above a well-loved pool table in the back. Ben immediately tries to forget the phrase "well-loved".

The crowd's a lot younger than normal, revealing again the hazard of Saturday night bar-going. Ben finds a corner table and pre-

221

pares to sip the least toxic beer he can find merely to wish Randy well during their hopefully brief ritual, but something about the scene marches into his mind and bivouacs. The few obvious regulars are mostly tired-looking blue collar workers in their forties, with one or two as young as thirty-seven. They roll their eyes at the rest of the crowd, mostly twenty-somethings with the irrational exuberances of youth and having discovered something authentic. The latter group soaks in the place with the same joy they might devote to making a rediscovered box of long-forgotten video game tie-in cereal the centerpiece of a serious conversation.

Randy beams, returning with two mugs. "Here's to 28!" They clink, then drink. Ben grimaces. Watery.

"I never thought I'd live this long," admits Randy. "I have no idea what I'm doing."

"Aren't you having fun?"

"Yeah, but I'm starting to feel the urge, you know, maybe to settle down. I've had a good run, a few laughs, but maybe it's time to stop before it's too much fun altogether. I mean, if I had a million dollars right now I'd still build a house with a combination art museum and disco and call it Vincent Van Go-Go, but I might think that famous paintings are an investment, too." He's not gulping the first beer; he traces lines in the condensation with his thumb between sips.

Ben shakes his head. "I'm not hearing this correctly. You're asking for responsibility?"

Randy shrugs. "Maybe everybody born in December gets depressed this time of year, but I look at you and Emily and think that that's something I never had. Yeah, I have fun, but there's more to life than fun. There's understanding someone deeply and profoundly and being understood. Maybe I never really thought I could have that or thought I would want that until I saw it with you two. You and I, we're more alike than you think."

What Happens in the Past...

Ben closes his eyes and sighs.

"Look at that guy over there. You don't think I pay attention to these things, but I do. You're thinking that he's, what, so wrapped up in how ironic it is to enjoy a throwback to the middle-of-the-road pub interior decorated in the '70s that he wouldn't appreciate real irony if it, what's the phrase, '...danced a Busby Berkeley number on the bar in front of him'? He's probably 21 or 22—born in the '80s, and to him the '70s are something that he can't possibly take seriously. It's something that no one could take seriously.

"Look at us; we were born then. Maybe it's time we started taking things seriously too."

Ben opens his eyes and really looks around the room. It's dark; he feels crowded. Clusters of would-be couples huddle together in pools of light. He speeds up the movie in his mind, time-lapse, to watch the temporary couples break apart again and rejoin the darkness.

"Ben? That was a compliment. Come on. I'm being *genuine* here."

He finally notices what disturbed him earlier. In the corner of the bar—in the corner of the room—a pretty little blonde girl with freckles and big blue eyes and straight white teeth tucks a loose strand of chin-length hair behind her ear in a gesture so familiar that it pulls his heart toward her. She smiles at some generically handsome and bland guy he's never seen before.

Ben watches himself stand and slam his mug on the table. Foam splatters. He's shaking. He takes one step, then another, and then he's halfway across the bar, not knowing what he's doing and not thinking about what he has to say. The red bar across his vision fades for just a moment and he watches the guy turn away, unsuccessfully, and he catches a better glimpse of her and realizes that it's not, it's not Emily. Then he's outside and crouching by the brick by the door underneath the empty unfaded rectangle where the sign used to be. His breath puffs out in huge, unfurling clouds.

223

He's not sure what just happened.

One moment he felt dizzy and disoriented as if the ground were shifting underneath him—normal for at least the past couple of weeks. He'd grudgingly accepted his complete powerlessness and, to his mind, accepted the sinkhole of grief slowly scarring over where he'd kept his heart.

In a moment, thinking he'd have the opportunity to force a confrontation, he...doesn't know what he would have done. The flashing rage still recedes from the edges of his vision and his pulse slows. Adrenaline dilutes and his muscles feel cold and loose, and ache weakly. A nausea grows in his stomach as beer and pain mix, and he stares at the sidewalk between his feet for a moment to will it away, wishing that he had more control over his body, his emotions, his thoughts, his anything.

Ben stands, lashing out his right hand to steady himself on cold, rough bricks. His vision swirls. The world goes liquid. He can't hear anything for a moment, and then it returns with a rush of wind and the sound of tension on a string somewhere, growing and increasing and finally pulling into a snap and a twang. Everything shifts a degree clockwise and snaps into clearer focus.

An epiphany grabs his shoulder and forces him to turn, but then the moment is gone. He almost had it. He almost saw it. He almost touched it. He almost said it. He closes his eyes and sighs, feeling something in his chest go soft and afraid. Why?

Then Randy is clasping his shoulder and saying something.

"Ben, are you okay? Ben, talk to me. Ben?"

He chokes and coughs. "I...just needed some fresh air."

"When was the last time you ate anything, Ben? Want me to get you a sandwich?"

His vision remains blurred. Somewhere straight ahead an outline remains, just beyond the ghostly remains of her face. He recognizes the shape of the words but can't pronounce them. He can't read them.

If he sees them again he'll recognize them. He clings to that.

"Go on inside. I'll be back in in a minute."

Randy's concern fills his vision. Ben watches him give in to the unbelievable lie. "Alright. I'll be inside. You do what you have to do." He squeezes Ben's shoulder and leaves him alone again.

The night is cold and dark. Thin clouds wisp across the stars. For a moment, he had it. He saw the whole thing: the world and his place within it. For a moment the bonds that lashed him to the ground loosened. He saw how to escape the gravity that held him. He saw his escape—the secret of how to skim across the surface of events, never letting them draw him down. It brushed his fingertips but he fell short, unable to hold onto it.

Now that he knows that it's possible, he won't find rest until he holds it again.

o o o

Epilogue

Levity

EVEN still, two years later, he turns his head in dreams and sees her face, hears her voice, and watches the expression on her face turn sometimes to grief and others to rage, but it never softens into what he used to understand as love. He resolves never again to flip through phone books online for various combinations of names and initials, trying to pin down first a likely state and second a likely address. It never works.

The desire fades. Time salves over rough and raw edges. Other griefs distract him from his most beautiful pain. Still, in the night and in the quiet he can't identify the color of nameless longing as grief or loss or even indignation.

There's no time to think of that now, though. There's his job to consider. Now that Randy's off of strong painkillers and back on boring, over-the-counter analgesics, they brainstorm options for forming their own software business or finding Ben another job or, as Randy always votes, planning a Che- and Fidel-style motorcycle tour of at least the southwestern United States.

For the second year in a row, late February turns temperate. It feels important to leave the house on such a lovely winter day. They wind through the neighborhood as fast as Randy on his crutches can hobble, breathing in humid air and drinking in uncharacteristic sunlight. Deciduous trees haven't yet started to bud, but zealous daffodils and crocuses peek their way from the soil. It's quiet and calm, with a hum in the earth below. Surprised by early thaws, spring wastes no time.

"The scary part is that I don't know what's going to happen," Ben offers. "Ned's the only one who really wants to switch. The customer's happy, we found a good balance, and everything's back to normal. At least, that's what we thought."

"Plans change. I don't let it get to me. We restructure every three or four months and the managers shuffle jobs and responsibilities and spend the next three or four months learning their new positions before they switch all over again. That leaves people like me to do the real work. You get used to it." Randy's words tumble out between pants in twos and threes; he sets the pace of the walk.

Ben scoffs. "You're a terrible devil's advocate. When was the last time you took your work seriously?"

"Maybe that's the problem—not mine, yours. When was the last time you took anything lightly? You're in a ridiculous situation. You fix it or you don't. You face it or you don't. You leave, you stay, you wait for them to kick you out. Whatever you do, it's a choice and it's yours."

A cloud reaches across the sun to throw shadows in their path. "I don't like that. I liked my job. Isn't that enough?"

"Is it what you want?"

Ben faces Randy. "I don't want to have to think about it. I found the right job. I'm good at it. I enjoy it. Isn't that enough? Why do I have to keep asking myself what I like and what I want and what to do next?"

Randy's face flushes. "Hang on, I have to adjust my crutch." He hops on his good leg and rearranges the pad under his right armpit. "It's all wrinkled and starting to give me a blister. Ah, that's better. Anyway, you have the option not to think about these things.

"I knocked that kid into the road. Sure, he shouldn't have been playing there and yes, I know you think that in an ideal world there'd never be accidents and we'd never have moral dilemmas, but it happened and my only choice was to save him or to watch the bus hit him. I never had the choice not to choose."

"Would you do it differently if you knew the bus would hit you?"

"I can't answer that. I wish I could, but that's not the point. You want a luxury that you don't have. No wonder it drives you crazy. It doesn't exist."

Ben starts walking again. Randy fumbles his crutch back into place and hobbles after him. "You don't believe me, do you?"

"No. I don't accept that. I chose once already. Isn't that enough?"

"What's the point, then? You bang around for a while and hope you find a role that fits and you stick with it for the rest of your life and that's it? You don't change? You don't grow? You don't make mistakes?"

Ben whirls, waving his finger. "You're the last person who should talk about making mistakes." He stands and sighs, watching Randy watch him with sad and curious eyes, then slumps against a nearby brick wall. It's cold and rough and filthy and sends a familiar itch down his back.

"Maybe so," Randy agrees, "but if you're not happy, isn't that a mistake too?" He lowers himself to his haunches, clinging to the crutch on one side and sticking his cast straight out ahead. "How is it a loss if you never really had it in the first place? You're not talking only about your job, are you?"

"No."

They sit in silence. Ben draws his knees to his chest and folds his arms over them, making a cradle for his head. "I want to be able to count on something, maybe connect to something that's not going to disappear someday. I don't want to skip through life on the surface, flitting between distractions. I want something that means something, you know?"

"Maybe that's not work. Maybe it's not this job. Maybe you don't have to find it today."

"But when?"

Randy grimaces and shifts his weight, pulling himself up with his good leg and leaning back against the wall. Ben's calves ache in sympathy as his friend points his toe toward and away, toward and away.

Ben rails silently against the unfairness of the universe. He'd had good things in his hand; they slipped away. He'd recognized them as good things. He'd built plans around them. He'd wanted them, knowing enough about himself and adulthood and endocrinology and emotions to be able to look at his heart and his mind and make rational choices about what is good. Then the universe took them away. Why? What lesson could there be? What cruelty is this, time after time?

A muffled thumping escapes from the building. Again a bad cover band performs its warm-up exercises in a futile attempt to tune its sound for the poor acoustics of a dive bar, all wood paneling and hard corners and soft bodies moving about.

He counts again the beats the drummer misses and calculates the time signature the bassist must have intended. Something seems familiar, yet distant. Then the world shifts, and he's inside himself.

"You know what it's like?" he asks.

"What?"

"You ever see things, in your head? Like when you're upset or nervous, you get an image of people walking around or talking to you?"

Randy raises an eyebrow, though his eyes remain closed. "A dream? A vision?"

"No, not exactly. Maybe a daydream?"

"Not a clue. I'm really not following you here, Ben."

"I'm in a room full of pictures. It's cramped. It's circular. There's no door. They're memories. I'm jumping off of the diving board by myself while Dad watches, or graduating from college, or starting my job and buying a house. It smells really stale, like an attic.

"There are windows on the other side, and they look out on a beach, a wedding, a library, and a forest full of sunlight and trees and rosebuds about to open. Then I hear this noise, like a great giant bird flapping its wings, and I have to get out of the room."

He doesn't say that at this point the portrait of Emily speaks, asking, "Don't you want to know what happened?" It pushes her hair back behind her left ear and he watches the soft curve of her jaw move. It's her voice.

"So I jump out of one of the windows and it feels like I'm having a heart attack; my chest hurts so much. Then I land, hard, and that's when I wake up." At least, that's how it ends this time. He's never made it to the window before, never died in his sleep before.

Yet he's awake and alive now.

Randy opens an eye and turns his head. "Can't say I know what that's like." An English setter's nose peeks around the corner and the rest of the dog takes Randy for a likely target. "Oh, hey!" He scratches the dog behind his ears. "Hi there!"

Ben stretches. "Just curious. Who's your friend?"

Randy shrugs. "It's like he knows me or something. Whoa, look out!" The dog brushes past him on his way to Ben, whipping its tail back and forth. Randy moves his cast out of the way just in time. "Careful!"

The last time Ben saw Matthew, it was dark and the dog was much more of a puppy. The traditional markings have grown more distinct now. Even without the nametag, he's still obviously the same dog. "Hey, I know this guy. He lives just down the street." Ben knows where he is now. He hasn't been here in *months*, but it's almost the same as he left it—same bar, same bad cover band, probably the same people inside.

There's dried blood and mud in the dog's fur, but that doesn't diminish his exuberance. Matthew splits his time between jumping up at Ben and Randy and ducking his head under their hands and whining for ear-scratching.

"No collar," Randy wonders. "How did you know that?"

"I met him before, the last time I was this way. Let's walk him home." Ben brushes off his pants and, despite Matthew's help, stands.

"Are you sure you're okay? That dream stuff sounds pregnant with psychological demon babies."

"It's a long story, maybe not worth telling. It feels good to get that much out though. Don't worry. I'm good. I really am."

They walk, and Ben repeats that in his head. It's not perfect. It's not even easy. Yet sunlight washes him clean and the weekend stretches out in front of him, and he realizes that he can and ought to say that, whatever happens next, it really is good.

o   o   o

About the Author

S. Christopher left the world of software development for writing in 2002. He has also unloaded dry ice, framed houses, written certification tests for box-making factories and database administrators, worked simultaneously at two newspapers, taught preschool, played in a rock band, driven an ambulance (once), and helped burn through a million dollars at a dot-com company.

He lives in the Pacific Northwest where he tries to keep his cats off of the keyboard when he types. This is his first novel.

www.ingramcontent.com/pod-product-compliance
Lightning Source LLC
Chambersburg PA
CBHW070101260626
47160CB00004B/1271